MUD VEIN

Cover Designer: Sarah Hanson, Okay Creations, www.okaycreations.com

Interior Designer: Jovana Shirley, Unforeseen Editing, www.unforeseenediting.com

ISBN-13: 978-1497455047

ISBN-10: 1497455049

Visit my website at www.tarrynfisher.com

For Lori

Who saved me when I was drowning

CONTENTS

Part Three: Anger and Bargaining

PART ONE

SHOCK AND DENIAL

DAY 1

I wrote a novel. I wrote a novel and it was published. I wrote a novel and it cruised onto the *New York Times Bestseller* List. I wrote that novel and then I watched it play out in a movie theater with a large, buttery bag of popcorn in my lap. My novel. That I wrote. I did it all alone, because that's how I like it. And if the rest of the world wants to pay for a peek into my discombobulated mind, so be it. Life is too short to hide your wrongs. So I hide myself instead.

It's my thirty-third birthday. I wake up in a cold sweat. I am hot. No, I am cold. I am freezing. The blankets tangled around my legs feel unfamiliar—too smooth. I pull at them, trying to cover myself. My fingers feel thick and piggy against the silky material. Maybe they're swollen. I can't tell because my brain is sluggish, and my eyes are glued shut, and now I'm getting hot again. Or maybe I'm cold. I stop fighting the blankets, letting myself drift … *backwards* …. *backwards*…

When I wake up, there is light in the room. I can see it through my eyelids. It is dim—even for a rainy Seattle day. I have floor-to-ceiling windows in my bedroom; I roll in their direction and force open my eyes only to find myself facing a wall. A wall made of logs. There are none of those in my house. I let my eyes travel the length of them, all the way up to the ceiling before I bolt upright, coming fully awake.

I am not in my bedroom. I stare around the room in shock. Whose bedroom? I think back to the night before. *Had I—*

No way. I haven't even looked at a man since … there is no way I went home with someone. Besides, last night I had dinner with my editor. We'd had a couple glasses of wine. Chianti doesn't make you black out. My breathing is shallow as I try to remember what happened after I left the restaurant.

Gas, I'd stopped for gas at the Red Sea Service Station on Magnolia and Queen Anne. What after that? I can't remember.

I look down at the duvet clutched between my white knuckles. Red … feather … unfamiliar. I swing my legs over the side of the bed and the room wobbles and tilts. I feel sick right away. Day after a huge drinking binge sick. I gasp for air, trying to breathe deeply enough to quell my nausea. Chianti doesn't do this, I tell myself again.

"I'm dreaming," I say out loud. But I'm not. I know that. I stand up and I am dizzy for a good ten seconds before I am able to take my first step. I bend over and vomit … right on the wood floor. My stomach is empty, but it heaves anyway. I lift my hand to wipe my mouth and my arm feels wrong—too heavy. This isn't a hangover. I've been drugged. I stay bent over for several more seconds before I straighten up. I feel like I'm on the Tilt-A-Whirl at the fair. I stumble forward, taking in my surroundings. The room is round. It's freezing. There is a fireplace—with no fire—and a four-poster bed. There is no door. *Where is the door?* Panic kicks in and I run in a clumsy circle, grabbing onto the bed to steady myself when my legs buckle.

"Where is the door?"

I can see my breath steaming into the air. I focus on that, watch it expand and dissipate. My eyes take a long time to re-focus. I'm not sure how long I stand there, except my feet start to ache. I look down at my toes. I can barely feel them. I have to move. Do something. Get out. On the wall in front of me there is a window. I amble forward and rip aside the flimsy curtain. The first thing I notice is that I'm on the second floor. The second thing I notice—oh God! My brain sends a chill down the rest of my body—a warning. *You are done, Senna,* it says. *Over. Dead. Someone took you.* My mouth is slow to respond, but when it does, I hear my intake of breath fill the dead silence around me. I didn't believe people actually gasped in real life until the moment I hear myself do it. This moment—this gasping, heart-stopping moment, when all that fills my eyes is snow. So much snow. All the snow in the world, piled right below me.

I hear my body crack against the wood, then I fall into darkness. When I wake up, I am on the floor lying in a pool of my vomit. I moan and a sharp pain shoots through my wrist when I try to push myself up. I cry out and shove my hand over my mouth. If someone is here I don't want them to hear me. *Good one, Senna,* I think. *You should have thought of that before you started fainting all over the room and making a racket.*

I grip my wrist with my free hand and slide up the wall for support. It is then that I notice what I am wearing. Not my clothes. A white linen pajama set—expensive. Thin. No wonder I'm so damn cold.

Oh God.

I shut my eyes. Who undressed me? Who brought me here? My hands are stiff as I reach across my body to examine myself. I touch my chest, pull my pants down. No bleeding, no soreness, except I am wearing white cotton panties that someone put on me. Someone had me naked. Someone touched my body. Closing my eyes at the thought, I start to shiver. Uncontrollably. *No, please, no.*

"Oh, God," I hear myself say. I have to breathe—deep and steady.

You're freezing, Senna. And you're in shock. Get it together. Think.

Whoever brought me here had more sinister plans than having me freeze to death. I look around. There is wood in the fireplace. If this sick fuck left me wood, perhaps he left me something to light it with. The bed I woke up in is in the center of the room; it is hand carved with four posters. Sheer chiffon is draped across the posts. It's pretty, which makes me sick. I take inventory of the rest of the room: a heavy wooden dresser, an armoire, a fireplace and one of those thick animal fur rugs. Throwing open the wardrobe, I rifle through clothes … too many clothes. Are they here for me? My hand lingers on a label. The realization that they are all in my size sickens me. *No*—I tell myself. *No, they can't be mine. This is all a mistake. This can't be for me, the colors are wrong. Reds … blues … yellows…*

But my brain knows it's not a mistake. My brain is acquainted with grief and so is my body.

Task at hand, Senna.

I find an ornate silver box on the top shelf of the armoire. I pull it down, shake it. It's heavy. Foreign. Inside is a box of lighters, a key, and a small silver knife. I want to question the contents of the box. Stare at them, touch them—but I need to move fast. I use the knife to cut a strip of material from the bottom of a shirt, then I loop it and tie it into a knot with my teeth and good hand. Slipping my wrist into my makeshift sling, I flinch.

I pocket the knife and fumble for one of the lighters. My hand hovers above the box. Eight pink Zippos. If I didn't already have chills, I'd get them now. I blow it off. I can't blow it off. I can and I have to, because I'm freezing. My hand is shaking as I reach for the lighter. *It's a coincidence.* I laugh. Can anything tied to a kidnapping be coincidence? I'll think later. Right now I need to get warm. My fingers are numb. It takes six tries before I can get the wheel on the Zippo to spin. It leaves indentations on my thumb The wood is hard to catch. *Damp.* Had he put it here recently? I look for something to feed the flames, but there is nothing I can burn that I might not need later.

I am already thinking survival, and it scares me. Kindling. What can I use for kindling? My eyes search the space until I see a white box in the corner of the armoire with a red medical cross on the top. A first-aid kit. I run to it and flip the lid. Bandages, aspirin, needles—*God.* I finally find single use packages of alcohol prep wipes. I grab a handful and run back to the fireplace. I rip the first one open and hold the lighter to its tip. It catches and flares. I tuck the burning pad against the log and rip open another package, repeating the process. I pray to whoever is in charge of fire and blow gently.

The wood catches. I pull the thick comforter off the bed and wrap myself in it, crouching in front of the meager flames. It is not enough. I am so cold I want to dive into the fire and let it burn this cold off of me. I stay like that, a lump on the floor, until I stop shaking.

Then I move.

There is a trapdoor under the rug with a heavy, metal handle. It is locked. I yank on it for five minutes with my good hand until my shoulder burns and I want heave up my guts again. I stare at it for a moment before I run to get the key from the silver box. What kind of sick game is this? And why do I take so long to realize the thing about the key? I don't know what to do. I pace around the trapdoor in my bare feet, smacking the key against my thigh. It is an abnormally large key, old fashioned and bronze. The keyhole in the trapdoor looks large enough to fit it. I get another chill and this time I know it's not just the cold. I stop my pacing to examine the key more closely. It takes up my entire hand, fingertips to wrist. There is a question mark in the center of the handle, the metal curling around the character in an ornate design. I drop the key. It clanks heavily against the floor not far from where I threw up. I back up until my shoulder blades are pressed against the wall.

"What. Is. This?" There is no one to answer, of course, unless they're waiting just below that trap door to tell me exactly what *this* is. I shiver and my fingers automatically close around the knife in my pocket. The blade is sharp. I feel really good about that. I have a penchant for sharp knives and I sure as hell know how to carve skin. If I have a key, they have a key. I can wait here for them to come up, or I can go down. I prefer the second option; it feels like it affords me a little more power.

I walk quickly, sidestepping the vomit and snatch up the key. Before I can think about what I am doing, I crouch over the trapdoor and plunge it into the keyhole.

Metal against metal and then … *click*.

I use my good hand to heave it open. It's damn heavy. I'm careful not to make noise when I set it down. I peer into the darkness. There is a ladder. At the bottom of the ladder are a round rug and a hallway. I cannot see past a few feet. I am going to have to go down. I place the knife between my teeth and count the rungs as I climb.

One … two … three … four … five … six. My feet hit the rug. The floor is cold. The cold shoots up my legs. Why hadn't I thought to look for shoes?

I hold my knife at arm's length, ready to stab anyone who jumps out at me. I'll go for the eye socket, and if I can't reach that—the balls. Just one sharp jab, and when they're bent over, I'll run. Now that there is a plan, I take a look around. There is a skylight above me, laser-thin rays of sunlight pierce through it and hit the wood floor. I step through them, my eyes darting around for a hidden attacker.

I am at the end of a corridor: wood floors, wood walls, wood ceiling. There are three doors: two on the left side, one on the right. All of them are closed. There is a wall directly behind me, as well as the ladder I just climbed down. Beyond the hallway I can see a landing. I decide that's where I'll go first. If someone jumps out of one of those doors, I'll be past them and on my way to the front door. Something is whispering in the back of my brain that it won't be that easy. I walk on my tiptoes past the doors and stop on the landing. The knife is clutched in my hand, though it seems small compared to the situation.

I am obviously in a cabin. I can make out a large, open kitchen down the stairs and to the left. To the right is a living room with thick, cream-colored carpet. Everything is eerily quiet. I creep down the stairs, my back to the wall. If I can make it to the front door, I can run. Get help. My mind goes to the endless snow I saw out the window in the round room. I push the thought away. There will be someone … a house … or a store, maybe. *God, why had I not thought to take shoes?* I am all action and no brains. I am going to have to run through three feet of snow with nothing on my feet. The front door is directly at the bottom of the staircase. I glance up to the top floor to make sure no one is following me, and then dive for it. It is locked. A keypad sits next to the door. It opens electronically. I am going to have to find another way out. I am shaking again. If someone attacked me now, I wouldn't be able to hold the knife steady enough to defend myself. I could break a window. The kitchen is in front of me and to my left. I try that first. It is rectangular. Shiny, stainless steel appliances. They look brand new.

God, where am I? A window runs the length of the kitchen, its continuity broken only by the fridge. In the corner there is a heavy circular table with two curved benches on either side. I walk to the drawers and pull them open until I find the one with the knives. I pluck out the largest one, testing its weight in my hand before leaving my baby knife on the counter. I think twice and slip it in my pocket instead.

Now that I have a weapon, a real weapon, I head for the living room. Books line one wall; on the other is the fireplace. A sofa and a loveseat are arranged around the coffee table. There is no way out. I look for something to break a window with. The coffee table is too heavy for me to lift—especially with a sprained wrist. When I look more closely I see that it is bolted to the floor. There are no chairs. I go back to the kitchen, open every cabinet and drawer, my desperation increasing with every second I risk being discovered. There is nothing large enough or heavy enough to break a window. With a sinking feeling, I realize I'm going to have to go back upstairs. This could be a trap. There could be someone hiding behind one of the doors. But, why give me a key to the room I was locked in if they wanted me trapped? Were they playing games? My whole body is shaking as I climb back up the stairs. I haven't cried in years, but I feel as close to tears as I've ever come. *One foot in front of the other, Senna, and if someone jumps out at you, you use your knife and cut them in half.* I am between the doors. I choose the one to my left, put my hand on the knob and turn. I can hear myself breathing: ragged, cold, terrified breaths.

It opens.

"Oh my God."

I slap my hand over my mouth and clutch my weapon tighter. I don't lower my knife, I keep it up and ready. I step onto the carpet, my toes curling around the shag like they need to hold onto something. A canopy bed sits against the far wall, facing me. It looks like a child's bed in design but it is larger than an adult king. Two of its posters are life-sized carousel horses, their poles disappearing into the wooden beams of the ceiling. There is a fireplace to my left, a window seat to my right. I am having trouble breathing. First the lighters, then the key, then … this.

I can't get out of there fast enough. I close the door behind me. One more door. This one feels more frightening than the last. Is it just my intuition or is this the last place my kidnapper could be hiding? I stand facing it for the longest time, my breath curling into the air, and the frozen fingers of my good hand clutching my little knife. I reach for the knob with my injured hand and flinch when pain shoots up my arm. I push it open and wait. The room is dark, but so far no one has jumped out at me. I take a step forward, feel for a light switch. Then I hear it; a man's moan—deep and guttural. I back out of the room, pointing my knife at the sound. I want to run, climb back up the ladder and lock myself in the round room. I don't. If I do not go looking for what brought me here, it will come looking for me. I will not be a victim. Not again. My heart is beating erratically. The moaning suddenly stops as if he's realized I'm there. I can hear him breathing. I wonder if he can hear me. The noise starts again, muffled words this time as if he's speaking through something. Words … words that sound like *HELP ME!* This could be a trap. What do I do? I walk right into it.

No one attacks me, but my body is wound up and ready to spring. The deep cries of *Eeeel, eeeeel* become more persistent. I search for a light switch, which means I have to transfer my knife to my injured hand. It doesn't matter—if someone comes at me, I'll take every bit of pain to cut them open. I find it: a broad, flat square that I have to push down with two fingers. In the time it takes for the lights to turn on, I quickly switch the knife back to my good hand. The room is suddenly washed in a urine-yellow glow. It flickers before gripping whatever power it's using, and starts to hum. I blink at the sudden change. My knife hand extends as I stab at air. There is nothing in front of me—no attacker—but there is a bed. In it is a man, his arms and legs bound to the four posters with bright white rags. He is blindfolded and gagged with the same white cloth. I watch in shock as his head thrashes from side to side. The muscles in his arms are pulled so taut I can see the outlines of where each one starts and ends. I start to rush forward to help him, then stop. I could still be in danger. This could be a trap. He could be the trap.

I walk cautiously, keeping my eyes on the corners of the room as though someone might emerge from the wood walls. Then I spin toward the door from which I entered, to make sure no one is sneaking up behind me. I continue this cycle until I reach the side of the bed, and my heart is racing painfully. I rotate the wrist that is clutching the knife in a circle. There is a door next to the bed. I kick it open and he goes perfectly still, his face angled toward me, his breathing coming hard. He has dark hair … lots of scruff on his face. The bathroom is empty, the shower curtain pulled back as if my captor had thought—at the last minute—to reassure me he wasn't there. I leave the bathroom. The man is no longer struggling. Angling my back to the wall, I reach over and yank away his blindfold and gag. I am half leaning over him when we see each other for the first time. I can see his shock. He can see mine. He blinks rapidly as if he's trying to clear his vision. I drop my knife.

"Oh my God." That's the second time I've said that. I don't want to make a habit of it. I don't believe in God.

"Oh my God," I say again. I bend slowly at the knees, keeping my eyes on him and the door until I've retrieved my weapon. I back up. I need distance between us. I'm moving toward the door, but then I realize I could be ambushed from behind. I spin. I extend my knife. There is nothing behind me. I spin again—point my knife at the man in the bed. This can't be happening. This is crazy. I'm acting crazy. I press my back to the nearest wall. This is the only way I feel relatively safe, when I can survey the room and not feel like someone is sneaking up from behind.

"Senna?" I hear my name. I look back at his face. Any minute I expect to wake from this nightmare. I will be in my own bed, underneath my white comforter, wearing my own pajamas.

"Senna," he chokes. "Cut me loose … please…"

I hesitate.

"Senna," he says again. "I'm not going to hurt you. It's me."

He leans his head back against the pillow and closes his eyes like he can't stand the pain.

I hold the knife tightly and chop at the white fabric that is binding his arms. I can barely breathe—never mind see. I slice his skin with the tip of the knife. He flinches, but doesn't make a sound. I watch his blood pool in fascination before it streams down his arm.

"I'm sorry," I say. "My hands are shaking. I can't—"

"It's all right, Senna. Take your time."

Funny, I think. *He's the one tied up and he's reassuring me.*

I make it through his other hand binding, and he takes the knife from me, cutting his own legs free. I silently panic. I shouldn't have handed over my knife. *He could be … he could be the one…*

It doesn't make sense.

When he's through, he springs off the bed, massaging his wrists. I take a step away from him … toward the door. The only thing he has on is a thin pair of pajama pants. *Someone put those on him too,* I think.

And then I say his name in my mind: *Isaac Asterholder.*

When he looks at me he narrows his eyes. "Is anyone else here? Have you seen—"

"No," I cut him off. "I don't think anyone is here."

He immediately makes for the door. I flinch as he passes me. I want my knife. I linger in the doorway, not sure what to trust. Then I follow him. He searches the rooms while I cradle my wrist. If someone attacks us, he will be their first target. I need something sharp to hold in my hand. We descend the stairs and Isaac tries the front door, yanks hard when it won't open, slams his fist against the wood and swears. I see him eye the keypad, but he doesn't touch it. A keypad on the inside of the house. Whoever put us here gave us the option of getting out.

After he's made a thorough search of both floors, he looks for something to break a window.

"We could both lift the bench," I offer, motioning toward the heavy wooden table in the kitchen. Isaac rubs his temples.

"Okay," he says. But when we try to lift it, we find that there are smooth, bronze bolts locking it to the floor. He checks the rest of the furniture. It's all the same. Anything heavy enough to break a window is bolted to the floor.

"We need to get out," I insist. "There may be tools to lift those bolts. We can find help before whoever brought us here comes back. There has to be something near here, somewhere we can go..."

He turns toward me suddenly angry. "Senna, do you really think that someone would go through all the trouble to abduct us, lock us in a house and then make it easy to get away?"

I open and close my mouth. *Abducted.* We'd been abducted.

"I don't know," I say. "But we have to at least try!"

He's opening and closing drawers, rifling through their contents. He swings open the fridge and his face visibly pales.

"What? What is it?" I rush forward to see what he's seeing. The refrigerator is large, industrial-sized. Every shelf is stocked without an inch of space to spare. The freezer is the same: meat, vegetables, ice cream, cans of frozen juice. My head spins as I take it all in. There is enough food for months. I grab a large can of tomatoes and throw it at the window as hard as I can. I throw it with my left hand, but fear propels it forward at an impressive speed. It hits the window with a muted thud, and drops to the counter, rolling backward toward the floor. We stare at it, dented on one side, for several minutes before Isaac bends to pick it up. He tries, pulling his arm back like a pitcher and letting it shoot from his fingertips. This time the thud is louder, but the result the same. I run back to the front door, throwing myself at the handle. I scream, slamming my fists against the wood, ignoring the searing pain in my injured hand. I need to feel pain, I want to. I pound and kick for a solid minute before I feel Isaac's hands on my arms. He pulls me away.

"Senna! Senna!" He shakes me. I stare up at him, my breath coming quickly. He must see something in my eyes, because he wraps me in a hug. I shiver against his warmth until he pulls away from me.

"Let me see your wrist," he says gently. I hold it out to him, flinching as he pokes at it gently with his cold fingertips. He nods in approval at my makeshift sling. "It's a sprain," he says. "Did you have it before you woke up?"

I shake my head. "I fell … upstairs."

"Where did you wake up?"

I tell him about the room at the top of the ladder, how I found the key.

"I think I was drugged."

He nods. "Yes, we both were. Let's go take a look at this room. Also, if there is power, there should be heat. We need to find the thermostat."

We make our way back up the stairs.

I look at his face. His dark eyes look bleary like he's coming down from a high—except he doesn't take drugs. Not even for a headache. I know a lot about this man. That's what's shocking me the most. Why am I here? Why am I here with him?

His head swivels to look at me. It's as if he's really seeing me for the first time. I can see the up and down movement of his chest as he struggles for breath. This was me, fifteen minutes ago. His eyes search my face, before he says, "What do you remember?"

I shake my head. "I had dinner in Seattle. I left around ten. I stopped for gas on my way home. That's it. You?"

He stares at the ground, his brows drawn together. "I was at the hospital, just leaving my shift. The sun had just come up. I remember stopping to look at it. Then nothing."

"This doesn't make sense. Why would someone bring the two of us here?"

I think about the lighters and the key and the carousel room, and then I push it from my brain. A coincidence. But I want to laugh even as I think it.

"I don't know," Isaac says. I don't think I've ever heard him say that. I think about all the times in my life I've counted on him for answers—demanded answers—and he always has them.

But that was then…

He runs his hand over the stubble on his jaw, and I notice the deep purple bruises on his wrists where his bindings dug into his skin. How long had he been tied up like that? How long had I been unconscious?

"We need to get warm," Isaac says.

"I made a fire … in the room up the ladder."

We search for the thermostat. I notice how white his knuckles are around the handle of the knife. We find it in the carousel room, behind the door. He turns on the heat.

"If there is power, we must be close to something," I say hopefully. He shakes his head.

"Not necessarily. It could be a generator. This might not last."

I nod, but I don't believe him.

We climb up to the round room to sit by the fire and wait for the house to heat. He makes me go first. Once I am up, he glances over his shoulder one last time and then quickly climbs up to join me. We close the trapdoor and lock it. We try to scoot the armoire over it, but that's bolted too. The fire I built is puttering out. There are three extra logs. I reach for one and place it on the flames while Isaac takes a look around.

"Where do you think we are?" I ask when he comes to sit on the floor next to me. He sets the knife down between us. This makes me feel better. I don't trust anything yet. If he's not hiding his weapons from me, that's a good thing.

"This much snow? Who knows? We could be anywhere."

We are nowhere, I think.

"How did you get out of your bindings?"

"What?" I don't understand what he's saying, then I realize that he thinks I was tied up too.

"I didn't have any," I say.

He turns his head to look at me. We are so close the vapors of our breath are mingling mid-air. He has dark stubble on his face. I want to rub my palm across it just so I can feel something sharp and real.

His eyes, always intense, are two dark thinking pools. He hardly ever blinks. It unnerved me in the beginning when I first met him, but after a while I grew to appreciate it. It was like he was afraid to miss something. His patients, who also noticed it, used to say they appreciated his lack of blinking in surgery.

You know Doctor Asterholder is never going to nick a vein, was the running joke in the hospital.

Why wasn't I gagged and blindfolded, with my arms tied to the posts of my bed?

"So you could free me," he says, reading my thoughts.

A chill runs up my spine.

"Isaac, I'm afraid."

He shifts closer, puts an arm around my shoulders. "Me too."

When the house is warmer and our limbs feel like they can move again, we unlock the trap door and go downstairs. We sit facing each other at the table in the kitchen. Our eyes have the glazed vacant look of two people in shock. Though I have no doubt we'd spring, quick as cats, if we needed to. I touch the handle of my knife. Both Isaac and I have set our knives on the table in front of us; the knives are pointed in a face off. He doesn't have to say anything for me to know that there is suspicion on his face. I wear it too. We look silly; abducted and locked in a house, waiting for whoever did this to return.

"Ransom," I say. My voice is raspy. It catches in my throat before I can say anything else. I swallow and look up at Isaac.

His eyes dart to the corners of the room. His leg is bouncing up and down, I can feel the vibrations of it in the wood. Every few minutes his eyes move to the window, then back to the door.

"Maybe…"

I catch the pause after *maybe*. He wants to say more, but he doesn't trust me. And if I were to really examine my theory it would most likely fall apart. Kidnappings made for ransom were fast and messy; guns pointed at your head, urgent demands. Not keypads on the door and enough food to last through one of George R.R. Martin's long winters. I lay my hands flat on the table, fingertips pointing inward, and rest my chin over them. My pinkie is touching the handle of my knife.

We wait.

The cabin is so eerily silent we would hear a car or person approaching from a mile away, but we keep checking anyway. *Waiting … waiting.* Finally, Isaac gets up. I hear him walking from room to room. I wonder if he is looking for something or if he just needs to move. I realize it's probably the latter. He can't sit still when he's nervous. When he comes back in the kitchen, I break the silence.

"What if they're not coming back?"

He doesn't answer me for the longest time.

"There is a pantry, there—" he nods toward a narrow door to the left of the table. "It's stocked with enough food to last for months. There is a fifty-pound bag of flour. But the wood closet only has enough wood to last a few weeks. Four at most if we ration it."

I don't want to think about the gargantuan bag of flour, so I pretend I didn't hear him. The wood, however, bothers me. I'd rather not freeze to death. There are plenty of trees outside. If we could get outside, that is. We'd have wood.

"The carousel room," he says. "Do you find it strange?" His voice is clear, precise. It's the one he uses with his patients. I'm not one of his patients and I don't appreciate being spoken to like one.

"Yes," I say simply.

"The book?" His voice moves to gruff. "There was nothing in there about the carousel, was there?"

"No," I say. "There wasn't"

There didn't need to be.

"Do you think this could be one of your fans? Someone obsessed?"

I don't want to think about that, but it has already crossed my mind. I didn't want to be the one responsible for this.

"It's possible," I say cautiously. "But that doesn't explain you."

"Have you been getting any threats, strange letters?"

"No, Isaac."

He looks up when I say his name.

"Senna, you need to think carefully. This could make a difference."

"I have!" I snap. "There have been no letters out of the norm, no e-mails. Nothing!"

He nods, walks to the fridge.

"What are you doing?" I ask, spinning in my seat to watch him.

"Making us something to eat."

"I'm not hungry," I say quickly.

"We don't know how long we've been out. You need to eat and drink something or you'll dehydrate."

He starts taking things out of the fridge and putting them on the counter. He finds a glass, fills it with water from the faucet, and brings it to me. It's a funny color.

I take it. How can I eat or drink at a time like this? I force the water down because he's standing in front of me, waiting.

I stare blindly at the snow outside as he stands at the stove. The stove is gas; brand new from the looks of it.

When he comes back to the table he's carrying two plates, each piled with scrambled eggs. The smell makes me sick. He sets it down in front of me and I pick up the fork.

Weapons, we have so many: forks, knives … you'd think if someone were coming back, they wouldn't provide us with these things to attack them with. I voice my thoughts, and Isaac nods.

"I know."

Of course he had already thought of this. Always two steps ahead…

"Your hair is different," he says. "It took me a minute to recognize you … upstairs."

I blink at him. Are we really talking about my hair? I feel self-conscious about my white streak. I make sure it's tucked away, behind my ear.

"I grew it out."

Put food in mouth, chew, swallow, put food in mouth, chew, swallow.

We don't speak about my hair anymore. When I am finished eating, I announce that I need to use the restroom. I ask him to come with me. The only bathroom in the house is the one in the bedroom where I found Isaac. He waits outside the door, knife in hand. Before we leave the kitchen he upgrades to a larger one. It is almost funny, but not. Big knife, big wound. I had settled for a steak knife myself. They are easy to handle and sharp as hell.

I relieve myself and step over to the sink to wash my hands. There is a mirror hanging above it. I look at myself and flinch. My hair is limp and greasy, the inch-wide streak of grey that showed up when I was twelve is startling against my pale face. I have done everything to rid myself of it: dying it, cutting it, pulling it out strand by strand. Color won't take to the grey. I have sat in dozens of chairs over the years and every stylist has said the same thing. "It doesn't make sense … it won't take the color." No matter what I do, it always comes back like a stubborn weed. Eventually, I let it be. The old part of me won out.

I turn on the water, it sputters like the croup for several seconds before a weak brown stream comes dribbling out. I splash it over my face, drink some. It tastes funny—like rust and dirt.

When I walk out of the bathroom, Isaac hands me his butcher knife. I have to put my knife down to hold it, since my wrist is a gimp.

"Me too," he says. "Don't let the bad guys get us."

I grin—I actually grin—as he closes the door. His humor always shows up at the oddest moments. I thought I was the bad guy, I didn't think I'd ever be at the mercy of one.

When he comes out, his face has been washed, too, and his hair is damp. There is a trickle of water running from his temple.

"Now what?" I say.

"Are you tired? We could take turns. Do you want to sleep?"

"Hell no!"

He laughs. "Yeah, I get ya."

There is a long awkward pause.

"I'd like to take a shower," I say. What I don't add is, *in case the sick fuck touched me…*

He nods. I climb up the ladder to get something clean to wear. It makes me sick, putting on clothes that someone chose and put here for me. I wish I had my own, but not even the pajamas I'm still wearing are mine. I study the contents of the wardrobe. Almost every article of clothing is something I would have chosen for myself—except for the color. There is too much of that. This is creepy. Who would know me well enough to buy me clothes? Clothes that I actually like? I pluck a long sleeve yoga top from a hanger and find the matching pants underneath it. In a drawer are a variety of panties and bras.

Oh God!

I decide to go without either. I can't wear underwear that some sicko bought and folded into a drawer. It would feel like was touching me … there. I slam the drawer closed.

Isaac helps me down the ladder. Since my attack on the door, my wrist has swollen to twice its size.

"Keep it elevated and out of the hot water," he says before I go into the bathroom.

I find soap and shampoo under the sink. Generic stuff. The soap is white and smells like laundry. I keep the shower to five minutes even though I want to stay longer. The brownish water never gets really hot and it has a strange smell.

I get out and dry myself with the lemon-colored towel that is hanging on the towel rack. Such a cheerful color. Such an ironic color. And so thoughtfully hung here for us. I rub at my arms and legs trying to capture all of the drops. Yellow to soften the blow of the snow and the prison and the abduction. Maybe whoever brought us here thought that the color of this towel would stave off depression. I drop it on the floor, disgusted. Then I laugh, hard and shrill.

I hear Isaac knock lightly on the door.

"You okay, Senna?"

His voice is muffled. "I'm fine," I call out. Then I laugh so hard and loud he opens the door and lets himself in.

"I'm fine," I say to his concerned face, trying to stifle my laughter. I catch the laughter behind my hand as tears begin to leak from my eyes. I'm laughing so hard I have to hold myself up by the sink.

"I'm fine," I gasp. "Isn't that the craziest thing you've ever heard? Like I can be fine. Are you fine?"

I see the muscles in his cheek flicker. His eye color is metallic, like a tin can.

He reaches for me, but I bat his hand away. I've stopped laughing.

"Don't touch me." I say it louder and harsher than I intended.

He tucks his lips in and nods. He gets it. I'm crazy. No new revelations there. I sit on the bed with the knife and stare at the door while he takes his turn. If someone were to walk into the room right now, I'd be useless—knife or not. I feel like my body is here, but the rest of me is down a deep hole. I can't reconcile the two.

Isaac takes an even shorter shower than I do. I wake up a little when he gets out. He walks out in a towel and heads to the wardrobe. I see him looking at the clothes the same way I did. He doesn't say anything, but he rubs the cotton of a black shirt between his thumb and forefinger. I shiver. Even if this did have something to do with one of my fans, why Isaac? I stare at the knife while he gets dressed in the bathroom. It's brand new; the blade shiny spotless. *Bought just for us*, I think.

For lack of anything better to do we go back downstairs to wait. Isaac heats up two cans of soup and puts some frozen rolls in the oven. I am actually hungry when he hands me the bowl.

"It's still light outside. It should be dark by now."

He looks down at his food, purposefully avoiding my eyes.

"Why Isaac?"

Still, he doesn't look at me.

"Do you think we're in Alaska? How they hell did they get across the Canadian border with us?"

I get up and pace the kitchen.

"Isaac?"

"I don't know, Senna." His voice is terse. I stop pacing and look at him. He keeps his head bent toward his food, but lifts his eyes to my face. Finally, he sighs and sets his spoon down. He spins it slowly counter clockwise until it's come full circle.

"It's possible we're in Alaska," he says. "Why don't you get some rest? I'll stay up and keep watch."

I nod. I'm not tired. Or maybe I am. I lie down on the couch and curl my legs up to my chest. I am so afraid.

No one comes. Not for two days, then three. Isaac and I barely speak. We eat, we shower, we move from room to room like restless shadows. As soon as we walk into a room, our eyes go to the spot where we've hidden the knives. *Will we need to use them? How soon? Who will live and who will die?* It's the worst form of torture a person can imagine—the wait to die. I see the not knowing in the dark circles that have developed around Isaac's eyes. He sleeps less than I do. I know I can't look any different; it's eating at us.

Fear

Fear

Fear

We quench our worry with futile trying; trying to break the windows, trying to open the front door, trying to not lose our minds. We are so exhausted from trying that we stare at things … for hours at a time: a drawing of two sparrows that hangs in the living room, the bright red toaster, the keypad at the front door which is the portal to our freedom. Isaac stares at the snow more than anything else. He stands at the sink and looks out the window where it falls slowly.

On day four I am so tired of staring at things that I ask Isaac about his wife. I notice that his wedding ring is missing, and I wonder if *he* took it off, or if *they* did. Almost instinctively his fingers reach for the ghost of the ring. *'They' took it off*, I think.

We are sitting at the kitchen table, our breakfast of oatmeal recently consumed. My nails—bitten down to the quick—are stinging. He's just commented on how large and awkward the table is: a big, round block of wood supported by a circular base thicker than two tree trunks.

Initially he looks alarmed that I've asked. Then something breaks open in his eyes. He doesn't have time to hide it. I see every last speck of emotion, and it hurts me.

"She's an oncologist," he says. I nod, my mouth dry. That's a good fit for him.

"What's her name?"

I already know her name.

"Daphne" he says. *Daphne Akela.* "We've been married for two years. You met her once."

Yes, I remember.

He scratches his head, right above his ear, then smooths what he's disturbed with the heel of his hand.

"What would Daphne be doing right now … with you missing?" I ask, folding my legs underneath me.

He clears his throat. "She's a mess, Senna."

It's a matter-of-fact statement with an obvious answer. I don't know why I asked, except to be cruel. No one is looking for me, except maybe the media. *Bestselling Author Vanishes.* Isaac has people. People who love him.

"What about you?" he says, turning it on me. "Are you married?"

I tug on my grey, wind it around my finger, slide it behind my ear.

"Do you really need to ask me that?"

He laughs coldly. "No, I suppose not. Were you seeing anyone?"

"Nope."

He folds in his lips, nods. He knows me, too … sort of. "What happened to—"

I cut him off. "I haven't spoken to him in a long time."

"Even after you wrote the book?"

I put my crusty oatmeal spoon in my mouth and suck off the hardened oats. "Even after the book," I say, not meeting his eyes. I want to ask if he read it, but I'm too chicken.

"He probably has a Daphne, too, by now. You're not human unless you pair off with someone, right? Find your soulmate or the love of your life—or whatever." I wave it away like I don't care.

"People have a need to feel connected to someone else," Isaac says. "There is nothing wrong with that. There is also nothing wrong with being too burned to stay away from it."

My head jerks up. What? Does he think he's the soul whisperer?

"I don't need anyone," I assure him.

"I know."

"No you don't," I insist.

I feel bad for snapping at him, especially since I initiated the conversation. But I don't like what he's insinuating—that he *knows* me or something.

Isaac looks down at his empty bowl. "You're so self-assured, sometimes I forget to check on you. Are you okay, Senna? Have you been—"

I cut him off. "I've been fine, Isaac. Let's not go there." I stand up. "I'm going to mess with the keypad."

I can feel his eyes on me as I leave. I stand at the door and start pressing random number combinations. We have been taking turns trying to guess the four-digit code, a pretty stupid idea since there are ten thousand possible combinations, except there is nothing else to do, so why not? Isaac found a pen and we write the codes we try on the wall next to the door so we don't use repeats.

We have hidden knives in every room of the house: a steak knife under each mattress, a serrated knife the length of my forearm underneath the couch cushions in the little living room, a butcher knife in the bathroom under the sink, a carving knife in the upstairs hallway on the windowsill. *We have to find a better place for the upstairs hallway knife*, I keep thinking. Anyone can grab it. A*nyone. Grab … it…*

My finger is suspended over the button that reads 5. I can feel my chest constricting slowly, like there is an invisible boa constrictor giving me a snake hug. My breath is coming quickly, too quickly. I turn until my back is against the door and slide down the wall until I'm sitting on the floor. I can't catch my breath. I am drowning in a sea of air; it is all around me but I can't get enough of it into my lungs to live.

Isaac must hear my wheezing. He shoots around the corner and crouches in front of me.

"Senna … Senna! Look at me!" I find his face, try to focus on his eyes. If I can only catch my breath…

He takes my hand, his voice imploring me. "Senna, breathe. Nice and slow. Can you hear my voice? Try to match your breathing to my voice."

I try. His voice is distinct. I could pick it out in a lineup of voices. It's an octave above an alto. Deep enough to lull you to sleep, lilting enough to keep you awake. I follow the patterns of his speech as he speaks to me—the dragged out consonants, the slight rasp over his "e's". I watch his mouth. His incisors slightly overlap his front two teeth, which also overlap; a perfectly imperfect flaw. Gradually, my breathing slows. I focus on his hands, which are holding mine. Surgeon's hands. The best hands to be in. I trace the veins that run along the backs of them. His thumbs are rubbing circles on the skin between my thumb and forefinger. He has square nails. Manly. So many of the men I've dated have had oval nail beds. Square is better. I feel my lungs open. I take in air hungrily. He's helping me. *Square is better*, I say over and over again. It is my mantra. *Square is better.*

I am exhausted. Isaac doesn't skip a beat. He picks me up and carries me to the sofa. He's good at taking care of people. He takes care of you without you having to ask. He disappears into the kitchen and comes back a minute later with a glass of water.

I take it from him. "He knew to buy the exact clothes sizes that we wear, but he didn't know I have asthma?"

Isaac frowns. "Have you checked in all of the cabinets for an inhaler?"

"Yes. The first day."

He looks at the floor between his feet.

"Maybe he didn't want you to have an inhaler."

I grunt. "So, this sicko kidnaps me and brings me out here to die of an asthma attack? Anti-climactic."

"I don't know," he says. It's hard for a doctor to say those words. He told me that once. Doctors were supposed to have the answers. "None of this makes sense," he says. "Why someone would take me … put me here with you. How did they even make the connection between us?"

I don't know the answers to any of this. I turn my head away. Look at the picture of the sparrows.

"You need to take it easy. Be—"

I cut him off.

"I'm okay, Isaac." I place a hand on his arm and immediately pull it away. He looks at the spot where I touched him, then stands up and walks out of the room. I press everything together—my eyes, my palms, my lips, the hole inside of me that will never be sewn back together.

"Isaac," I breathe. But he doesn't hear me.

I start sleeping in the room with the trapdoor after the first week. It's warmer up there. Isaac makes me lock it as soon as my feet disappear up the ladder. "Just in case," he says. "They have a key too, but it will buy you time." *Sure. Great.*

He checks it after I turn the key, to make sure no one can get in. I always wait for the rattle before I move to the bed. I sleep with a butcher knife in my hand. Dangerous, but not as dangerous as your kidnapper coming into the prison he made for you and…

Every morning I wake up and feel fear, though I am never sure when it's morning or night or midday. The sun shines continuously. I am always afraid that when I climb down the ladder Isaac won't be there. He always is—ruffled and gaunt standing by the coffee machine. There is always fresh coffee in the pot when I come down. I can smell it as I descend the stairs. I always know Isaac is fine, and alive, and still there from the smell of the coffee. One morning when I climb down the ladder I don't smell it. I run for the stairs almost breaking my neck as I jump down in twos. When I get to the kitchen I find him asleep at the table, his head resting on his arms. I make the coffee that day. My hands are steady, but my heart won't stop racing.

One day (evening?), Isaac climbs up the ladder and lowers himself next to where I am sitting, cross-legged in front of the fire. I have been thinking about suicide. Not my own, just suicide. There are so many ways. I don't know why people are so uncreative when they kill themselves.

We usually don't leave the front door unguarded, but I can tell he wants to talk. I unfold my legs and stretch them toward the fire, wiggling my toes. We are running out of firewood, and Isaac says he's not sure how big the generator is, but we could be running out of fuel in that too.

"What are you thinking?" I ask, watching his face.

"The carousel room, Senna. I think it means something."

"I don't want to talk about the carousel room. It freaks me out."

His head snaps sharply toward me. "We're gonna talk about it. Unless you'd like to stay locked up here forever."

I shake my head, twist my skunk streak around my finger. "It's a coincidence. It doesn't mean anything."

He pulls his lips back from his teeth and his head rocks from side to side. "Daphne is pregnant."

It's that silent moment when you hear the rushing of water in your eyes. My eyes jerk to his face.

"Eight weeks the last time I saw her." He licks his lips and turns to look at me. "We did three rounds of in vitro to get pregnant, had two miscarriages." He rubs his forehead. "Daphne is pregnant and I need to talk about the carousel room."

I nod dumbly.

I feel something. I push it away. Bury it.

"Who knows about what happened?" he asks, gently. I watch the fire eat the logs. For a minute I'm not sure which instance he's referring to. There were so many. *The carousel,* I remind myself. It's such a strange memory. Nothing fancy. But private.

"Only you. That's why it seems unlikely…" I look at him. "Did you—?"

"No … no, Senna, never. That was our moment. I didn't even want to think about it after."

I believe him. For a long second our eyes are locked and the past seems to float between us—a frail soap bubble. I break eye contact first, looking down at my socks. Patterned socks, not white. I searched for white, but all that was stocked for me were knee length patterned socks. A deviation from my character. I wear my new, colorful socks over my tights. Today, they are purple and grey. Diagonal stripes.

"Senna…?"

"Yes, sorry. I was thinking about my socks."

He laughs through his nose, like he'd rather not laugh. I'd rather he not laugh, too.

"Isaac, what happened on the carousel was … personal. I don't tell people things. You know that."

"Okay, let's forget how this … this … person knows. Let's assume he does. Maybe it's a clue."

"A clue?" I say in disbelief. "To what? Our freedom? Like this is a game?"

Isaac nods. I study his face, look for a joke. But, there are no jokes in this house. There are just two stolen people, clutching knives as they sleep.

"And they call *me* the fiction writer," I say it to make him angry, because I know he's right.

I make to stand up, but he grabs my wrist and gently pulls me back down. His eyes travel across the span of my nose and my cheeks. He's looking at my freckles. He always did that, like they were works of art rather than screwed up pigment. Isaac doesn't have freckles. He has soft eyes that dip down at the outer corners and two front teeth that overlap slightly. He's average looking and beautiful at the same time. If you look close enough, you see how intense his features are. Each one speaks to you in a different way. Or maybe I'm just a writer.

"We are not here for ransom," he insists. "They want something from us."

"Like what?" I sound like a petulant child. I lift the back of my hand to my lips and bite the skin on my knuckles. "No one wants anything from me—except more stories, maybe."

Isaac raises his eyebrows. I think of Annie Wilkes and her rooty-patooties. *No way.*

"They didn't leave me a typewriter," I point out. "Or even a pen and paper. This isn't about my writing."

He doesn't look convinced. I'd rather steer him toward the carousel, especially if it mean he'll stops looking at me like I have the magical key to get out of here.

"The carousel is creepy," I say. That's all it takes to get his theory fuel going. I half listen to his surmisings—no, I don't listen at all. I pretend to listen and count the knots in the wood walls instead. Eventually, I hear my name.

"Tell me how you remember it," he urges me.

I shake my head. "No. What good will that do?"

I am not in the mood to revisit those instances of my life. They trudge up the other stuff. The stuff that landed me in the plushy couch of a therapist.

"Fine." He stands up this time. "I'm going to make dinner. If you're staying up here, lock the trapdoor."

This time he doesn't stay to check if I do. He's all over the place. I hate him.

We eat in silence. He defrosted hamburgers and opened a can of green beans. He's rationing our food. I can tell. I push the beans around and eat hamburger by using the side of my fork to cut it into pieces. Isaac eats with a knife and a fork, slicing with one, spearing with the other. I asked him about it once, and he said, "There are tools for everything. I am a doctor. I use the right tool for the right purpose."

He is aggravated with me. I shoot him a look every few bites, but his eyes are on his food. When I am finished, I stand up and take my plate to the sink. I wash and dry it. Put it back in the cabinet. I stand behind him as he finishes up his meal, and watch the back of his head. I can see grey in his hair, it's mostly at his temples. Just a little bit. The last time I saw him there had been no grey. Maybe in vitro put it there. Or his wife. Or surgery. I was born with mine, so who knows? When he pushes back from the table, I turn around quickly and busy myself with wiping the counter. Three wipes in and the chore seems foolish. *I'm cleaning my captor's house.* It feels a little like betrayal: *live in filth or clean your prison.* I should burn it to the ground. I finish wiping, rinse the rag, fold it neatly and hang it over the faucet. Before I go back upstairs, I grab an armful of wood from the wood closet. We all but collide at the foot of the stairs.

"Let me carry it for you."

I cling to my wood.

"Don't you have to stay to guard the door?"

"No one is coming, Senna." He looks almost sad. He tries to take the wood from me. I yank my arms out of reach.

"You don't know that," I retort. He looks at my freckles.

"Hush," he says, softly. "They would have come by now. It's been fourteen days."

I shake my head. "It hasn't been that long…" I mentally do the calculations. We've been here for … fourteen days. He's right.

Fourteen. My God. Where are the search parties? Where are the police? Where are we? But, most importantly, where is the person who brought us here? I yield my wood. Isaac half smiles at me. I follow him up the stairs and climb the ladder to the attic room so he can hand me the logs.

"Night, Senna."

I look at the bright sun streaming into the window behind me.

"Morning, Isaac."

We are nowhere.

Isaac is losing it. Most days he paces in front of the kitchen window for hours, his eyes on the snow like it's speaking to him. It looks like he's seeing something, but there is nothing to see—only mounds of white in the middle of white, spread out over white, covered in white. We are nowhere and snow doesn't speak. I hide from him up in my attic bedroom, and sometimes when I'm tired of that I lie on the floor in the carousel room and stare at the horses. He doesn't come in here, says it creeps him out. I try to hum songs, because that's what one of my characters would do, but it makes me feel nutty.

No matter where I am, I can feel him pulsing through the walls. He's always been intense. That's what makes him a good doctor. He's trying to figure out why we are here, why no one has come. I should, too, I guess, but I can't focus. Every time I start wondering why someone would do this my head starts throbbing. If I press at my thoughts I will implode. *Like a grapefruit in the microwave,* I think.

When we are in the same room his eyes press on me. They press like fingers into my flesh—harder and harder until I pull away, run to my trapdoor and hide. He doesn't come up to my room anymore. He started sleeping in the room where I found him tied up, instead of on the couch. It happened after the six-week mark. He just moved in there one night and stopped guarding the door.

"What are you doing?" I said, following him to the bed. He pulled off his shirt and I quickly averted my eyes.

"Going to bed."

I watched in bewilderment as he tossed his shirt aside.

"What if … what about…?"

"No one is coming," he said, ripping the sheets aside and climbing in. He wouldn't look at me. I wondered what he didn't want me to see in his eyes.

I hadn't argued with him. I'd carried my blankets and my knife downstairs and sat on the sofa, my eyes on the door. Isaac may be letting his guard down, but I wasn't going to. I wasn't going to trust my prison. I sure as hell wasn't going to accept this as permanent. I brewed a pot of coffee, grabbed some beef jerky and took watch. When he'd come downstairs the next morning, and found me still awake, he'd acted surprised. He brought me a fresh cup of coffee and some oatmeal, then sent me off to bed.

"Good morning, Isaac."

"Good night, Senna."

I hadn't slept. I could go ungodly amounts of time without sleep. Instead, I'd pulled a chair to the window that sat directly above the kitchen and watched the snow with him.

Now, a week later, I wake up with clarity as sharp and cold as the snow outside my window. Sometimes, when I am writing a book, I'll go to sleep with a plot hole in my story that I don't know how to fix. When I wake up, I know. It's as if it were there all along and I just needed the right sleep to access the answer.

I am on my feet in an instant, running to the trapdoor barefoot and dropping from the ladder before I reach the last rung. I take the stairs two at a time and come to a halt in the doorway of the kitchen. Isaac is sitting at the table, his head in his hands. His hair is spiked up like he's been running his fingers through it all night. I eye his knee bouncing beneath the table at jackrabbit speed. He's going through a kidnapped version of the seven stages of grief. By the look of his bloodshot eyes, I'd say he was well into *Acceptance.*

"Isaac."

He looks up. Despite my need to know what he is feeling, I avert my eyes. I lost my privilege to his thoughts long ago. My feet are freezing, I wish I'd put on socks. I walk to the window, and point at the snow.

"The windows in this house," I say, "they all face the same direction."

The fog in his eyes seems to clear a little. He pushes back from the table and comes to stand beside me.

"Yeah..." he says. Of course he knew that too. Just because I was in a haze didn't mean that he was.

He has more hair on his face than I have ever seen on him. I direct my eyes away from him, and we look at the snow together. We are so close I could extend a pinkie and touch his hand.

"What's behind the house?" he asks.

There is some silence between us before I say, "The generator..."

"Do you think...?"

"Yeah, I do."

We look at each other. I have goose pimples along my arms.

"He can refuel it," I say. "I think that as long as we stay put, he will refill the generator. If we figure out the code and get out, we will lose power and freeze."

He thinks long and hard about this. It sounds right. To me, at least.

"Why?" asks Isaac. "Why would you think that?"

"It's in the Bible," I say, and then automatically flinch.

"You're going to have to break this one down for me, Senna," he says, frowning. His voice is terse. He's losing patience with me, which isn't really fair since we are both sinking in the same ship.

"Have you seen the picture hanging next to the door?" He nods. Of course. How could he miss it? There are seven prints hanging on the walls of this house. When you spend six weeks locked up somewhere, you spend a lot of time examining the art on the walls.

"It's a painting by F. Cayley. It's supposed to be of Adam and Eve when they find out they have to leave Eden."

He shakes his head. "I thought it was just of two very depressed people on the beach."

I smile.

"We are like the first two people," I say.

"Adam and Eve?" He's already so full of disbelief I don't even want to tell him the rest.

I shrug. "Sure."

"Go on," he says.

"God put them in the garden and told them not to eat the forbidden fruit, remember?"

Now it's Isaac's turn to shrug. "Yeah, I guess. Sunday school one-o- one."

"Once they were tempted and ate the fruit they were on their own, exiled from God's provision and his protection in the place he created for them." When Isaac doesn't say anything, I go on. "They leave perfection and have to fend for themselves—hunt, garden, experience cold and death and childbirth."

I flush after the last word leaves my mouth. It was dumb of me to mention childbirth considering Daphne and their unborn baby. But Isaac doesn't skip a beat.

"So you're saying," he says, crinkling his eyebrows together, "that so long as we stay here—in the place our kidnapper provided for us—we will be safe and he will keep the heat and food coming?"

"It's just a wild guess, Isaac. I don't really know."

"So what's the forbidden fruit?"

I tap my finger on the tabletop. "The keypad, maybe…"

"This is sick," he says. "And if one painting means that much, what else is hidden in here?"

I don't want to think about it. "I'll make dinner tonight," I say.

I look out the window as I peel potatoes over the sink. And then I look down at the peelings, all piled up and gross looking. We should eat those. We will probably be starving soon, wishing we had a sliver of potato skin. I scoop up shreds and hold them in my palm, not sure what to do with them. I counted the potatoes before I chose four of the smallest ones out of the fifty-pound bag. Seventy potatoes. How long could we stretch that? And the flour, and rice and oatmeal? It seemed like a lot, but we had no idea how long we'd be imprisoned here. *Imprisoned. Here.*

I eat the skins. At least they won't go to waste that way.

God. I am grimacing and gagging on my potato skin when I drop the potato I'm holding into the sink and press the heel of my hand to my forehead. I have to focus. Stay positive. I can't let myself sink into that dark place. My therapist tried to teach me techniques to cope with emotional overload. Why hadn't I listened? I remember something about a garden … walking through it and touching flowers. Was that what she'd said? I try to picture the garden now, but all I see are the shadows that the trees make and the possibility that someone is hiding behind a hedge. I am so fucked up.

"Need help?"

I look over my shoulder and see Isaac. I'd sent him upstairs to take a nap. He looks rested. Surgeons are used to the lack of sleep. He's taken a shower and his hair is still wet.

"Sure." I point to the remaining potato and he picks up a knife.

"Feels like old times," I half smile. "Except I'm not catatonic and you don't have that perpetually worried look on your face."

"Don't I? This situation is kind of dire."

I put my knife down. "No, actually. You look calm. Why is that?"

"Acceptance. Embrace the suck."

"Really?"

I feel his smile. Across the two feet of air between us and a sink speckled with new potato skins. For a minute my chest constricts, then the peeling is done and he moves away, taking his soap smell with him.

I have a need to know where a person is in a room at all times. I hear him in the fridge, he crosses the room, sits down at the table. By the noises he's making I can tell that he has two glasses and a bottle of something. I wash my hands and turn away from the sink.

He is sitting at the table with a bottle of whiskey in his hands.

My mouth drops open. "Where did you find that?"

He grins. "Back of the pantry behind a container of croutons."

"I hate croutons."

He nods like I've said something profound.

We take our first shot as the meat is simmering in the skillet. I think it's deer. Isaac says it's cow. It really doesn't matter since this sort of situation steals most of your appetite. We don't really taste anything—deer or cow.

We both pretend that the drinking is fun instead of a necessity to cope. We click glasses and avoid eye contact. It feels like a game; click your glass, shoot whiskey, stare at the wall with a stiff smile. We eat our meal in near silence, faces hanging like limp sunflowers over our plates. So much for fun. We are coping willy-nilly. Tonight it's with whiskey. Tomorrow it might be with sleep.

When we are finished, Isaac clears the table and washes our plates. I stay where I am, stretching my arm across the wood and resting my head on the table to watch him. My head is spinning from the whiskey and my eyes are watering. Not watering. Crying. *You're not crying, Senna. You don't know how.*

"Senna?" Isaac dries his hands on a dishtowel and straddles the bench to face me. "You're leaking fluid otherwise known as tears. Are you aware of this?"

I sniff pathetically. "I just hate croutons so much…"

He clears his throat and squashes a smile.

"As your doctor I'd advise you to sit up."

I sniff and straighten myself until I am in a sort of upright slump.

We are both straddling the bench, now, facing each other. Isaac reaches out both thumbs and uses them to clear my cheeks of tears. He stops when he is cupping my face between his hands.

"It hurts me when you cry." His voice is so earnest, so open. I can't speak like this. Everything I say sounds sterile and robotic.

I try to look away, but he holds my face so that I can't move. I don't like being this close to him. He starts seeping into my pores. It tingles.

"I'm crying, but I don't feel anything," I assure him.

He pulls his lips into a tight line and nods.

"Yes, I know. That's what hurts me the most."

After the deal with the F. Cayley print, I take inventory of everything in the house. We could be missing something. I wish I had a pen, some paper, but our single Bic ran out of ink a long time ago… so I have to use my good ol' memory for this one.

There are sixty-three books scattered throughout the house. I've picked up each one, flipped through the pages, touched the numbers at the top right corners. I started reading two of them—both classics that I've already read—but I can't get my mind to focus. I have twenty-three light, colorful sweaters, six pairs of jeans, six pairs of sweatpants, twelve pairs of socks, eighteen shirts, twelve pairs of yoga pants. One pair of rain boots—in Isaac's size. There are six additional pieces of artwork on the walls, other than the F. Cayley; each of the others is by the Ukranian illusionist, Oleg Shuplyak. In the living room is "Sparrows" one of his milder pieces. But scattered across the rest of the house are the blurred faces of famous historical figures, blended almost indecipherably with landscapes. The one in the attic room disturbs me the most. I've tried to pry it from the wall with a butter knife, but it's cemented so firmly I can't get it to budge. It depicts a hooded man, his outstretched arms wielding two scythes. His mouth gapes and his eyes are two dark, empty holes. At first all you see is the eerie emptiness—the impending violence. Then your eyes adjust and the skull comes into view: the dark sockets of eyes between the scythes, the teeth, which seconds ago were simply a pattern on a garment. My kidnapper hung death in my bedroom. The sentiment makes me sick. The rest of the prints scattered throughout the house include: Hitler and the dragon, Freud and the lake, Darwin under the bridge with the mysterious cloaked figure. My least favorite is "Winter" in which a man is riding a yak over a snow-covered village while two eyes peer coldly at me. That one feels like a message.

When I have counted everything in my closet and Isaac's, I start counting things in the kitchen. I note the colors of the furniture and the walls. I don't know what I'm looking for, but I need to do something with my brain. When I run out of things to count, I talk to Isaac. He makes us coffee like he used to, and we sit at the table.

"Why did you want to fly away on your red bike?"

He raises his eyebrows. He's not used to questions from me.

"I don't know anything about you," I say.

"You never seemed to want to."

That stings. It's not entirely untrue. I have that whole *stay the hell away from me* thing going on.

"I didn't."

I count the kitchen cabinets. I forgot to do that.

"Why not?" He spins his coffee cup in a circle, and lifts it to his mouth. Before he can take a sip he sets it down again.

I have to take a moment to think about that one.

"It's just who I am."

"Because you choose to be?"

"This conversation was supposed to be about you."

He finally takes a sip of his coffee. Then he pushes his mug across the table to me. I've already finished mine. It's a peace offering.

"My dad was a drinker. He used to rough up my mom. Not so much a unique story," he shrugs. "What about you?"

I consider pulling my usual stunts of avoid and retreat, but I decide to surprise him instead. It gets boring always being the same.

"My mom left before I hit puberty. She was a writer. She said my dad sucked all of the life out of her, but I think suburban life did. After she left, my dad went a little crazy."

I take a sip of Isaac's coffee and avoid his eyes.

"What kind of crazy?"

I purse my lips. "Rules. Lots of rules. He became emotionally volatile." I finish off his coffee and he stands up to get the whiskey. He pours us each a shot.

"You trying to keep me talking, Doctor?"

"Yes, ma'am."

"Tequila works better."

He smiles. "I'll just run down to the liquor store and grab a bottle."

I take my shot and spill my guts. I'm not even drunk. Saphira would be so proud of me. I crinkle my nose when I think of her. What does she think about all of this? She probably thinks I dipped out of town. She was always accusing me of ... what was the word she used? Running?

"Tell me something about your life with him," Isaac urges. I purse my lips. "Hmmm ... so much fuckedupness. Where should I start?"

He blinks at me.

"A week before I graduated from high school he found a chip in one of our drinking glasses. He came storming into my room, demanding to know how it got there. When I couldn't give him an answer he refused to talk to me. For three weeks. He didn't even come to my graduation. My dad. He can make a drinking glass feel like a teen pregnancy."

I hold out my mug and Isaac refills me.

"I hate whiskey," I say.

"Me too as well."

I cock my head.

"Hush," he says. "You don't get to judge my turn of phrase."

I lay my arm across the table and rest my head on it.

He looks less and less like a doctor nowadays with his scruffy face and long hair. Come to think of it, he's acting less like one too. Maybe this is rockstar Isaac. I don't ever remember him drinking during the time we spent together. I lift my head and rest my chin on my arm.

I want to ask if he had a drinking problem back in the day—when he was actually living his tattoo. But it's none of my business. We all medicate with something. He notices me looking at him funny. He's on his fifth shot.

"Something you want to ask me?"

"How many more bottles of that stuff do we have?" I ask. The one he's holding has a third left. I'm thinking we might have some darker days. We need to save the happy juice for sadder times.

He shrugs. "What does it matter?"

"Hey," I say. "We are sharing family memories. Bonding. Don't be depressing."

He laughs, and sets the bottle on the counter. I wonder if he'd notice if I hid it. I watch him walk into the living room. I'm not sure if I should follow him or give him space. In the end, I go upstairs. It's not my business what Isaac is struggling with. I barely know him. No, that's not entirely true. I just don't know this side of him.

I wrap myself in my comforter and try to sleep. The whiskey has made my head spin. I like it. I'm surprised I never got addicted to alcohol. It's such a nice way to check out. Maybe I should find a new addiction. Maybe I should find Isaac.

Maybe…

When I wake up I feel sick. I just barely make it down the ladder and into Isaac's room. The bathroom door is closed. I don't think twice before flinging it open and throwing myself at the toilet. Isaac opens the shower curtain just as I do. I have a moment where the vomit is halfway up my esophagus and Isaac is naked in front of me, everything stands still, then I push him aside and hurl.

It's a terrible feeling, everything coming up from your stomach. Bulimics should get a medal. I use his toothbrush because I can't find mine. The one thing I'm not is a germaphobe. When I walk out of the bathroom, he's lying on the bed. Dressed, thank God.

"How come you didn't get sick?"

He looks up at me. "I guess I'm an old pro."

I have a fleeting thought, one where I wonder if he's the one who brought us here. I narrow my eyes and scan my mind for motive. Then I come to my senses. Isaac has no reason for wanting to be here. There is no reason for him to be here at all.

"Do me a favor," I say, against my better judgment. "If in your past life—the one where you tattooed emotion all over your body—you had a drinking problem, don't drink."

"Why do you care, Senna?"

"I don't," I say quickly. "But your wife and baby do."

He looks away.

"We are going to get out of here eventually." I sound way more sure than I actually am. "You can't go back to them all messed up."

"Someone left us here to die," he says, blandly.

"Bullshit." I shake my head and squeeze my eyes shut. I'm feeling queasy again. "All the food … the supplies. Someone wants us to survive."

"Limited food. Limited supplies."

"It doesn't make sense," I say. We both stopped messing with the keypad the day I spilled all that nonsense about Adam and Eve.

"Maybe we should get back to breaking out of here," I say.

Then I run back to the bathroom and throw up.

Later as I lie in my bed, still green-faced and queasy, I decide not to try to help anymore. It's not my forte. I want to be left alone, I should therefore leave others alone. We pick up our code breaking again, for lack of anything else to do.

To stave off boredom I try my hand at reading again. It doesn't work; I have kidnapped ADD. I like the feel of paper beneath my fingertips. The sound a page makes when it turns over. So I don't see the words, but I touch the pages and turn them until I've finished the book. Isaac sees me doing it one day, and laughs at me.

"Why don't you just read the book?" he asks.

"I can't focus. I want to, but I can't."

He comes over and takes it from my hands. The sofa yields as he sits down next to me and opens it to the first page. He's sitting so close our legs are touching.

Whether I shall turn out to be the hero of my own life, or whether that station will be held by anybody else, these pages must show.

I close my eyes and listen to his voice. When he reads the words, "I was destined to be unlucky in life…" my eyes shoot open. I want to say *Jinx*. Maybe I'll like *David Copperfield* after all. This isn't the first time Isaac's read to me. The last time was under very different circumstances. Very different and very much the same. He reads until his voice becomes hoarse. Then I take the book from him and read until mine gives, too. We mark the spot and set it down until tomorrow.

Nothing happens for weeks. We develop a routine, if you can call it that. It's more of a day-to-day stay sane and survive kind of thing. I call it Sanity Circulation. When you're caged up you need somewhere to send your hours, or you start getting prickly, like when you sit in the same position for too long and your legs get pins and needles. Except when you get them in your brain, you're pretty much on your way to the nuthouse. So we try to circulate. Or, I do at least. Isaac looks like he's two blinks away from needing Haloperidol and a padded room. He makes coffee in the morning, that's consistent. There is a huge sack of coffee beans in the pantry and several industrial sized cans of instant. He uses the beans, saying that when we run out of juice in the generator we can heat water for the instant over the fire. *When* … not *if*.

We drink our coffee at the table. Usually in silence, but sometimes Isaac talks to fill the space. I like those days. He tells me about cases that he's had … difficult surgeries, the patients who lived and ones who didn't. We eat breakfast after that: oatmeal or powdered eggs. Sometimes crackers with jam spread on them. Then we part ways for a few hours. I go up, he stays down. Usually I use that time to shower and sit in the carousel room. I don't know why I sit in there except to focus on the bizarre. We switch after that. He comes up to take his shower and I go down to sit for a while in the living room. That's when I pretend to read the books. We meet up in the kitchen for lunch. We know it's lunch by our hunger, not by the position of the sun, or by a clock. Tick-tock, tick- tock.

Lunch is canned soup or baked beans cooked with hot dogs. Sometimes he defrosts a loaf of bread and we eat that with butter. I clean the dishes. He watches the snow. We drink more coffee, then I go to the attic room to sleep. I don't know what he does during that time, but when I come downstairs again he's restless. He wants to talk. I climb up and down the stairs for exercise. Every other day I jog around the house and do sit-ups and push-ups until I feel as if I can't move. There are a lot of hours between lunch and dinner. Mostly we just wander around from room to room. Dinner is the big event. Isaac makes three things: meat, vegetable and starch. I look forward to his dinners, not just because of the food, but the entertainment as well. I come downstairs early and perch myself on the tablet to watch him cook. Once I asked him to verbalize everything he was doing so I could pretend I was watching a cooking show. He did, only he changed his voice and his accent and spoke in the third person.

Isseeec veel sautee zees undetermined meat over ze stove veeth butter and....

Every few days when the mood is lighter I request a different Isaac cook me dinner. My favorite being Rocky Balboa, in which Isaac calls me Adrian and mimics Sylvester Stallone's awful attempt at a Philly accent. Those are the better nights—little slivers in between the very bad ones. On the bad ones we don't speak at all. On those days the snow is louder than the kidnapped houseguests.

Sometimes I hate him. When he does the dishes, he shakes off each one before setting it in the drying rack. Water flies everywhere. A couple of drops always hit me in the face. I have to leave the room to avoid smashing a plate against his head. He hums in the shower. I can hear him from all the way downstairs, mostly AC/DC and Journey. He wears mismatched socks. He squints his eyes when he reads and then insists that there is nothing wrong with his eyesight. He closes the lid of the toilet. He looks at me funny. Like, really funny. Sometimes I catch him doing it and he doesn't even bother to look away. It makes my face and neck get this tingly burn feeling. He barely makes any noise when he moves. He sneaks up on me all the time. When you've been kidnapped it's never a good idea to be too quiet when entering a room. He's received countless elbows in the ribs and loose-handed slaps as a result.

"Is there anything I do that irritates you?" I ask him one day. We are both in irritable moods. He's been lurking; I've been stalking. We bump into each other as I come from the kitchen and he comes from the little living room. We stand in limbo in the space between the two rooms.

"I hate it when you go comatose."

"I haven't done that in a while," I point out. "Four days at least. Give me something more tangible."

He looks up at the ceiling. "I hate it when you watch me eat."

"Gah!" I throw my hands up in the air—which is completely unlike me. Isaac snickers.

"You eat with too many rules," I tell him. There is humor in my voice. Even I can hear it. He narrows his eyes like something is bothering him, then he seems to shake it off.

"When I met you, you didn't listen to music with words, " he says, folding his arms across his chest.

"What does that have to do with anything?"

"Why don't we discuss this over a snack." He points to the kitchen. I nod but don't move. He takes a step forward, placing us impossibly close. I step back twice, allowing him room to move into the kitchen. He sets crackers on a plate with some beef jerky and dried bananas and puts it between us. He makes a show out of eating a cracker, hiding his mouth behind his hand in mock embarrassment.

"You live by rules. Mine are just more socially appropriate than yours," he says.

I snicker.

"I'm trying really hard not to watch you eat," I tell him.

"I know. Thanks for making the effort."

I pick up a piece of banana. "Open your mouth," I say. He does without question. I toss the banana at his mouth. It hits his nose, but I lift my hands in triumph.

"Why are you celebrating?" He laughs. "You missed."

"No. I was aiming for your nose."

"My turn."

I nod and open my mouth, tilting my head forward instead of back so I can make it harder for him.

The banana lands directly on my tongue. I chew it sulkily.

"You're a surgeon. Your aim is impeccable."

He shrugs.

"I can beat you," I say, "at something. I know I can."

"I never said you couldn't."

"You imply it with your eyes," I wail. I chew on the inside of my cheek while I try to cook something up. "Wait here."

I sprint up the stairs. There is a metal chest in the carousel room at the foot of the bed. I found games in there earlier, a couple of puzzles, even some books on human anatomy and how to survive in the wild. I rifle through its contents and pull out two puzzles. Each one has a thousand pieces. One depicts two deer on a cliff. The other is a "Where's Waldo at the Zoo." I carry them downstairs and toss them on the table. "Puzzle race," I say. Isaac looks a little taken back.

"Seriously?" he asks. "You want to play a game?"

"Seriously. And it's a puzzle, not a game."

He leans back and stretches his arms over his head while he considers this. "We stop at the same time for bathroom breaks," he says firmly. "And I get the deer."

I extend my hand and we shake on it.

Ten minutes later we are sitting across from each other at the table. It is so large in circumference that there is plenty of room for both of us to spread out with our respective thousand pieces. Isaac sets two mugs of coffee between us before we start.

"We need some rules," he announces. I slide my mug over and hook a finger in the handle. "Like what kind?"

"Don't use that tone with me."

My face actually feels stiff when I smile. Other than my manic laughing the first day we woke up here, it's probably the first time my face has moved in the upward direction.

"Those there are the laziest muscles on your body," Isaac announces when he sees it. He slides into his chair. "I think I've seen you smile one other time. Ever."

It feels awkward to even have it on my face, so I let it drop to sip the coffee.

"That's not true." But I know it is.

"Okay, the rules," he says. "We take a shot every half hour."

"A shot of liquor?"

He nods.

"NO!" I protest. "We'll never be able to do this if we are drunk!"

"It levels the playing field," he says. "Don't think I don't know about your puzzle love."

"What are you talking about?" I drag a piece of my puzzle around the table with my fingertip. I make figure eights with it—big ones then small ones. How could he possibly know something like that? I try to remember if I had puzzles in my house when…

"I read your book," he says.

I flush. *Oh yeah.* "That was just a character..."

"No," he says, watching the path my puzzle piece is making. "That was you."

I glance at him from beneath my lashes. I don't have the energy to argue, and I'm not sure I can make a compelling argument anyway. *Guilty,* I think. *Of telling too much truth.* I think about the last time we took shots and my stomach rolls. If I get a hangover I'll sleep through most of the following day and be too sick to eat. That saves food and kills at least twelve boring hours. "I'm in," I say. "Let's do this."

I pick up the piece underneath my fingertip. I can make out colorful pant legs and a tiny bulldog on a red leash. I set it back down, pick up another, roll it between my fingertips. I'm bothered by what he said, but I also just found Waldo. I set him underneath my coffee mug for safekeeping.

"I'm an artist, Senna. I know what it is to put yourself into what you create."

"What are you talking about?" I fake confusion.

Isaac already has a small corner put together. I watch his hand travel over the pieces until he plucks up another. He's getting a good head start on me. He has at least twenty pieces. I'll wait.

"Stop it," he says. "We're being fun and open tonight."

I sigh. "It's not fun to be open." And then, "I was more honest in that book than I was in any of the others."

Isaac hooks another piece onto his growing continent. "I know."

I let spit pool in my mouth until I have enough of it to hang a really good lugie, then swallow it all at once. He'd read my books. I should have known. He's at thirty pieces now. I tap my fingers on the table.

"I don't know that side of you," I say. "The artist." I collect more spit. Swirl it, push it between my teeth. Swallow.

He smirks. "Doctor Asterholder. That's who you know."

This conversation is pricking where it hurts. I am remembering things; the night he took off his shirt and showed me what was painted on his skin. The strange way his eyes burned. That was my peek down the rabbit hole. The *other* Isaac, like the other mother in *Coraline*. He's at thirty- three pieces. He's pretty good.

"Maybe that's why you're here," he says, without looking up. "Because you were honest."

I wait awhile before I say-"What do you mean?"

Fifty

"I saw the hype around your book. I remember walking into the hospital and seeing people reading it in waiting rooms. I even saw someone reading it at the grocery store once. Pushing her cart and reading like she couldn't put it down. I was proud of you."

I don't know how I feel about him being proud of me. He barely knows me. It feels condescending, but then it doesn't. Isaac isn't really a condescending guy. He's equal parts humble and slightly awkward about receiving praise. I saw it in the hospital. As soon as anyone started saying good things about him, his eyes would get shifty and he'd look for an escape route. He was all clickety-clack, don't look back.

Sixty two pieces.

"So how did that get me here?"

"Thirty minutes," he says.

"What?"

"It's been thirty minutes. Time for a shot."

He stands up and opens the cabinet where we keep the liquor. We keep finding hidden bottles. The rum was in a Ziploc bag in the sack of rice.

"Whiskey or rum?"

"Rum," I say. "I'm sick of whiskey."

He grabs two clean coffee mugs and pours our shots. I drink mine before he's even had time to pick up his mug. I smack my lips together as it rolls down my throat. At least it's not the cheap stuff.

"Well?" I demand. "How did it get me here?"

"I don't know," he finally says. He finds the piece he's looking for and joins it to the ear of his deer. "But I'd be stupid to think this wasn't a fan. It's that or there is one other option."

His voice drops off and I know what he's thinking.

"I don't think it was him," I rush. I pour myself a voluntary shot.

I don't have much of an alcohol tolerance and I haven't eaten anything today. My head does a little flipsy doosey as the alcohol runs down my throat. I watch his fingers slide, clip into place, slide, search, slide…

100 pieces.

I pick up my first piece, the one with the bulldog.

"You know," Isaac says. "My bike never did grow wings."

The rum has curbed my vinegar and loosened the muscles in my face. I fold my features into a version of shock mock and Isaac cracks up.

"No, I don't suppose it did. Birds are the only things that grow wings. We're just left to muck through the mire like a bunch of emotional cave men."

"Not if you have someone to carry you."

No one wants to carry someone when they're heavy from life. I read a book about that once. A bunch of drivel about two people who kept coming back to each other. The lead male says that to the girl he keeps letting get away. I had to put the book down. No one wants to carry someone when they're heavy from life. It's a concept smart authors feed to their readers. It's slow poison; you make them believe it's real, and it keeps them coming back for more. Love is cocaine. And I know this because I had a brief and exciting relationship with blow. It kept my knife-to-skin addiction at bay for a little while. And then I woke up one day and decided I was pathetic—sucking powder up my nose to deal with my mommy issues. I'd rather bleed her out than suck her in. So I went back to cutting. Anyway … love and coke. The consequences for both are expensive: you get a mighty fine high, then you come barreling down, regretting every hour you spent reveling in something so dangerous. But you go back for more. You always go back for more. Unless you're me. Then you lock yourself away and write stories about it. Boo-hoo. Boo fucking hoo.

"Humans weren't made to carry someone else's weight. We can barely lift our own." Even as I say it, I don't entirely believe it. I've seen Isaac do things that most wouldn't. But that's just Isaac.

"Maybe lifting someone else's weight makes yours a little more bearable," he says.

We catch eyes at the same time. I look away first. What can you say to that? It's romantic and foolish, and I don't have the heart to argue. It would have been kinder if someone had broken Isaac Asterholder's heart at some point. Being stuck on love was a real bitch to cure. Like cancer, I think. Just when you think you're over it, it comes back.

We take another shot right before I snap my last piece of the puzzle into place. It's the Waldo piece from underneath my coffee cup. Isaac is only half finished. His mouth gapes when he sees.

"What?" I say. "I gave you a good head start." I get up to go take my shower.

"You're a savant," he calls after me. "That wasn't fair!"

I don't hate Isaac. Not even a little bit.

The days melt. They melt into each other until I can't remember how long we've been here, or if it's supposed to be morning or night. The sun never stops with the damn light. Isaac never stops with the damn pacing. I lie still and wait.

Until it comes. Clarity, bleeding through my denial, warm against my numb brain. Warm—it's a word I'm becoming less and less familiar with. Isaac has become increasingly worried about the generator lately. He calculates how long we've been here. "It's going to run out of gas. I don't know why it hasn't already…"

We turned off the heat and used the wood from the closet downstairs. But now we are running out of wood. Isaac has rationed us down to four logs a day. Any day now the generator could run out of fuel. It is Isaac's fear that we will no longer be able to get water through the faucet without the power. "We can burn things in the house for heat," he tells me. "But once we run out of water we're dead."

My feet are cold, my hands are cold, my nose is cold; but right now, my brain is cooking something. I press my face into the pillow and will it away. My brain is sometimes like a rogue Rubik's cube. It twists until it finds a pattern. I can figure out any movie, any book within five minutes of starting it. It's almost painful. I wait for it to pass, the twisting. My mind can see the picture that Isaac has been looking for. While he, no doubt, paces the kitchen, I get up and sit on the floor in front of my dwindling fire. The wood is hard against my legs, but wood absorbs heat and I'd rather be warm and uncomfortable than cold and cushioned. I'm trying to distract my thoughts, but they are persistent. *Senna! Senna! Senna!* My thoughts sound like Yul Brynner. Not girl voice, not my voice, Yul Brynner's voice. Specifically in *The Ten Commandments.*

"Shut up, Yul," I whisper.

But, he doesn't shut up. And no wonder I didn't see it before. The truth is more twisted than I am. If I am right, we will be home soon; Isaac with his family, me with mine. I giggle. If I am right, the door will open and we can walk to a place where there is help. All of this will be over. And it's a good thing, too, we are down to a dozen logs. When my toes are thawed, I stand and head downstairs so that I can tell him.

He's not in the kitchen. I stand for a moment at the sink where I usually find him looking out the window. The faucet has a drip. I watch it for a minute before turning away. The whiskey we were drinking a few nights ago is still on the counter. I screw off the cap and take a swig straight from the bottle. The lip feels warm. I wonder if Isaac was in here doing the same thing. I flinch, lick my lips and take two more deep sips. I walk boldly up the stairs, swinging my arms as I go. I've learned that if you move all of your limbs at once you can chase some of the cold away.

Isaac is in the carousel room. I find him sitting on the floor staring up at one of the horses. This is unusual. It's typically my spot. I slide down the wall until I am sitting next to him and stretch my legs out in front of me. I am already feeling the effects of the whiskey, which makes this easier. "The carousel day," I say. "Let's talk about it."

Isaac turns his head to look at me. Instead of avoiding his eyes, I catch and hold them. He has such a piercing gaze. Steely.

"I haven't told anyone that story. I can't for the life of me figure out how someone would know. That's why this room seems more like a coincidence," I say.

He doesn't reply, so I carry on. "You told someone though, didn't you?"

"Yes."

He lied to me. He told me he hadn't told a soul. Maybe I lied, too. I can't remember.

"Who did you tell, Isaac?"

We are breathing together, both sets of eyebrows drawn.

"My wife."

I don't like that word. It makes me think of frilly aprons with apple pattern and blind, submissive love.

I look away. I look instead at the death that adorns the horses' lacquered manes. One horse is black and one is white. The black has the flared nostrils of a racehorse, its head tossed to the side, eyes wide with fear. One leg is furled up like it was mid-stride when sentenced to eternal fiberglass. It is the more striking of the two horses: the determined, angry one. I am endeared to it. Mostly because there is an arrow piercing its heart.

"Who did she tell?"

"Senna," he says. "No one. Who would she tell that to?"

I push myself to my feet and walk barefoot to the first horse—the black one. I trace the saddle with my pinkie. It is made of bones.

I am not fond of the truth; it's why I lie for a living. But I am looking for someone to blame.

"So, then this is a coincidence, just like I initially said." I no longer believe that, but Isaac is withholding something from me.

"No, Senna. Have you looked at the horses—I mean really looked at them?" I spin around to face him.

"I'm looking at them right now!" *Why am I shouting?*

Isaac jumps up and rounds on me. When I won't look at him he grabs my shoulders and spins me 'til I'm facing the black horse again. He holds me firmly. "Hush and look at it, Senna."

I flinch. I look just so he won't say my name like that again. I see the black horse, but with new eyes: non-stubborn, just plain old Senna eyes. I see it all. I feel it all. The rain, the music, the horse whose pole had a crack in it. I can smell dirt and sardines … something else, too … cardamom and clove. I pull out of it, pull out of the memory so fast my breath stops. Isaac's hands loosen on my shoulders. I'm disappointed; he was warm. I am free to run, but I curl my toes until I can feel them gripping carpet, and I stay. I came here to solve one of our problems. One of our many problems. These are the same horses. The very same. I trace the crack with my eyes. Yul says something about me repressing my memories. I laugh at him. *Repressing my memories.* That's a Saphira Elgin thing to say. But he's right, isn't he? I'm in a fog and half the time I don't even realize it.

"The date that it happened," I say softly. "That's what will open the door."

The air prickles, then he runs. I hear him taking the stairs two at a time. I didn't even have to remind him of the date. It's cut into the fleshy part of our memories. I wait with my eyes closed; praying it works, praying it doesn't. He comes back a minute later. Much slower this time. *Plunk, plunk, plunk* up the stairs. I feel him standing in the doorway looking at me. I can smell him too. I used to bury my head in his neck and breath in his smell. *Oh God, I'm so cold.*

'Senna," he says, "want to come outside?"

Yes. Sure. Why not?

PART TWO

PAIN & GUILT

It was December twenty-fifth. Consequently, that day came every year, and I wished to hell it wouldn't. You couldn't get rid of Christmas. And even if you could, all of the hopeful people in the world would find a new day to celebrate, with their cheap tinsel and stuffed turkeys and lawn ornament bullshit. And I'd be forced to hate that day, too. Turkey was disgusting anyway. Anyone with taste buds could tell you that. It tasted like sweat and had the texture of wet paper. The entire holiday was a joke; Jesus had to share it with Santa. The only thing worse was that Jesus had to share Easter with a bunny. That was just creepy. But at least Easter had ham.

My annual tradition on Christmas was to wake up with the fog and jog along Lake Washington. It helped me deal. Not just with Christmas, with life. Plus, jogging was a shrink-approved activity. I didn't see shrinks anymore, but I still jogged. It was a healthy way to produce enough endorphins to keep my demons in their respective cages. I thought there were drugs for that—but, whatever. I liked to run.

On the morning of that Christmas, I didn't feel like jogging my usual route along the lake. A person might hate Christmas, but still feel the necessity to do something significant on it. I wanted to be in the woods. There is something about trees the size of skyscrapers, their bark dressed in moss, that makes me feel hopeful. I'd always thought that if there was a god, the moss would be his fingerprints. Grabbing my iPod, I headed out the door around six a.m. It was still dark, so I took my time walking to the trail, giving the sun some time to rise. To get to the trail I had to cut through a neighborhood of cookie cutter houses called The

Glen. I was resentful of The Glen. I had to drive past it to get to my house, which was at the top of the hill.

I glanced in windows as I passed the houses, eyeing the Christmas lights and trees, wondering if you'd be able to hear the children from the sidewalk while they were opening presents. I stretched just outside of the woods, turning my face toward the winter drizzle. That was my routine; I'd stretch, will myself to live for another day, secure my ponytail, and let the beat of my legs begin. The trail is bumpy and precipitous. It borders the cookie cutter Glen, which I find ironic. The whole thing has been rutted by time and rain, woven with rogue tree roots and sharp flints. It took concentration just to make it through in the daylight without a sprained ankle, which was precisely the reason it had few joggers. I don't know what I was thinking running it while it was still dark. I realized that I should have stuck to the plan of jogging around the lake. I should have stayed home. I should have done anything but jog that trail, on that morning, at that time.

At 6:47 he raped me.

I know this because seconds before I felt arms wrapping around my upper body, crushing the breath from my lungs, I glanced at my watch and saw 6:46. I figure it took him thirty seconds to drag me backward off the trail, my legs kicking the air uselessly. Another thirty seconds to throw me down at the base of a tree and rip off my clothes. Two seconds to hit me hard across the face. A minute to turn the sum of my life into a violent stained memory. He took what he wanted and I didn't scream. Not when he grabbed me, not when he hit me, not when he raped me. Not even after, when my life was irrevocably soiled.

After, I stumbled out of the woods, my pants half pulled up and blood trickling into my eyes from a cut on my forehead. I ran looking over my shoulder, and right into another jogger who had just gotten out of his car. He caught me as I fell. I didn't need to say anything, because he immediately pulled out his phone and called the police. He opened his passenger side door and helped me sit, then turned the heat on full blast. He had an old blanket in the trunk that he said he used for camping. He said lots of things in the ten minutes we waited for the police. He was trying to set me at ease. I didn't really hear him, though the sound of his voice was a soothing constant. He wrapped the blanket around my shoulders and asked if I wanted water. I didn't but I nodded. He announced that he was opening the back door to get it. He told me everything he did before he did it.

I was taken to the hospital in an ambulance. Once there I was wheeled to a private room and handed a hospital gown by an orderly. A nurse came in a few minutes later. She looked harried and distracted, the hair above her ears sticking out in tufts. "We're going to administer an SOEC kit, Ms. Richards," she said, without looking at me. When I asked what that was, she told me it was Sexual Offense Evidence Collection.

My humiliation was high as she pried my legs open. The SOEC kit was on a metal table that she'd wheeled next to the bed. I watched her unpack it, laying each item out on a tray. There were several small boxes, microscope slides and plastic bags, and two large white envelopes, which she slipped my clothes into. I started shaking when she took out a small blue comb, a nail pick and cotton swabs. That's when I averted my eyes to the ceiling, squeezing them shut so tight I saw gold stars on the inside of my eyelids. *Please no, God. Please no.* I wondered if the words *sexual assault* made women feel less victimized. I hated it. I hated all the words people were using. The cop who had brought me in whispered the word *raped* to the nurse. But to me it had been sexual assault. They were off brands of the real deal.

The kit took two hours. When she was finished, I was told to sit up. She handed me two white pills in a little paper cup. "For the discomfort," she said. *Discomfort.* I repeated the word in my head as I dropped the pills on my tongue and took the paper cup of water she was now extending. I was too shocked to be offended. A female officer came in when the nurse was finished to talk to me about what happened. I gave her a description of the man: heavyset, mid-thirties, taller than me, but shorter than the officer, a skull cap pulled over his hair, which might have been brown. No tattoos that I could see … no scars. When the nurse was finished, she asked if there was anyone they could call. I said, *No.* An officer would give me a ride home. I stopped short when I saw the man at the nurses' station. The jogger—the one who'd helped me—was wearing a white doctor's coat over his sweatpants and t-shirt, and flipping through what I presumed was my chart. It's not like he didn't already know what happened to me, but I still didn't want him to read it on my chart.

"Ms. Richards," he said. "I'm Doctor Asterholder. I was there when—"

"I remember," I said, cutting him off.

He nodded. "I'm not on duty today," he confessed. "I came in to check on you."

To check on me? I wondered what he saw when he looked at me. A woman? A soiled woman? Sorrow? A face to pin pity on?

"I understand you need a ride home. The police can take you," he glanced at the uniformed officer who was standing off to the side. "But I'd like to drive you if that's okay."

Nothing was okay. But, I didn't say that. Instead, I thought about the way he knew exactly what to do and what to say to keep me calm/ He was a doctor; in hindsight it all made sense. If I could choose my ride home, I choose not to ride in the back of a police cruiser.

I nodded.

He glanced at the cop who seemed more than happy to hand me off. A rape case on Christmas Day, who wanted to be reminded that there was evil in the world while Santa and his reindeer were still leaving contrails in the sky?

Dr. Asterholder walked me out a side door and into a staff parking lot. He'd offered to pull around the front of the building to pick me up, but I'd shaken my head firmly. His car was nondescript. The unflashy hybrid. It looked a little self-righteous. He opened the door for me, waited until my feet were tucked in … closed it … walked around to his side. I stared out the window at the rain. I wanted to apologize for ruining his Christmas. For getting raped in the first place. For making him feel as if he had to drive me home.

"Your address?" he asked. I pulled my eyes away from the rain.

"1226 Atkinson Drive." His hand hovered over the GPS before moving back to the steering wheel.

"The stone house? On the hill—with the vines on the chimney?"

I nod. My house was noticeable from all across the lake, but he must live near if he'd seen it close enough to know about the vines.

"I live in the area," he said a moment later. "It's a beautiful house."

"Yes," I said absently. I suddenly felt cold. I lifted my hands to my arms to catch the goose bumps, and he turned up the heat without me asking. I saw a family crossing the parking lot, each with an armful of presents. All four of them were wearing Christmas hats, from the toddler to the beer-bellied father. They looked hopeful.

"Why aren't you with your family on Christmas?" I asked him.

He pulled out of the lot and turned onto the street. It was one o'clock on Christmas Day so, for once, there was no traffic.

"I moved here from Raleigh two months ago. My family is back East. I couldn't get enough time off to go see them. Plus hospitals are short staffed on Christmas. I was scheduled to come in later today."

I looked out the window again.

There was silence for a few miles, and then I said, "I didn't scream … maybe if I'd screamed—"

"You were in the woods, and it was Christmas morning. There was no one to hear you."

"But I could have tried. Why didn't I try?"

Dr. Asterholder looked at me. We were at a light, so he could. "Why didn't I get there sooner? Just ten minutes and I could have saved you…"

My shock drew me out. For a minute I was a different Senna. Appalled, I said, "It's not your fault."

The light turned green, the truck ahead of us pulled forward. Before Dr. Isaac Asterholder put his foot on the gas, he said, "It's not yours either."

The drive from the hospital to my house is roughly ten minutes. There are three traffic lights, a brief stint on the highway, and a steep, winding hill that makes even the toughest car have bad labor pains. Chopin was playing softly from the speakers as the doctor drove me home the rest of the way in silence. His car interior was cream; soothing. He pulled into my driveway and immediately got out to open my door. I had to remind myself to move, to walk, to put my keys into the lock. It all took conscious effort, as if I was controlling my limbs from outside my body—a puppet master and a puppet at the same time. And maybe I was not in my body. Maybe the real me kept running on that trail, and what he grabbed was a different part. Maybe you could detach from the ugly things that happened to you. But even as I opened the door I knew it wasn't true. I felt too much fear.

"Do you want me to check the house?" Dr. Asterholder asked. His eyes moved past me into the foyer. I looked at him, grateful for the suggestion and also afraid of letting him in. In all respects, he was the man who saved me, yet I was still looking at him like he could attack me at any minute. He seemed to sense that. I cast my own glance into the darkness behind me, and suddenly felt too afraid to even flick on the light switch. What would be there? The man who raped me?

"I don't want to make you uncomfortable." He took a voluntary step back, away from me and the house. "I'm fine with just dropping you off."

"Wait," I said. I was ashamed of my voice, swollen with panic. "Please check." It took everything for me to say that, to ask for help. He nodded. I stepped aside to let him in. When you allow someone into your house to check for the boogey man, you are unwittingly letting him into your life as well.

I waited on a barstool in my kitchen while he inspected the rooms. I could hear him moving around from the bedrooms to the bathrooms, then to my office, which hung over the kitchen. *You are in shock,* I told myself. He checked each window and door. When he finished he pulled out a card from his wallet and slid it on the counter toward me.

"Call me anytime you need me. My house is a mile away. I'd like to check on you tomorrow, if that's okay."

I nodded.

"Do you have someone that can come over? Stay with you tonight?"

I hesitated. I didn't want to tell him that I didn't.

"I'll be fine," I said.

When he was gone, I pushed the sofa to the front door and wedged it between the jamb and the wall. It was no more a barrier against someone intruding than my small, ineffective fists, but it made me feel better. I undressed in the foyer, kicking off the lightweight pants and shirt the nurse gave me at the hospital after she bagged mine for evidence. Naked, I carried them to the fireplace, setting them on the floor next to me as I opened the grate and arranged the logs. I lit a fire and waited until it was hot and hungry. Then I threw everything in, and watched the worst day of my life burn.

Carrying a Brillo pad and a half-full jug of bleach to the downstairs bathroom, I turned the water to the hottest setting. The bathroom filled with steam. When the mirrors were hazed, and I couldn't see myself, I climbed into the shower and watched my skin turn red. I scrubbed my body until my skin bled and the water turned pink around my feet. Screwing the cap off the bleach, I lifted it above my shoulders, and poured. I cried out and had to hold myself up while I did it again. Then I lay on the floor with my knees spread apart and my hips raised, and poured it into my body. They'd given me a pill, told me it would take care of an unwanted pregnancy. *Just in case,* the nurse said. But, I wanted to kill everything he touched—every skin cell. I needed to make sure there was nothing left of him on any part of me. I walked naked to the kitchen and pulled a knife from the block I kept next to the fridge. Using the tip, I ran it up and down the inside of my arm, tracing my favorite vein. Too many windows; my house had too many ways to break in. What if he'd been watching me? If he knew where I lived?

I pierced the skin with that last thought and dragged the tip about two inches. I watched the blood trickle down my arm, mesmerized by the sight. When my doorbell rang, the knife clattered to the floor.

I was so afraid, I couldn't move. It rang again. Grabbing a dishtowel I held it over the cut on my arm and looked toward the door. If they were here to hurt me, they probably wouldn't ring the doorbell. I grabbed for laundry basket that was resting on my kitchen counter, pulling out a clean t-shirt and jeans. They dragged stubbornly over my damp skin as I rushed to put them on. I took the knife with me. I had to push the couch aside to reach the door. When I looked through the peep hole, my hands were shaking so badly I could barely hold the knife. What I saw was Doctor Asterholder, in different clothes.

I opened the deadbolt and swung the door wide. Wider than a woman who'd experienced my day should have. I wouldn't have even done that before what happened today. We stared at each other for a good thirty seconds, before his eyes found the dishtowel and my fresh blood.

"What did you do?"

I stared at him blankly. I couldn't seem to speak; it was like I'd forgotten how. He grabbed my arm and ripped the cloth from the wound. It was then I realized he thought I was trying to kill myself.

"It's not—it's not in the right spot," I said. "It's not like that." He was blinking rapidly when he looked up from the cut.

"Come," he said. "Let's get you cleaned up."

I followed him into the kitchen and slid onto a barstool, not quite sure what was happening. He took my arm, more gently this time, and turned it over, peeling back the dishrag.

"Bandages? Antiseptic?"

"Upstairs bathroom, under the sink."

He left to retrieve my little first-aid kit and came back with it about two minutes later.

I only realized I was still clutching the knife when he gently pried it from my fingers and set it on the counter.

He didn't speak as he cleaned and bandaged my wound. I watched his hands work. His fingers were deft and agile.

"It won't need stitches," he said. "Flesh wound. But, keep it clean."

His eyes traced the rawness on my exposed skin, left from the Brillo pad.

"Senna," he said. "There are people, support groups—"

I cut him off. "No."

"Okay." He nodded. It reminded me of the way my shrink used to say *okay*, like it was a word you swallowed and digested instead of one you spoke. Somehow, from him, it seemed less condescending.

"Why are you here?"

He hesitated briefly then said, "Because you are."

I didn't understand what he meant. My thoughts were so contorted, choppy. I couldn't seem to…

"Go to bed. I'll sleep right there." He pointed to the couch, still angled across the front door.

I nodded. *You're in shock*, I told myself again. *You're letting a stranger sleep on your couch.*

I was too tired to over think it. I went upstairs and locked the door to my bedroom. It still didn't feel safe. Picking up my pillow and blanket, I carried them to my bathroom, locked that door, too, and lay down on the mat. My sleep was that of a woman who had just been raped.

I woke up and stared at my ceiling. Something was wrong … something … but I couldn't figure out what it was. A weight pressed down on my chest. The kind that comes when you feel dread, but you can't quite place your finger on why. Five minutes, twenty minutes, two minutes, seven minutes, an hour. I have no idea how long I lay like that, staring up at the ceiling … not thinking. Then I rolled onto my side and a nurse's word came back to me: *discomfort.* Yes, I felt discomforted. *Why?* Because I was raped. My mind recoiled. I'd once seen a neighbor boy pour salt on a snail. I'd watched in horror as its tiny body disintegrated on the pavement. I'd run home crying, asking my mother why something we seasoned our food with had the power to kill a snail. She'd told me that salt absorbs all of the water that their bodies are made of, so they essentially dry out or suffocate because they can't breathe. That's what I felt like. Everything had changed in a day. I didn't want to acknowledge it, but it was there—between my legs, in my mind … oh God, on my couch. Suddenly, I couldn't breathe. I rolled over, reaching for the inhaler in my nightstand and knocking the lamp over. It crashed to the floor as I struggled to sit up. When had I even come back to my bed? I'd gone to sleep in the bathroom, on the floor. A second later, Dr Asterholder came crashing through my bedroom door. He looked from me to the lamp, then back to me again. "Where is it?" he barked. I pointed, and he was across the room in two steps. I watched him rip open the drawer and rummage around until he found it. I grabbed it from his hand, biting down on the spacer and feeling the albuterol fill my lungs a second later. He waited until I'd caught my breath to pick up the lamp. I was embarrassed. Not just about the asthma attack, but about the night before. That I'd let him stay.

"Are you all right?"

I nodded without looking at him.

"From the asthma?"

Yes. As if sensing my discomfort, he took leave of my room, closing the door behind him. It jerked into place as if it didn't sit against the seam so well anymore. I'd locked the door the night before, and he'd managed to get in with a hard shove of his shoulder. That didn't make me feel very good.

I showered again, this time forgoing the Brillo pad for a bar of plain, white, soap with a bird cut delicately into its skin. The bird irritated me, so I scratched it away with my fingernail. My skin, still fresh and pink from the night before, tingled under the hot water. *You're fine, Senna,* I told myself. *You're not the only one this has happened to.* I dried off, patting my tender skin, and stopped to look at myself in the mirror. I looked different. Though I couldn't put my finger on how. Maybe less soul. When I was a child my mother would tell me that people lost soul in two ways: someone could take it from you, or you'd surrender it willingly.

You're dead, I thought. My eyes said it was true. I dressed, covering every inch of my body in clothing. I wore so many layers someone would have to cut me out of them to get to my body. Then I walked downstairs, flinching at the discomfort between my legs. I found him in my kitchen sitting on a barstool and reading the paper. He had brewed coffee and was sipping out of my favorite mug. I don't even get the paper. I hoped he stole it from my neighbors; I hated them.

"Hello," he said, setting his mug down. "I hope you don't mind." He gestured to the coffee setup and I shook my head. He got up and poured me a mug. "Milk? Sugar?"

"Neither," I said. I didn't want coffee but I took it when he handed it to me. He was careful not to touch me, not to get too close. I took a tentative sip and set my mug down. This was awkward. Like the morning after a one night stand when no one knows where to stand and what to say, and where their underwear is.

"What type of doctor are you?"

"I'm a surgeon."

That's about as far as I went with questions. He stood up and carried his mug to the sink. I watched him rinse it and place it upside down in the draining rack.

"I have to get to the hospital."

I stared at him, unsure why he was telling me this. Were we a team now? Was he coming back?

He pulled out another card and set it on the counter. "If you need me."

I looked at the card, plain white card stock with block lettering, then back to his face.

"I won't."

I spent the rest of the day on my back porch, staring at Lake Washington. I drank the same cup of coffee Dr. Asterholder handed me before he left. It stopped being hot a long time ago, but I cradled it between both of my hands like I was using it for heat. It was an act, a piece of body language that I'd learned to imitate. Hell itself could unfurl in front of me, and chances are I wouldn't feel it.

I didn't have thought. I saw things with my eyes and my brain processed the colors and shapes without matching them to feelings: water, boats, sky and trees, plump loons and grebes that glided over the water. My eyes traced everything, across the lake and in my yard. The heaviness in my chest kept pressing. I didn't acknowledge it. The sun set early in Washington; by four-thirty it was dark and there was nothing left to look at but the tiny lights from houses across the water. Christmas lights that would be stripped down soon. My eyes hurt. I heard the doorbell, but I was unable to stand up and answer it. They'd go away eventually, they usually did. They always did.

I felt pressure on my upper arms. I looked down and saw hands gripping me. Hands, as if there were no body attached to them. Solitary hands. Something snapped and I started screaming.

"Senna! … Senna!"

I heard a voice. It was a clogged sound, like words said through a mouthful of cheese. My head rolled back and suddenly I realized that someone was shaking me.

I saw his face. He touched a finger to the pulse on my neck.

"I'm here. Feel me. See me." He grabbed my face and held it between his hands, forcing me to look at him.

"Hush … hush," he said. "You're safe. I've got you."

I wanted to laugh, but I was too busy screaming. Who is safe? No one. There is too much bad, too much evil in the world to ever be safe.

He wrestled me into what must have been a hug. His arms encircled my body, my face was pressed against his shoulder. Five years, ten years, one year, seven—how long had it been since I was hugged? I didn't know this man, but I did. He was a doctor. He helped me. He spent the night on my couch so I wouldn't be alone. He broke down my bedroom door to get my inhaler.

I heard him shushing me like a child. I clung to him—a solid body in the darkness. I was seeing my attack as he held me … feeling the panic, the disbelief, the numbness all at once until they tangled together in a fray. I wailed, an ugly, guttural noise like a wounded animal. I don't know how long I was like that.

He took me inside. Picked me right up and carried me through the French doors and set me gently on the couch. I lay down and curled up, tucking my knees under my chin. He tossed a blanket over me and started a fire, then he disappeared into the kitchen and I could hear him moving around. When he came back he made me sit up handing me a mug of something hot.

"Tea," he said. He had a few pieces of cheese and a slice of homemade bread on a plate. I'd made the bread on Christmas Eve. *Before.* I pushed the plate away, but took the tea. He watched me drink it from his haunches. It was sweet. He waited for me to finish and took the cup.

"You need to eat."

I shook my head. "Why are you here?" My voice was raspy—too much screaming. My white streak dangled in front of my eye, I tucked it and looked at the flames.

"Because you are."

I didn't know what he meant. Did he feel responsible for me because he found me? I lay back down and curled up.

He sat on the floor in front of the couch where I was lying, facing the fire. I closed my eyes and slept.

When I woke he was gone. I sat up and stared around the room. Light was creeping in through the kitchen window, which meant I'd slept straight through the night. I had no reference for what time he carried me inside. I wrapped the blanket around my shoulders and walked barefoot to the kitchen. Had he taken off my shoes after he carried me inside? I didn't remember. I might not have been wearing shoes. There was fresh coffee in the pot and a clean mug sitting next to it. I picked up the mug and underneath he had left another card. *Clever.* He'd written something along the bottom.

Call me if you need anything. Eat something.

I crumpled the card in my fist and tossed it in the sink.

"I won't," I said out loud. I turned on the faucet and let the water smear the words.

I took a shower. Got dressed. Started another fire. Stared at the fire. I added a log. I stared at the fire. Around four o'clock I wandered into my office and sat behind my desk. My office was the most sterile room in the house. Most authors filled their writing space with warmth and color, pictures that inspire, chairs that allow them to think. My office consisted of a black lacquered desk in the center of an all white room: white walls, white ceiling, white tile. I needed emptiness to think, a clear white canvas to paint on. The black desk grounded me. Otherwise I'd just float around in all the white. Things distracted me. Or maybe they complicated me. I didn't like to live with color. I wasn't always like that. I learned to survive better.

I opened my MacBook and stared at the cursor. One hour, ten minutes, a day … I'm not sure how much time passed. The doorbell rang, jarring me. When did I come in here? I felt stiff as I stood up. A long time. I walked down the stairs and stopped in front of the door. Every one of my movements was robotic and forced. I could see Doctor Asterholder's car through the peephole; charcoal sitting atop my wet, brick driveway. I opened the door and he blinked at me like this was normal—him being on my doorstep. He had both arms around paper bags loaded to the brim with groceries. He brought me groceries.

"Why are you here?"

"Because you are." He stepped passed me and walked to the kitchen without my permission. I stood frozen for several minutes, looking at his car. It was drizzling outside, the sky covered in a thick fog that hung over the trees likes a burial shroud. When I finally closed the door, I was shivering.

"Doctor Asterholder," I said, walking into the kitchen. *My kitchen.* He was unpacking things on my counter: cans of tomato paste, boxes of rigatoni, bright yellow bananas and clear cartons of berries.

"Isaac," he corrected me.

"Doctor Asterholder. I appreciate … I … but—"

"Did you eat today?"

He fished his soggy business card out of the sink and held it between two fingers. Not knowing what else to do, I wandered over to my barstool and took a seat. I wasn't used to this sort of aggression. People gave me space, left me alone. Even if I asked them not to—which was rare. I didn't want to be anyone's project and I definitely didn't want this man's pity. But for the moment I had no words.

I watched him open bottles and chop things. He took out his phone and set it on the counter and asked me if I minded. When I shook my head, he put it on. Her voice was raspy. It had both an old and new feel to it, innovative, classic.

I asked him who she was and he told me, "Julia Stone." It was a literary name. I liked it. He played her entire album, tossing things into a pot he found by himself. The house was dark aside from the kitchen light he stood underneath. It felt quaint, like a life that didn't belong to me, but I enjoyed watching. When was the last time I had someone over? Not since I bought the house. That was three years ago. There was a long window above my sink that stretched the length of the room. My appliances were all on the same wall, so no matter what you were doing you had a panoramic view of the lake. Sometimes when I was washing dishes I'd get so caught up looking outside, my hand would still and the water would turn cold before I realized that I'd been staring for fifteen minutes.

I saw him peering into the darkness as he stood at the stove. The lights from the houses floated like fireflies in ink behind him. I let my eyes leave him and I watched the darkness instead. The darkness comforted me.

"Senna?" I jumped.

Isaac was next to me. He put a placemat and utensils in front of me, along with a bowl of steaming food, and a glass of something bubbly. I never even noticed.

"Soda," he said, when he saw me looking. "My vice."

"I'm not hungry," I said pushing the bowl away.

He pushed it back and tapped his forefinger on the counter. "You haven't eaten in three days."

"Why do you care?" It came out harsher than I intended. Everything I said did.

I watched his face for a lie, but he just shrugged.

"It's who I am."

I ate his soup. Then he made himself comfortable on my couch and went to sleep. In his clothes. I stood on the stairs and watched him for a long time, his socked feet sticking out of the bottom of the blanket he was using. Eventually I crawled into my bed. I reached out before I closed my eyes, and touched the book on the nightstand. Just the cover.

He came every night. Sometimes as early as three o' clock in the afternoon, sometimes as late as nine. It was alarming how quickly a person could acquiesce to something—something like a stranger in your house, sleeping and scooping grounds into your Mr. Coffee. When he started buying groceries and cooking meals it felt permanent. Like I suddenly had a roommate or a family member I never signed up for. But on the nights he came late I found myself anxious, pacing the hallways in three pairs of socks, unable to stay in one room for more than a few seconds before I moved to the next. The worst part was, when he arrived, I immediately retreated to my bedroom to hide. None of the relief I felt at seeing the lights of his car reflected through my windows was allowed to show. It was cold, but it was survival. I wanted to ask him why he was late. Was it surgery? Did they make it? But I didn't dare.

Every morning I woke up to find another of his business cards on the counter. I stopped throwing them away after a few days and let them pile up near the fruit bowl. The fruit bowl that was always filled with fruit, because he bought it and put it there: red and green apples, yellow pears, the occasional fuzzy kiwi. We didn't speak much. It was a silent relationship, which I was fine with. He fed me and I said thank you, then he went to sleep on my couch. I started to wonder how well I'd be sleeping if he wasn't guarding the door. If I'd sleep at all. The couch was short—too short for his six-foot frame; it was the smaller of the two that I owned. One day while he was at the hospital I took a break from staring at the fire to push the longer couch in front of the door. I left him a better pillow and a warmer blanket.

There was one particular night that he didn't arrive until almost eleven. I'd given up on him coming altogether, thinking our strange relationship had finally run its course. I was on my way up the stairs when I heard a quiet knock on the door. Just a *rap rap rap*. It could have been a gust of wind it was so light. But in my hope I heard it. He didn't look at me when I opened the door. Or wouldn't. Or couldn't. He seemed to be finding my pavers particularly interesting, and then the spot just above my left shoulder. He had dark crescents under his eyes, two hollow moons cradling his lashes. It would have been a hard call to decide who looked worse—me in my layers of clothing or Isaac with his droopy shoulders. We both looked beat up.

I tried to pretend I wasn't watching him as he walked to the bathroom and splashed cold water on his face. When he came out, the top two buttons of his shirt were undone and his sleeves were rolled to his elbows. He never brought a change of clothes. He slept in what he wore and left early in the morning, presumably to go home and shower. I didn't know where he lived, how old he was, or where he went to medical school. All the things you found out by asking questions. I did know that he drove a hybrid. He wore aftershave that smelled like chai tea spilled on old leather. Three times a week he grocery shopped. Always paper bags; most of Washington is composed of people trying to save the planet, one Coke can at a time. I always chose plastic just to be defiant. Now I had mounds of paper grocery bags stacked on my pantry floor, all neatly folded. He'd started wheeling the green recycling can to the curb on Thursdays. I was officially and unwillingly part of the green people cult. On Sundays he'd steal my neighbor's paper. It's the only thing I really liked about him.

Isaac opened the fridge and stared inside, one hand rubbing the back of his neck.

"There's nothing here," he said. "Let's go out for dinner." Not what I was expecting.

I immediately felt like I couldn't breathe. I backed up until my heels were pressing against the stairs. I hadn't left the house in twenty-two days. I was afraid. Afraid that nothing would be the same, afraid that everything would be the same. Afraid of this man who I didn't know, and who was speaking to me with so much familiarity. *Let's go out to dinner.* Like we did this all the time. He didn't know anything. Not about me, at least.

"Don't run," he said, coming to stand in the spot where the kitchen met the living room. "You haven't left the house in three weeks. It's just dinner."

"Get out," I said, pointing to the door. He didn't move.

"I won't let anything happen to you, Senna."

The silence that followed was so loud that I could hear my faucet dripping, my heart beating, the scratchy feet of fear as it crawled out of my pores.

Thirty seconds, two minutes, one minute, five. I don't know how long we stood there in a silent standoff. He hadn't really said my name since the night he found me outside. We'd been two strangers. Now that he'd said it, it made everything feel real. *This is really happening*, I thought. *All of it.*

He moved in for the kill. "We'll walk to the car," he said. "I'll open the door for you, because that's what I do. We will drive to a great Greek place. Best gyros you've ever tasted-open twenty-four hours. You get to choose the music in the car. I'll open your door, we'll go inside, get a table by the window. We want the table by the window because the restaurant is across the street from a gym, and the gym is next door to a doughnut shop. And we'll want to count how many gym goers stop for doughnuts after they work out. We'll talk or we can just watch the doughnut shop. Whatever you want. But you have to leave the house, Senna. And I'm not going to let anything happen to you. Please."

I was shaking by the time he finished. So violently I had to sit down on the bottom stair, my fingernails bending against the wood. That meant I was considering what he was saying. Actually thinking about leaving the house, wanting to taste the gyros … see the doughnut shop. But not just that, there was something in his voice. He needed to do this. When I looked up, Isaac Asterholder was still where he was. Waiting.

"Okay," I said. It wasn't like me, but everything had changed. And if he kept showing up for me, I could show up for him. Just this once.

It was raining. I liked the cover that rain provided. It protected you from the hard brutality of the sun. It brought things to life, made them flourish. I was born in the desert where the sun and my father almost killed me. I lived in Washington because of the rain, because of how it made my life feel washed of my past. I stared out the window until Isaac handed me his iPod. It was beat-up looking. Well loved.

He had the *Finding Neverland* soundtrack. I pressed play, and we drove without words, from our lips or from our music.

The restaurant was called Olive and smelled like onions and lamb. We sat by the window, just as Isaac promised, and ordered gyros. Neither of us spoke. It was enough to be out among the living. We watched people amble on the sidewalk across the street. Gym goers and doughnut shop goers, and just as he promised, sometimes they were one and the same. The shop was called The Doughnut Hole. It had a large picture of a pink frosted doughnut on the storefront with an arrow pointing to the hole in the center. There was a large flashing blue sign that said, *Open 24/7*. People in the city didn't sleep. I should live there.

Some people had a stronger will than others, they only looked lovingly into The Doughnut Hole's window before racing to their cars. Their cars were mostly hybrids. Generally, hybrid drivers had a nose in the air to things that weren't good for them. But most couldn't resist the temptation. It seemed like a cruel joke, really. I counted twelve people who resisted the call to be healthy and followed the smell of white flour and sticky glaze. I liked those people better—the hypocrites. I could relate.

When the meal was over, Isaac slipped his credit card out of his wallet.

"No," I said. "Let me…"

He looked ready to kick up a fuss. Some men don't like female gendered credit cards. I gave him a fierce look, and after about five seconds he tucked his wallet back into his back pant pocket. I handed over my card. It was a power move and I'd won—or he'd let me. It's good to have a little power either way. When he saw me staring across the street at the doughnut shop, he asked if I wanted one. I nodded.

He led me to the store and bought a half dozen. When he handed me the bag it was hot … greasy. My mouth started to water.

I ate one as he drove me home and we listened to the rest of the *Finding Neverland* soundtrack. I didn't even like doughnuts; I just wanted to see what turned all of those people into hypocrites.

When we pulled into my driveway I wasn't sure if he was going to come in or leave me at the door. The rules changed tonight. I willingly went somewhere with him. It felt datish or, at the very least, friendish. But when I opened the front door he followed me inside and turned the deadbolt. I was headed up the stairs when I heard his voice.

"I lost a patient today." I stopped on the fourth stair, but I didn't turn around. I should have. Something like that was worth turning around for. His voice was clotted. "She was only sixteen. She coded on the table. We couldn't bring her back."

My heart was racing. I gripped the banister until the veins in my hands popped and I thought the wood was going to snap beneath the pressure.

I waited for him to say more, and when he didn't I climbed the rest of the stairs. Once I was in my bedroom I shut the door and leaned with my back against it. Almost as quickly I turned around and pressed my ear against the wood. I couldn't hear any movement. I took seven reverse steps up until the backs of my knees were touching the bed, then I spread my arms wide and fell backwards.

When I was seven my mother left my father. She also left me, but mostly she left my father. She told me that before she carried her two suitcases out the front door and climbed in the cab. *I have to do this for myself. He's killing me slowly. I'm not leaving you, I'm leaving him.*

I never had the courage to ask her why she wasn't taking me. I watched her leave from the living room window with my hands pressed against the glass in a silent *STOP*. Her parting words to me had been, *You'll feel me in the fall backwards.* She'd kissed me on the mouth and walked out.

I never saw her again. I never stopped trying to figure out what she meant. My mother had been a writer, one of the obscure artsy types who surround themselves with color and sound. She published two novels in the late seventies and then married my father, who she claimed sucked all the creativity out of her.

Sometimes I felt like I became a writer just to make her see me. Consequently, I was very good at it. I'd yet to feel her in the fall backwards.

I stared at the ceiling and wondered what it would feel like to have someone's life in your hands, and then to watch that life slip away like Isaac had. And when had I started to call him Isaac? I felt myself drifting off and I closed my eyes, welcoming it. When I woke up, I was screaming.

Someone was holding me down, I writhed left and then right to get away. I screamed again and I felt hot breath on my face and neck. A crash and my bedroom door swung open. *Thank God! Someone is here to help me.* And that's when I realized that I was alone, lying in the residue of a dream. No one was here. No one was attacking me. Isaac leaned over where I lay, saying my name. I could hear myself screaming and I was so ashamed. I squeezed my eyes closed, but I couldn't stop. I couldn't make it go away—the feel of cruel, relentless hands on my body, tearing, pressing. I screamed louder until my voice grew fingernails and tore into my throat.

"Senna," he said, and I don't know how I heard him above the noise I was making, "I'm going to touch you."

I didn't fight as he climbed in bed behind me, and stretched both of his legs on either side of mine. Then he pulled me back until I was leaning against his chest, and wrapped both arms around my torso. My hands were curled into fists as I screamed. The only way to deal with the pain was to move, so I rocked back and forth and he rocked with me. His arms anchored me to what was real, but I was still halfway in the dream. He said my name. "Senna."

The sound of his voice, the tone, calmed me a little. His voice was a slow thunder.

"When I was a little boy, I had a red bike," he said. I had to stop screaming to hear him. "Every night when I went to bed I begged God to give my bike wings so that in the morning, I could fly away. Every morning I'd crawl out of bed and run straight to the garage to see if he answered my prayers. I still have the bike. It's more rusted then red now. But I still check. Every day."

I stopped rocking.

I was still shaking, but the pressure of his arms wrapped around my torso caused the trembling to taper off.

I fell asleep in a stranger's arms, and I was not afraid.

Isaac breathed like he had trust. He pulled in his air steady and deep and exhaled it like a sigh. I wished I could be like that. But that was all gone. I listened to him for a long time, time enough for the sun to come up and try to press through the clouds. The clouds won, in Washington they always won. I was still wrapped in him, leaning against his chest—this man I didn't know. I wanted to stretch my muscles, but I stayed still because there was something good about this. His hands were draped across my abdomen. I studied them since my eyes were the only things I dared move. They were average looking hands, but I knew that the twenty-seven bones in each of this man's hands were exceptional. They were surrounded by muscle and tissue and nerves that together saved human life with their dexterity and precision. Hands could bruise or they could fix. His hands fixed. Eventually, his breathing lightened and I knew he was awake. It felt like a standoff to see who would make the first move. His arms left my body, and I crawled forward and stepped out of bed. I didn't look at him as I walked to the bathroom. I washed my face and took two aspirin for my headache. When I came out he was gone. I counted the cards on the counter. He didn't leave one that day.

He didn't come back that night, or the next.

Or the next.

Or the next.

Or the next.

There were no more dreams, but not for lack of horror. I was afraid to sleep, so I didn't. I sat in my office at night, drinking coffee and thinking of his red bike. It was the only color in the room—Isaac's red bike. On January thirty-first my father called me. I was in the kitchen when the phone vibrated on the counter. There was no house phone, just my cell. I answered without looking.

"Hello, Senna." His voice always distinct, nasally with an accent he tried not to have. My father was born in Wales and moved to America when he was twenty. He retained the European mentality and accent and dressed like a cowboy. It was one of the saddest things I'd ever seen.

"How was your Christmas?"

I immediately felt cold.

"Fine. How was yours?"

He began a detailed minute-by-minute account of how he spent Christmas Day. I was, for the most part, grateful I didn't have to speak. He wrapped things up by telling me about his promotion at work; he said the same thing he repeated every time we spoke.

"I'm thinking about taking a trip out there to see you, Senna. Should be soon. Bill said I get an extra week's vacation this year because I've been with the company twenty years."

I'd lived in Washington for eight years and he'd never come to visit me once.

"That'd be great. Listen Dad, I've got some friends coming over. I should go."

We said our goodbyes and I hung up, resting my forehead on the wall. That would be it from him until the end of April, when he would call again.

The phone rang a second time. I almost didn't answer it, but the area code is from Washington.

"Senna Richards, this is the office of Dr. Albert Monroe."

I racked my brain trying to place the doctor and his specialty, and then for the second time that day, my blood ran cold.
"Something came up on your scan. Dr. Monroe would like you to come in to the office."

I was leaving my house the next morning, walking to my car when his hybrid pulled into my horseshoe driveway. I stopped to watch him climb out and pull on his jacket. It was casual, almost beautiful in its grace. He'd never come this early before. It made me wonder what he did on the mornings of his days off. He walked toward me and stopped just in time to keep two solid feet between us. He was wearing a light blue fleece, pushed up past his elbows. I was shocked to see the dark ink of tattoos peeking out. What type of doctor had tattoos?

"I have a doctor's appointment," I said stepping around him.

"I'm a doctor."

I was glad to be turned away from him when I smiled.

"Yes, I know. There are quite a few others in the state of Washington."

His head jerked back like he was surprised I was anything but the stoic, expressionless victim he'd been cooking for.

I was opening the driver's side door to my Volvo when he held out his hand for my keys.

"I'll drive you."

I dropped my eyes into his hand and snuck another look at the tattoos.

Words—I could just make out the tip of them. My eyes slid up the sleeves of his shirt and rested on his neck. I didn't want to look in his eyes when I handed him my keys. A doctor who loved words. Imagine that.

I was curious. What did a man who had held a screaming woman all night have written on his body? I sat in the passenger seat and instructed Isaac where to go. My radio was on the classical station. He turned it up to hear what was playing and then lowered it back down.

"Do you ever listen to music with words?"

"No. Turn left here."

He turned the corner and shot me a curious look.

"Why not?"

"Because simplicity speaks the loudest." I cleared my throat and stared straight ahead. I sounded like such a chump. I felt him looking at me, cutting into me like one of his patients. I didn't want to be dissected.

"Your book," he said. "People talk about it. It's not simple."

I don't say anything.

"You need simplicity to create complexity," he said. "I get it. I suppose too much can clog up your creativity."

Exactly.

I shrugged.

"This is it," I said softly. He turned into a medical complex and pulled into a parking spot near the main entrance.

"I'll wait for you right here."

He didn't ask where I was going or what I was here for. He simply parked the car where he could see me walk in and out of the building and waited.

I liked that.

Dr. Monroe was an oncologist. In mid December I found a lump in my right breast. I forgot about the worry of cancer in the wake of a more immediate and needier pain. I sat in his waiting room, my hands pressed between my knees, a strange man waiting in my car, and all I could think about were Isaac's words. The ones on his arms and the ones that came out of his mouth. A red bicycle in a stark white room.

A door opened next to the reception window. A nurse said my name.

"Senna Richards."

I stood. I went.

I had breast cancer. I could talk about the moment Dr. Monroe confirmed it, the emotions I felt. The words he said to me afterwards, meant to comfort, reassure; but the bottom line was, I had breast cancer.

I thought about his red bike as I walked to the car. No tears. No shock. Just a red bike that could fly. I didn't know why I wasn't feeling anything.

Maybe a person could only deal with one dose of mental atrophy at a time. I slid into the passenger seat. He'd changed the radio station, but he switched it back to the classical one before he put the car in reverse. He didn't look at me. Not until we arrived at my house and he opened the front door with my keys. Then he looked at me, and I wanted to disappear into the cracks between my brick driveway. I didn't know what color his eyes were; I didn't want to know. I pushed past him into the foyer and stopped dead. I didn't know where to go—the kitchen? The bedroom? My office? Everywhere seemed stupid. Pointless. I wanted to be alone. I didn't want to be alone. I wanted to die. I didn't want to die.

I went to my barstool, the one positioned to get the perfect view of the lake, and I sat. Isaac moved into the kitchen. He started to make coffee and then stopped, turning to look at me.

"Do you mind if I put on some music? With words?"

I shook my head. His eyes were grey. He set his phone on top of the breadbox while he spooned grinds into the filter.

This time he played something more upbeat. A man's voice. The beats were so strange I stopped my incessant ability to not feel and listened.

"Alt-J," he said, when he saw that I was listening. "The song is called *Breezeblocks.*"

He glanced at my face. "It's different, right? I used to be in a band. So I get a kick out of their beats."

"But, you're a doctor." I realized how stupid that sounded when it was already out. I pulled an inch-wide chunk of grey hair free, and wound it around my finger twice, right by the roots. I left it there, with my elbow resting on the counter. My security blanket.

"I wasn't always a doctor," he said, grabbing two mugs out of my cabinet. "But when I became one, my love of music remained ... and the tattoos remained."

I glanced at his forearms where they peeked out of his shirtsleeves. I was still looking when he brought me my coffee. I caught the tips of the words that faced me.

After he handed me the coffee, he started making food. I didn't have an appetite, but I couldn't remember the last time I'd eaten. I didn't want to, but I listened to the words of the song he was playing. The last time I listened to this type of music the boy bands had just taken the world by storm and filled every radio with their cliché-licked songs. I wanted to ask him who was singing, but he beat me to it.

"Florence and the Machine. Do you like it?"

"You're fixated on death."

"I'm a surgeon," he said, not looking up from where he was dicing vegetables.

I shook my head. "You're a surgeon because you have a fixation on death."

He didn't say anything, but slightly hesitated as he cut into a zucchini—barely noticeable, but my eyes caught mostly everything.

"We all do don't we? We are consumed with our own mortality. Some people eat right and exercise to preserve their lives, others drink and do drugs daring fate to take theirs, and then there are the floaters—the ones who try to ignore their mortality altogether because they're afraid of it."

"Which are you?"

He set down his knife and looked at me.

"I've been all three. And now I'm undecided."

Truth. When was the last time I heard such stark truth? I stared at him for a long time as he spooned food onto plates. When he set a plate down in front of me, I said it. It was like a sneeze ejecting from my body without permission, and when it was out I felt mildly embarrassed.

"I have breast cancer."

Every part of him stopped moving except his eyes, which dragged slowly to mine. We stayed like that for … one … two … three … four seconds. It was like he was waiting for the punch line. I felt compelled to say something else. A first for me.

"I don't feel anything. Not even fear. Can you tell me what to feel, Isaac?"

His throat spasmed, then he licked his lips.

"It's emotional Morphine," he said finally. "Just go with it."

And that was it. That's all we said for that night.

Isaac drove me to the hospital the next day. It was only my third time leaving the house and the thought of going back there made me sick to my stomach. I couldn't eat the eggs or drink the coffee he put in front of me. He didn't push me to eat like most people would, or give me the concerned eyes that most people would. It was all matter of fact; if you don't want to eat—don't. The moment you are diagnosed with cancer a gavel comes down on life, you start being afraid. And since I was already afraid, it felt compounded; fear pressing against fear. And just like that you inherit a cancer gremlin. I imagined it looked mutated, like my genes. It was sinister. Lurking. It kept you awake at night, gnawing on your insides, turning your mind into a distillery of fear. Fear trumps good sense. I wasn't ready to go back to the hospital; it was the last place I was really afraid, but I had to because cancer was eating at my body.

The tests and scans started around noon. My first consult was with Dr. Akela, an oncologist Isaac went to medical school with. She was Polynesian and so strikingly beautiful my mouth hung open when she walked in. I could smell fruit on her skin; it reminded me of the bowl Isaac kept filling on my counter. I expelled the smell from my nostrils and breathed through my mouth. She spoke about chemotherapy. Her eyes had a heart and I was under the impression that she was an oncologist because she cared. I hated people who cared. They were prying and nosy and made me feel less human because I didn't care.

After Dr. Akela, I saw a radiation oncologist, and then a plastic surgeon who pressured me to make an appointment to see a grief counselor. I saw Isaac in between each appointment, each scan. He was on his rounds, but he came to walk me to my next appointment. It was awkward. Though each time his white coat emerged, I became a little more familiar with him. It was a weird form of brand recognition—Isaac the Good. His hair was brown, his eyes were deep-set, the bridge of his nose was wide and crooked, but the most telling part of him was his shoulders. They moved first, then the rest of his body followed.

I had a tumor on my right breast. Stage II cancer. I was a candidate for a lumpectomy with radiation.

Isaac found me in the cafeteria sipping on a cup of coffee, staring out the window. He slid into the chair across from me and watched me watch the rain.

"Where is your family, Senna?"

Such a hard question.

"I have a father in Texas, but we're not close."

"Friends?"

I looked at him. Was he kidding? He had spent every night for a month in my house and my telephone hadn't rung once.

"I don't have any." I left off the *haven't you figured that out yet?* bit.

Dr. Asterholder shifted in his seat like the topic made him uncomfortable, and then, as an afterthought, folded his hands over the crumbs on the tabletop.

"You're going to need a support system. You can't do this alone."

"Well what would you suggest I do? Import a family?"

He continued as if he hadn't heard me. "There might be more than one surgery. Sometimes, even after radiation and chemotherapy, the cancer comes back…"

"I'm having a double mastectomy. It's not going to come back."

I wrote about shock on people's faces: shock when they find out their love has been cheating on them, shock when they discover faked amnesia—heck, I even wrote about a character who constantly wore a look of shock on his face, even when there was nothing to be shocked about. But I couldn't say that I'd ever seen true shock before. And here it was, written all over Isaac Asterholder. He dove in immediately, his eyebrows drawing together. "Senna, you don't—"

I waved him off.

"I have to. I can't live every day in fear, knowing it might come back. This is the only way." He searched my face, and I knew then that he was the type of man who always considered what someone else was feeling. After a while the tension left his shoulders. He lifted his hands from where they'd been resting on the table, and placed them over mine. I could see the crumbs sticking to his skin. I focused on them so I wouldn't pull away. He nodded.

"I can recommend—"

I cut him off for the third time, jerking my hands out from beneath his. "I want you to do the surgery."

He leaned back, put both hands behind his head and stared at me.

"You're an oncologic surgeon. I Googled you."

"Why didn't you just ask?"

"Because I don't do that. Asking questions is at the forefront of developing relationships."

He cocked his head. "What's wrong with developing relationships?"

"When you get raped, and when you get breast cancer, you have to tell people about it. And then they look at you with sad eyes. Except they're not really seeing you, they're seeing your rape or your breast cancer. And I'd rather not be looked at if all people are seeing are the things I do, or the things that happen to me instead of who I am."

He was quiet for a long time.

"What about before those things happened to you?"

I stared at him. Maybe a little too fiercely, but I didn't care. If this man wanted to show up in my life, and put his hands over mine, and ask why I didn't have a best friend—he was going to get it. The full version.

"If there was a God," I said, "I'd say with confidence that he hates me. Because my life is the sum of bad things. The more people you let in, the more bad you let in."

"Well, there you have it," Isaac said. His eyes weren't wide; there was no more shock. He was a cucumber.

It was the most I'd ever said to him. It was probably the most I'd said to any person in a long time. I pulled my cup up to my mouth and closed my eyes.

"All right," he said, finally. "I'll do the surgery on one condition."

"What's that?"

"You see a counselor."

I started shaking my head before the words were out of his mouth.

"I've seen a psychiatrist before. I'm not into it."

"I'm not talking about medicating yourself," he said. "You need to talk about what happened. A therapist—it's very different."

"I don't need to see a shrink," I said. "I'm fine. I'm dealing." The idea of counseling petrified me; all of your inner thoughts put in a glass box, to be seen by someone who spent years studying how to properly judge thoughts. How was that okay? There was something perverse about the process and the people who chose to do it for a living. Like a man being a gynecologist. *What's in this for you, you freak?*

Isaac leaned forward until he was uncomfortably close to my face and I could see his irises, pure grey without any flecks or color variations. "You have Post-Traumatic Stress Disorder. You were just diagnosed with breast cancer. You. Are. Not. Okay." He pushed away from the table and stood up. I opened my mouth to deny it, but I sighed instead, watching his white coat disappear through the cafeteria doors.

He was wrong.

My eyes found the scar from the night I cut myself. It was pink, the skin around it tight and shiny. He hadn't said anything when he found me bleeding, hadn't asked me how or why. He had simply fixed it. I stood up and walked in his wake. If someone was going to be digging around in my chest with a scalpel, I wanted it to be the guy who showed up and fixed things.

He was standing at the main entrance to the hospital when I found him, hands tucked into his pockets. He waited until I reached him and we walked in silence to his car. We were far enough apart that we couldn't touch, close enough together that it was clear we were together. I slid quietly into the front seat, folding my hands in my lap and staring out the window until he pulled into my driveway. I was about to get out—halfway suspended between car and driveway—when he put his hand on my arm. My eyebrows were drawn together. I could almost feel them touching. I knew what he wanted. He wanted me to promise I'd see a counselor.

"Fine." I yanked myself out of his reach and stalked toward my house. I had the key in the lock, but my hands were shaking so badly I couldn't turn it. Isaac came up behind me and put his hand over mine. His skin was warm like it had been sitting in the sun all day. I watched in mild fascination as he used both of our hands to turn the key. When the door swung open, I stood frozen on the spot, with my back toward him.

"I'm gonna go home tonight," he said. He was so close I could feel his breath moving tendrils of my hair. "Will you be all right?"

I nodded.

"Call me if you need me."

I nodded again.

I climbed the stairs to my bedroom and crawled into bed fully clothed. I was so tired. I wanted to sleep while I could still feel him on my hand. Maybe, I wouldn't dream.

The next morning it was snowing. A freak February snow that coated the trees and rooftops in my neighborhood with a butter cream frosting. I wandered from room to room, standing at the windows and staring out at the different views. Around noon, when I was tired of looking, and felt the slow thrumming of a headache starting behind my temples, I talked myself into going outside. *It'll be good for you. You need the fresh air. Daylight doesn't have teeth.* I wanted to touch the snow, hold it in my hand until it burned. Maybe it could clean me of the last few months.

I walked past where my jacket hung on the coat rack and swung open the front door. The cold air hit my legs and crawled under my t-shirt. The t-shirt was all I was wearing. No layers of sweaters, no tights underneath sweatpants. The thin beige t-shirt hung around me like a shedding second skin. I was barefoot as I stepped into the snow. It gave under my feet with a soft sigh as I took a few steps forward. My father would have freaked out if he saw me. My father who yelled at me to put my slippers on if I walked on the kitchen floor barefoot in the winter. I could see tire marks that led up one side of my horseshoe driveway to where Isaac parked. It could have been the mailman. I looked back over my shoulder to see if there was a package on my doorstep. There was none. It was Isaac. He was here. Why?

I walked to the middle of the driveway and scooped up some of the snow, cupping it in my palm, looking around. It was then that I saw it. A patch of snow had been cleared from my car's windshield. The car that I never park in the garage, though now I wish I had. There was something underneath my wiper blade. I carried my handful of snow over, stopping when I reached the driver's side door. Anyone could drive past my house and see me half undressed, cupping snow in my hand and staring limpidly at my snow-capped Volvo. There was a brown square underneath the blade. I dropped my snow, and it landed in a semi-hard clump on my foot. The package was thin, wrapped grocery bag paper I turned it over in my hands. He'd written something on it in blue sharpie. His handwriting flicked across the paper in messy, carefree lines. A doctor's scrawl, the kind you might find on a medical chart or a script. I narrowed my eyes, absently licking off drops of snow on the back of my hand.

Words. That's what he'd written.

I carried it inside, flipping it over in my hand. There was a slot on one side of the cardboard. I stuck my finger inside and pulled out a CD. It was black. A generic disk, something he'd burned himself.

Curious, I put the disk into my stereo and hit play with my big toe as I stretched out on the floor.

Music. I closed my eyes.

Heavy drum beat, a woman's words … her voice bothered me. It was emotive, going from warm cooing to hard with each word. I didn't like it. It was too unstable, unpredictable. It was bipolar. I stood up to turn it off. If this was Isaac's attempt at facilitating me into his music, he was going to have to try for something less…

The words—they suddenly picked me up and held me, dangling in the air; I could kick and writhe and I wouldn't have been able to come down from them. I listened, staring at the fire, and then I listened with my eyes closed. When it was over, I played it again and listened for what he was trying to convey.

When I ripped the CD from the player and stuffed it back in its envelope my hands were shaking. I marched it to the kitchen and shoved it in the back of my junk drawer, underneath the Neiman Marcus catalog and pile of bills bound by a rubber band. I was agitated. My hands couldn't stop moving— through my skunk streak, into my pockets, pulling on my bottom lip. I needed a detox so I retreated to my office to soak up the colorless solitude. I lay on the floor and stared up at the ceiling. Normally the white cleansed me, calmed me, but today the words to the song found me. *I'll write!* I thought. I stood up and moved to my desk. But even when the blank Word document was pulled up in front of me—clean and white—I couldn't splash any thoughts onto it. I sat at my desk and stared at the cursor. It seemed impatient as it blinked at me, waiting for me to find the words. The only words I could hear were the words of the song that Isaac Asterholder left on my windshield. They invaded my white thinking space until I slammed shut my computer and marched back downstairs to the drawer. I dug out the cardboard sleeve from where I'd shoved it underneath the catalogs and bills, and dropped it into the trash.

I needed something to distract myself. When I looked around, the first thing I saw was the fridge. I made a sandwich with the bread and the cold cuts Isaac kept stocked in my vegetable bin, and ate it sitting cross-legged on my kitchen counter. For all of his *save the earth with hybrids and recycling* bullshit, he was a soda fanatic. There were five variations of carbonated, stomach-eating, sugar-infested soda in my fridge. I grabbed the red can and popped the tab. I drank the whole thing watching the snow fall. Then I dug the CD from the trash. I listened to it ten times … twenty? I lost count.

When Isaac walked through the door sometime after eight, I was draped in a blanket in front of the fire, my arms wrapped around my legs. My bare feet were tapping to the music. He stopped dead in his tracks and stared at me. I wouldn't look at him, so I kept to the fire, focused. He moved to the kitchen. I heard him cleaning up my sandwich mess. After a while he came in with two mugs and handed me one. Coffee.

"You ate today." He sat down on the floor and leaned his back against the sofa. He could have sat on the couch, but he sat on the floor with me. With me.

I shrugged. "Yeah."

He kept staring at me and I squirmed, pressed down by his silver eyes. Then, what he said hit me. I hadn't fed myself since it happened. I would have starved if not for Isaac. That sandwich was the first time I'd taken action to live. The significance felt both dark and light.

We sat in silence drinking our coffee, listening to the words he left me.

"Who is it?" I asked softly. Humbly. "Who is singing?"

"Her name is Florence Welch."

"And the name of the song?" I sneaked a glance at his face. He was nodding slightly, like he approved of me asking.

"*Landscape.*"

I had a thousand words, but I held them tightly in my throat. I wasn't good at saying. I was good at writing. I played with the corner of my blanket. *Just ask him how he knew.*

I squeezed my eyes shut. It was so hard. Isaac took my mug and stood up to carry them to the kitchen. He was almost there when I called out.

"Isaac?"

He looked at me over his shoulder, his eyebrows up.

"Thanks … for the coffee."

He tucked his lips in and nodded. We both knew that was not what I was going to say.

I put my head between my knees and listened to *Landscape.*

Saphira Elgin. What kind of shrink goes by the name Saphira? It's a stripper's name. One with scabby track marks up her arm and greasy black roots growing inch-deep above brittle yellow hair. Saphira Elgin the MD has smooth slender arms, the color of caramel. The only things decorating them were thick gold bracelets that stacked from her wrist to the middle of her forearm. It was a classy show of wealth. I watched her write something on her notepad, the bracelets tinkling gently as her pen scratched across the paper. I categorized people by whichever one of the four senses they exhibited the strongest. Saphira Elgin would fall under sound. Her office made sounds, too. There was a fire to the left of us, snapping as it ate a log. A small water fountain behind her left shoulder trickled water down miniature rocks. And in the corner of the room, past the walnut bookcase and chocolate couches, there was a large, brass birdcage facing the window. Five rainbow finches hopped and chirped from tier to tier. Dr. Elgin looked up at me from her notepad and said something. Her lips were the color of beets and I watched them vapidly when she spoke.

"I'm sorry. What did you say?"

She smiled and repeated the question. Smoky voice. She had an accent that put heavy emphasis on her 'r's'. It sounded like she was purring.

"Yourrr motherrr."

"What does my mother have to do with my cancer?"

Saphira's leg bounced gently on her knee, making a swishing sound. I'd decided to call her Saphira rather than Dr. Elgin. That way I could pretend I wasn't being psychoanalyzed by Isaac's choice of shrink.

"Our sessions, Senna, arrrre not just about your cancerrrr. There is morrrrre to your composition as a perrrrson than a disease."

Yes, a rape. A parent who left me. A parent who pretended he didn't have a daughter. A slew of bad relationships. A lost relationship…

"Fine. My mother not only walked out on her family, she also probably passed this *disease* down to me. I hate her for both."

Her face was impassive.

"Has she trrrried to contact you afterrrr she left?"

"Once. After my last book published. She sent me an e-mail. Asked to meet with me."

"And? How did you respond?"

"I didn't. I'm not interested. Forgiveness is for Buddhists."

"What are you then?" she asked.

"An anarchist."

She considered me for a moment, and then said, "Tell me about your father." *Tell me about yourrrr fatherrrr.*

"No."

Her pen scratched on her notepad. It sounded itchy. Or maybe I was just aggravated.

I imagined her writing; *Will not talk about father. Abuse?* There was no abuse. Just nothingness.

"Your book, then." She reached under her notepad and pulled out a copy of my last novel, setting it on the table between us. I should have been surprised that she had a copy, but I wasn't. When it was made into a movie, I didn't think I would see it, but I did. Chances were they'd turn my book into some bastardized Hollywood knockoff. At least my book would get good publicity. They anticipated a small release, but on opening night the movie grossed three times the expected amount and then went on to top the box office for three weeks before it was knocked out by a tights-wearing superhero. My book became an overnight sensation. And I hated it. All of a sudden everyone was looking at me, looking into my life, asking questions about my art, which I had always deemed highly private. So, I bought a house with my money, changed my number and stopped answering my e-mails. For a while I was one of the most sought after interviews in the book world. Now I was a rape victim and I had cancer.

I hated Isaac for making me do this. I hated him for making this the condition for performing my surgery. I'd taken to the internet, searching other surgeons who could cut out my cancer. They were plentiful. Cancer was trending. There were websites you could go to where you could see their pictures, where they went to medical school, how their former patients rated them. *Five stars to Dr. Stetterson from Berkley! He took the time to know me as a person before dissecting me like a live specimen! Four stars to Dr. Maysfield. His bedside manner was stiff, but my cancer is gone.* It was like a damn dating site. Scary. I'd quickly closed the window and resolved to see the shrink Isaac was forcing on me.

The only peace I had at that point was knowing it was he who would cut the cancer from my body. Not any old stranger—the stranger who'd been sleeping on my couch and feeding me.

"Let's talk about your last relationship," Saphira said.

"Why? Why do we have to dissect my past? I hate it."

"To know who a person really is, I believe you have to know first who they were."

I hated where she put her words. A normal person would have said *you first have to know who they were.* Saphira mixed everything up. Threw me off. Used her dragged out 'r's' as a weapon. She was a purring dragon.

In my hesitation, her pen scratched on paper again.

"His name was Nick." I picked up my untouched coffee and spun the cup in my hands. "We were together for two years. He's a novelist. We met at a park. We broke up because he wanted to get married and I didn't." Some of the truth. It was like sprinkling artificial sweetener over bitter fruit.

I sat back, satisfied that I'd filled the session with enough information to keep Saphira the Dragon happy. She raised her eyebrows, which I figured was the prompt to keep talking.

"That's it," I snapped "I'm fine. He's fine. Life moved on." I pulled out my grey and smoothed it back behind my ear.

"Where is Nick now?" she asked. "Do you keep in contact?"

I shook my head. "We tried that for a while. It was too painful."

"For you, or him?"

I stared at her blankly. Weren't breakups always painful for everyone involved? Maybe not…

"He moved to San Francisco after he published his last book. Last I heard he was living with someone." I looked at the finches while she wrote on her notepad. I had to turn my back to her to do it, but it felt good, like passive-aggressive defiance.

"Did you read his book?"

I waited a second to turn back around, just enough time to rearrange my face. I lifted a hand to my throat, wrapping my forefinger and thumb under my chin. Nick used to say it looked like I was trying to strangle myself. I suppose subconsciously I was. I quickly pulled my hand away.

"He wrote it about me … about us."

I had thought that would be enough, that it would divert her attention and allow me to breathe. But she waited patiently for my answer. *Did you read his book?* Her chocolate eyes were unblinking.

"No, I didn't read it."

"Why not?"

"Because I can't," I snapped. "I don't want to read about how I failed him and broke his heart."

It felt okay to say. The problems I had two years ago with Nick felt welcome compared to what was lurking in the shallow tide pools of my memory.

"He mailed me a copy. It's been sitting on my nightstand for two years."

I glanced at the clock … hoping. And, yes! Our time was up. I jumped up and grabbed my purse.

"I hate this," I said. "But my stupid surgeon won't operate unless I talk to you."

She nodded. "I'll see you Thursday."

I was shrugging my coat on and opening the door when she called after me.

"Senna."

I paused, one arm not all the way in my sleeve.

"Read the book," she said.

I left without saying goodbye. Dr. Elgin was humming softly as the door quietly shut behind me.

It was the first time I'd driven myself anywhere. I brought Isaac's CD, and I played *Landscape* all the way home. It calmed me. Why? I'd love to know. Maybe Saphira could eventually tell me. It was the only song I owned that actually had words attached to it, and the beat wasn't particularly soothing. Quite the opposite.

When I got home, I carried the CD inside. I set it on the kitchen counter and climbed the stairs. I had no intention of listening to anything Saphira Elgin said, but when I saw the cover of Nick's novel lying next to my bed, I picked it up. It was a reflex—we'd been talking about the book, and now I was having a look. There was a fine layer of dust over the top. I wiped it off with my sleeve and studied the jacket for clues. The cover was not his style, but authors had little say over what cover went on their book. There is a team that does that at the publishing company. They brainstorm with cheap Flavia coffee, in a windowless conference room-that's what my agent told me at least. If I was looking for Nick in the cover, I would not find him. The cover looked like a close-up of bird feathers: greys and whites and blacks. The title is angled in chunky white letters: *Knotted.*

I opened it to the dedication page. That was as far as I'd gotten in the past before slamming it shut.

For MV

I breathed through my mouth, flexing my fingers across the open page like I was preparing to do something physical. My mind caressed the dedication again.

For MV

I turned the page.

Chapter One

She bought me with words; beautiful, promising and intricately carved words…

My doorbell rang. I closed the book, set it on my nightstand, and went downstairs. There was no way in hell I was reading that.

"We should just make you a key," I said to Isaac. He was standing on my doorstep, arms loaded with paper grocery bags. I stepped aside to let him in. It was a snarky comment, but I'd said it with familiarity.

"I can't stay," he said, setting the bags down on the kitchen counter. There was a brief sting, like a bee had wandered into my chest cavity. I wanted to ask him why, but of course I didn't. It wasn't my business where he went or who he went there with.

"You don't have to do this anymore," I said. "I saw Dr. Elgin today. Drove there myself. I—I'm better."

He was wearing a brown leather jacket and his face was scruffy. It didn't look like he came from the hospital. And on days he did there was always the faint smell of antiseptic around him. Today there was only aftershave. He rubbed his fingers across the hair on his face. "I scheduled your surgery for two weeks from Monday. That way you'll have a few more sessions with Dr. Elgin."

My first instinct was to reach a hand up to feel my breasts. I'd never been one of those women who prided themselves on their bra size. I had breasts. For the most part I ignored them. But, now that they were going to be taken, I felt protective.

I nodded.

"I'd like you to keep seeing her … after…" His voice dropped off, and I looked away.

"All right." But I didn't mean it.

He tapped the granite with his fingertip. "All right," he repeated. "I'll see you later, Senna."

I started unpacking the groceries. At first I felt nothing. Just boxes of pasta and bags of fruit being shelved … put away. Then I felt something. An itch. It nagged at me, tugging and pulling until I was so frustrated I threw a box of soup crackers across the room. They hit the wall and I stared at the spot where they'd landed, trying to find the sound of my emotion. *Sound.* I ran to the living room and hit play on Florence Welch. She'd been singing this song to me nonstop for days. Her real voice would be tired by now, but her recorded voice called out to me, unfailing. Strong.

How had he known this song, these words, this tormented voice would speak to me?

I hated him.

I hated him.

I hated him.

I didn't see Isaac until a few days before the surgery. I saw plenty of Dr. Elgin. I saw her three times a week upon my surgeon's demand. It was like trying to fit a lifetime's worth of therapy into six sessions. She commanded me to speak with her eyes and her tinkling bracelets: *tell me more, tell me more.* Each time I sank into her couch, I sank a little lower in esteem. This was not me. I was spilling my guts, as some people called it; divulging. It was word vomit and Saphira Elgin had her fingers down my throat. I discovered that private things were mostly sour. They sat spoiling in the corners of your heart for so long that by the time you acknowledged them you were dealing with something rancid. And that's what I did; I threw every rotting thing at her, and she absorbed each one. It seemed that the more Saphira Elgin absorbed of me, the less of me there was. Sometimes I tried to be funny, just so I could hear the dusty way she laughed. She laughed at the inappropriate, sometimes the crass. I liked her so much on some days, and on others I hated her.

At the end of every session the dragon would purr the same thing: "Read Nick's book. It will give you purrrrspective. Closurrrrre." I would drive home determined, but then I would get to the title page and see *For MV,* and quickly close the cover.

The dedication page was beginning to look worn and touched, rivets of fingerprints on the page.

I waited until our last session to tell her about the rape. I didn't know why except that other than the cancer, the rape was the last thing that happened to me. Maybe I had a chronological way of dealing with things; a writer's route to solving problems. Her insouciance over the matter was what finally won me over. It was as if the entire time I saw her I was counting down the days until I would have to tell her about the rape, dreading the pity I'd see appear her eyes. But there was none. "Life happens," she said. "Bad things happen because we live in a world with evil." And then she'd asked me the strangest thing. "Do you blame God?" It had never occurred to me to blame God since I didn't believe in him.

"If I believed in God, I would blame him. I suppose it's easier not to believe, then I have nothing to be angry at."

She smiled. A cat's curl smile. And then it was over, and I'd left a free woman, my purgatory served. Isaac would operate on me now. I would be free of cancer, free to move forward without fear. Without some of the fear.

That night I started having the dreams again, hands pushing and pulling at me. Sharp pain and humiliation. The feeling of helplessness and panic. I woke up screaming, but there was no Isaac. I got in the shower to wash away the dream, shivering under the scalding water. I couldn't fall back to sleep with those images so fresh in my mind, so I sat in my office and pretended to write the book my agent was waiting for. The book I had no words for.

At noon, five days before my surgery, I dressed to go to the hospital for my pre-op appointment. It was March and the sun had been fighting the clouds for a week. Today the sky was uninterrupted blue. I felt resentful of the sun. That thought made me think of the things Nick used to say about me. *You're all grey. Everything you love, the way you see the world.* I walked out to my car, stepping around puddles of rainwater from the day before. They were colored like an oyster shell, iridescent from the oil collected from my car or Isaac's. When I got to the driver's side door, I saw a cardboard square underneath my wiper blade. I darted a look over my shoulder before plucking it out. He had been here. Last night? This morning? Why hadn't he rung the bell?

I climbed into the car a little bit excited and slipped the CD from the sleeve. This time he'd written the name of the song on the disk in red permanent marker. Kill Your Heroes, *Awolnation.* My hands were shaking as I hit play.

I listened with my eyes closed, wondering if all people listened to music with words this way. When the last note played, I started my car and drove to the hospital fighting a smile. I'd expected something to strip me naked like the Florence Welch song had. The title and its tie to the great Oscar Wilde had been enough to make me smirk, but the words, which to anyone else fighting cancer would have felt insensitive, uplifted me. So gloriously morbid.

I hit play and listened one more time, drumming my fingers on the steering wheel as I drove.

I was sitting in the exam room in a hospital gown when Isaac walked in, followed by a nurse, Dr. Akela and the plastic surgeon I saw a few weeks earlier—I think his name was Dr. Monroe, or maybe it was Dr. Morton. Isaac was wearing black scrubs underneath his white lab coat. I had a moment to study him as he looked over my chart. Dr. Akela was smiling at me, standing almost too close to Isaac. Was that possession? Dr. Monroe/Morton looked bored. On television they called his kind *Plastics.*

Finally, Isaac looked up.

"Senna," he said. Dr. Akela glanced up at him when he used my first name. I wondered if she was where he went missing to when he wasn't with me. If I were a man, I'd go missing to Dr. Akela, too. She'd make a beautiful hiding place. Her sense was sight, I decided. Everything about her called loudly to the eyes: the way she moved, the way she looked, the way she spoke sentences with only her body.

Isaac asked me to sit up. "We're going to take a look." He gently untied the back of my hospital gown and stepped away so I could lower it myself. I made myself feel nothing, staring straight ahead as the cold air touched my skin.

"Lie back, Senna," he said softly. I did. I focused on the ceiling as I felt his hands on me. He examined each breast, his fingers lingering around the lump on the right side. His touch was gentle, but professional. If anyone else had been touching me, I would have bolted upright and run straight out of the room. When he was done, he helped me sit up and retied my gown. I saw Dr. Akela watching him again.

"Your labs look good," he said. "Everything is set for the surgery next week. Dr. Montoll is here to talk to you about reconstruction." *Montoll!* "And Dr. Akela would like to go over the radiation treatments with you."

"I won't be needing to speak with Dr. Montoll," I said.

Isaac's face jerked up from my chart. "You'll want to discuss reconstruction of—"

"No," I said. "I don't."

Dr. Montoll the Plastic stepped in, suddenly not looking quite as bored. "Ms. Richards, if we get the expanders in now, your reconstruction—"

"I'm not interested in reconstruction," I said, dismissively. "I'll have the mastectomy and then I'll go home without expanders. That's my decision."

Dr. Montoll opened his mouth to speak, but Isaac cut him off.

"The patient has made her decision, doctor." He was staring straight at me when he said it. I pulled my lips tight, in thanks.

"If my services aren't needed, you'll excuse me," Dr. Montoll said, before making his exit. I looked at my hands. Dr. Akela sat on the edge of my bed. We spoke for a few minutes about the radiation I'd have to go through after my surgery. Six weeks. I had to admire her bedside manner; she was warm and personal. On her way out she touched Isaac lightly on the back of his arm. *Mine.*

Isaac waited until the door clicked shut before he took a step forward. I braced myself for an influx of questions, but instead he said, "You can get dressed now. Are you free for lunch?"

I blinked up at him.

"Isn't that a conflict of interest? Eating lunch with a patient?"

He smiled. "Yes, we'd have to go somewhere other than the hospital cafeteria."

I was about to say *no*, when I heard the lyrics of the song he gave me this morning, playing in my head. Who gave someone a song that said, *No need to worry because everybody will die* when they had cancer?

I liked it. It was the honesty.

"All right," I said.

He glanced at his watch. "Meet you in the parking lot in ten?"

I nodded.

I got dressed and made my way downstairs. "I'm over this way," he said, once I found him in the parking lot. He'd changed out of his scrubs and was wearing a white shirt and grey pinstriped pants. I followed him to his car, and he opened the door for me. It was too much. I freaked.

"I can't do this," I said. I backed away from the car. "I'm sorry. I need to get home."

I didn't look back as I walked toward my car.

He probably thought I was losing my mind. There was a good chance I was.

Isaac was waiting for me when I got home a few hours later, leaning against his car with his face turned upward. *Soak it up, Isaac,* I thought. *Tomorrow my clouds will be back.* For a brief second, I thought about not turning into my driveway and heading up to Canada instead. But I'd been driving around for hours and the needle to my gas tank was pointing to E. I wanted to go home. I walked past him to the front door. We were barely past the foyer when I said, "Why didn't you ask me why I don't want reconstruction?"

"Because if you want to tell me, you will."

"We're not friends, Isaac!"

"No?"

"I don't have friends. Can't you see that?"

"I can see that," he said. I waited for him to say something more, but he didn't. I was wearing a navy blue jacket over my shirt. I took it off and flung it on the couch. Then I piled my hair on top of my head and tied it into a knot.

"So why are you here?"

He looked at me then. "I want you to be okay."

Too much. I ran upstairs. I was crazy. I knew that. Normal people didn't leave conversations right in the middle. Normal people didn't let strangers sleep on their couch.

Two years ago I purchased a stationary bike from an eighty-eight year old widower with pink hair named Delfie. She'd put an ad in the Penny Saver after she'd had hip replacement and couldn't *damn well use it,* as she'd said. I'd picked it up the same day I made the call. After all the hassle and tassle of hauling the thing up the stairs, I'd yet to sit on it. I walked over to where it was collecting dust in the corner of my bedroom and climbed on. I had to adjust Delfie's setting on the padded seat. I pedaled until my legs felt like jelly. I was panting when I climbed off, my bare feet sore from the plastic pedals. I walked on the sides of my feet to my night table. I flipped open the cover of *Knotted* with my pinkie.

For MV

I closed it, and went downstairs to see what Isaac was making for dinner.

Fortune favors the brave. That's what I repeated to myself as they prepped me for surgery. Except I didn't say it in English, I said the Latin words: *fortes fortuna juvat ... fortes fortuna juvat ... fortes fortuna juvat.* Mantras sounded better in Latin. Repeat any phrase in the educated fancy-pants language most of the ancient philosophers used, you sounded like a goddamn genius. Repeat the same phrase in English, you sounded like a loon. Who wrote that phrase? A philosopher. I should have remembered his name, but I couldn't. *Nerves,* I told myself. I searched for something else to focus on, something that could comfort my decision. I knew that the Bible said something about cutting out your eye if it offended you. I was cutting out my breasts. I thought that this was both my brave move and my offended one. It didn't matter; most bravery boiled down to nothing more than a strong sense of duty that piggybacked an even stronger sense of crazy. Everything brave was a little bit crazy. I tried to focus on something else so I wouldn't have to think about how crazy I was. There was a nurse taking my blood.

The nurses were very attentive even when they were sticking needles into my flesh. *Oh, sorry honey, you have small veins. This will only sting for a second.* They told me to close my eyes as if I were a child. This one didn't have any problems with finding the right vein in my arm. I wondered if Isaac admonished them to take good care of me. It seemed like something he would do. The hospital room was white. Thank God for that. I could think in peace without the colors breaking through. Isaac came in to examine me. I was trying to be strong when he sat on the edge of my bed and stared down at me with soft eyes.

"Why did you stop playing music?" My voice cracked on the last word. I needed something to distract myself. A truth from Isaac.

He considered my question for a minute, then he said, "There are two things that I love."

I stopped breathing. I thought he was going to tell me about a woman. Someone he'd loved and that he'd given up music for. Instead he surprised me. "Music and medicine."

I settled down in the bed with my head against the pillows to listen to him.

"Music makes me destructive—to myself and everyone around me. Medicine saves people. So I chose medicine."

So matter-of-fact. So simple. I wondered what it would be like to give up writing. To choose something else over what I craved.

"Music saves people too," I said. I don't know this personally, but I was a writer and it was my job to know how other people thought. And I'd heard them say it.

"Not me," he said. "It makes me destructive."

"But you still listen to it." I thought of his songs. The ones he'd left me, and the ones he played in his car.

"Yes. But I don't create it anymore. Or get lost in it."

I couldn't keep it out of my eyes, the desire to know more. Isaac caught it.

"How does a person get lost in music?"

He grinned and looked at the lines running from my veins into the IV a few feet away.

"What drugs do they have you on?" he teased.

I stayed quiet, afraid that if I responded to his joke he wouldn't tell me the answer.

"You let it live in you. The beat, the lyrics, the harmonies … the lifestyle," he added. "There is only room for one of you, eventually."

I was quiet for a bit. Processing.

"Do you miss it?"

He smiled. "I still have it. It's just not my focus."

"What did you play?"

He took my hand, turned it over until the inside of my wrist was facing up. Then with his pointer and middle finger began tapping a beat on my pulse. I let him for at least a minute. Then I said, "A drummer."

I had another question on the tip of my tongue, but I held it there when the nurse walked in. Isaac stood up and I knew our conversation was over. In my mind, I replayed the beat he'd played on my wrist as the nurse fit a cap over my hair. I wondered what song it belonged to. If it was one of the ones he'd left on my windshield.

"I'm going to walk you through the procedure," he said, lowering my gown. "Then Sandy is going to take you to surgery." He morphed from Isaac the man to Isaac the doctor in just a few seconds. He told me where he was going to make the incisions, outlining them on my breasts with a black marker. He spoke about what he was going to be looking for. His voice was steady, professional. While he spoke tears streamed down my face and fell into my hair in a silent but torrid emotional cacophony. It was the first time I'd cried since my childhood. I hadn't cried when my mother left, or when I was raped, or when I found out cancer was eating at my body. I hadn't even cried when I made the decision to cut out the very essence of what made me a woman. I cried when Isaac played drums on my pulse and told me he had to give it up before they destroyed him. Go figure. Or maybe that statement had just broken it all open. My cry felt anticlimactic. Like something more profound should have kicked the last stone out of the dam before it burst open.

He saw my tears, but he didn't acknowledge them. I was so, so grateful. They wheeled me into the OR and the anesthesiologist greeted me by name. I was asked to count backwards from ten. The last thing I saw before I lost consciousness was Isaac, staring intently into my eyes. I thought he was telling me to live.

"Senna … Senna…"

I heard his voice. My eyes felt weighted. When I opened them Isaac was standing over me. It was an alarming comfort to see him.

"Hi," he said softly. I blinked at him, trying to clear my vision.

"Everything went well. I need you to rest. I'll be back later to talk to you about the surgery."

"Is it gone?" My voice was just a scratch. He smelled like coffee when he leaned down. He spoke into my ear as if he were telling me a secret.

"I got it all."

I could barely nod before I closed my eyes again. I drifted off wanting coffee and wishing my eyelids weren't so heavy so I could see his face a little longer.

When I woke up there was a nurse in my room checking my vitals. She was blonde and had pink fingernails. They were smooth and shiny like little candies. She smiled at me and told me she was going to page Dr. Asterholder. He came back a few minutes later and sat on the edge of my bed. I watched as he poured water into a glass from a pitcher and held the straw to my lips. I drank.

"I took out three lymph nodes. We had them tested to see how far the cancer spread." He paused. "You made the right call, Senna."

My chest felt tight. How did he get the results that soon? I wanted to reach up and touch the bandages, but it hurt too much. "You just need to rest for now. Can I get you anything?"

I nodded. When I spoke my voice sounded charred. "There is a book on my nightstand, next to my bed. Can you get it for me next time you—"

"I'll bring it tomorrow," he said. "Your cell phone is there." He pointed to the table next to my bed. I had no need for a cell phone, so I didn't look. "I have to do rounds. Call me if you need anything." I nodded, half wishing he'd leave a business card like the old days.

True to his word, the next day Isaac brought me Nick's book. I held it in my hands for a long time before I had a nurse put it on my hospital nightstand. Old habits die hard.

Isaac came to check on me after his shift ended. He was out of his scrubs and wearing jeans and a white t-shirt. The nurses twittered when he walked in dressed that way. He looked closer to a drummer than a doctor. He sat on my bed. But he was not a doctor this time. He was a drummer. I wondered if drummer Isaac was very different than doctor Isaac. He reached for the book and picked it up, turning it over in his hands. My eyes followed the tattoos on his forearm. It felt strange to see Nick's book in Isaac's hands. He studied it for a while, then he said, "Do you want me to read it to you?"

I didn't answer him, so he opened it to the first chapter. He breezed right past the dedication page without even looking. *Bravo,* I thought. *Good for you.*

When he started reading, I wanted to scream at him to stop. I was tempted to cover my ears. To refuse the assault of a book written to make me hurt. But I did neither. I listened, instead, to Isaac Asterholder read the words that the love of my life wrote to me. And they went like this…

NICK'S BOOK

You don't have to be alone. We are mostly born that way, though. We grow up being nurtured to believe that the other half of our soul is somewhere out there. And since there are six billion people inhabiting our planet, chances are one of them is for you. To find that person, to find your soul-piece, or your great love, we must count on our paths diverging, the tangling of lives, the soft whispering of one soul recognizing another.

I found my piece. She wasn't what I was expecting. If you formed a woman's soul out of black graphite, bathed it in blood, and then rolled it around in the softest rose petals, you still wouldn't have touched on the complication that was my match.

I met her on the last day of summer. It felt appropriate that I would meet a daughter of winter as the last of the Washington sunshine sieved through the sky. Next week there would be rain, rain and more rain. But today, there was sun, and she stood underneath it, squinting even beneath her sunglasses as if she were allergic to the light. I was walking my dog through a busy park on Lake Washington. We'd just turned around to head home when I stopped to look at her. She was lean—a runner, probably. And she was wearing one of those things that's longer than a sweater and shorter than a dress. A sweater dress? I followed the line of her legs to camo boots. You could tell she loved those shoes by the worn creases and the way she stood so comfortably in them. I loved those boots for her. And on her. I wanted to be in her. A rough manly thought I'd be too ashamed to admit out loud. The straps of a messenger bag crossed over her chest and hung at her left thigh. Now, I consider myself a bold man, but not quite bold enough to approach a woman whose every body movement said she wanted to be left alone. I did that day. And the closer I got, the stranger she became.

She didn't see me; she was too busy looking at the water. Lost in it a little. How can a man be jealous of water? That's exactly what I wanted to explore.

"Hi," I said, when I was standing in front of her. She didn't raise her eyes right away. When she did, her look was a little indolent. I jumped right in. "I'm a writer, and when I saw you standing here, I was compelled to start putting words down on paper. Which makes me think you're my muse. Which makes me think I need to talk to you."

She smiled at me. It looked like it took effort, that perhaps maybe she didn't smile very often and her facial muscles were stiff.

"That's the best pickup line I've ever heard," she mused.

I wasn't sure if it was a pickup line. It was embarrassingly truthful. Just saying it made my lips pucker like I was holding in a mouthful of lemon pulp.

I eyed the worn leather messenger bag at her hip.

"What's in the bag?" I asked. I was starting to get a feeling about her. Like I knew what she was before she told me.

"A computer."

I didn't peg her as a college student. She had too much attitude to be a professional. Self-employed, I was guessing.

"You're a writer, too," I said.

She nodded.

"So we speak the same language," I offered. She had a strip of silver running through her brown hair. More proof, it seemed, that she was born for winter.

"You're John Karde," she said. "I've seen your picture. In Barnes and Noble."

"Well, that's embarrassing."

"Only if I don't like sappy women's fiction," she said. "Which I do."

"Do you write it?"

She shook her head, and I swear that sliver of silver glimmered in the dying sun. My nerdy writer mind immediately said *mithril.*

"I'm working on my first real novel. It feels pretty angry."

"Let's talk about it over dinner," I offered. I couldn't take my eyes off of her. I mean, sure she was stunning—but it was more than that. She was a house with no windows. You could go crazy in one of those. I wanted in. She eyed my dog.

"I can drop him off, my house is on the way to town."

She paused only to check her watch before nodding. We walked in silence for a few blocks. She kept her head down, choosing the sidewalk over the rest of the world. I wondered if she liked the cracks, or if she just didn't want to meet the eyes of the people we passed. It might have felt uncomfortable, our quiet walking, but it didn't. I suspected her to be a woman of few words. Muses often spoke with their eyes and their bodies. The power they supply is electrifying in itself. They set fire to your synapses.

She waited at the edge of my driveway, even though I invited her in, toeing a stray weed that had forced its way up through the concrete. I wasn't much of a gardener. My yard looked unloved. I walked Max back up to the house and opened the door I never locked. I stopped by his water bowl and topped it off under the faucet while he watched me. Max knew my routine with women. I'd take her to dinner, I'd say things about my writing and my passion, then we'd come back here. Before I went back outside, I ran my fingers through my hair, grabbed a piece of Juicy Fruit off the counter, and stepped into the chill. She was gone. It was then I realized that I had never asked her name. I never really told her mine—not my real one, anyway. I carefully unfolded the gum from its wrapper, sticking the yellow strip between my teeth. I pocketed the piece of wax paper, scanning the street for some sign of her. I'd just lost a girl I really wanted to know. It didn't feel good.

NICK'S BOOK

She came back. Two days later. I saw her from my living room window, standing in the same spot I'd left her, staring at my house as if it were something out of a bad dream. The last time I saw her she'd been standing in sunshine, this time it was rain. She had on a white slicker, the rim of it dripping water into her face. I could see the silver streak in her hair plastered to her cheek. I watched her from the window for a few minutes, just to see what she'd do. She seemed rooted to the spot. I decided to go get her. Walking barefoot down my driveway, I sipped my coffee casually, running my tongue over the chip in the rim. A few raindrops dripped into my mug. When I came within a few feet of her I stopped and looked up at the sky.

"You like this weather." It wasn't a question.

"Yes," she said.

I nodded. "Want to come in for some coffee?"

Instead of answering me she started walking up the driveway, helping herself to the door. It slammed behind her before I realized she was alone in my house.

Was it my imagination, or did she make sure to step on every weed on her way up?

She didn't stop to look around when she walked through the corridor that connected my foyer to the rest of the house. I had several pictures hanging on my walls—art and some family stuff. Normally women stopped to examine each one. I always thought they did it to ease their nerves. She took off her jacket and dropped it on the floor. Puddles formed around it as the rainwater skirted off. She was an odd bird. She walked right to the kitchen like she'd been there a hundred times before, stopping in front of my beat-up

Mr. Coffee. She pointed to the cabinet above it, and I nodded. She chose a Dr. Seuss mug—smart girl. I tended to stick to the Walt Whitman with the chip on the rim. I watched her lift the pot from the warmer and pour without looking. She was staring out my window. Right when the liquid reached the rim of the mug, her hand automatically pulled back. I breathed a sigh of relief. She had the weight and timing perfected in that strange little head of hers. When she was done, she leaned back against the counter and looked at me expectantly.

"So, the other day…"

"What?" I said. "You're the one that just left."

"It wasn't the right day."

What the hell type of thought was that?

"And today is the right day?"

She shrugged. "Maybe. I just felt like coming, I guess."

She ambled over and sat across from me at the worn dinette I'd taken through three relationships. If I ended up with this girl I was going to buy a new table. I'd had sex on it too many times for it to be relationship kosher.

"This is a stupid world," she said, and traced her finger along the edge of the table like she was reading brail.

I waited for her to go on but she didn't. My forehead was creased. I felt the skin wrinkling against itself. She was sipping her coffee, already thinking about something else.

"Do you ever have a complete thought?"

She seriously considered my question and languidly took another sip. "I have many."

"Finish the last one then."

"I don't remember what it was."

She drank the rest of her coffee, then stood up to leave.

"See you Tuesday," she said, heading for the door.

"What's Tuesday?" I called after her.

"Dinner at your house. I don't eat pork."

I heard the screen slam behind her. Max raced for the door, barking, his nails clicking against the tile as he scrambled past me. I leaned back in my chair, smiling. I didn't eat pork either. Except bacon, of course. Everyone eats bacon.

She showed up on Tuesday, right at six. I had no idea when to expect her, so I made sushi with the salmon I'd bought that morning from the market. I was busy wrapping my rolls in seaweed when she let herself in. I heard the screen door slam and Max's manic barking.

She slid a bottle of whiskey across the counter.

"Most people bring wine," I said.

"Most people are pussies."

I choked on my laugh.

"What's your name?"

"Brenna. What's yours?"

"You already know my name."

It was mostly true. She knew my pen name.

"Your real name," she said.

"It's Nick Nissley."

"So much better than John Karde. Who are you hiding from?"

She unscrewed the lid from the Jack and drank straight from the bottle.

"Everyone."

"Me, too."

I looked at her out of the corner of my eye as I poured soy sauce into two ramekins. She was young, much younger than me. What did she have to hide from? Probably an ex-boyfriend. Nothing serious. Just a guy who didn't want to let go, most likely. I had some exes who probably wanted to hide from me. It was a shallow thought, because if this woman was really that simple, she wouldn't have struck my interest. I saw her standing still and quiet, and she caused movement in my brain. I'd already written over sixteen thousand words since she'd walked with me to my house and then disappeared. A feat, considering I'd been claiming writer's block for the last year of my life.

No, if this woman said she was running away, she was.

"Brenna," I said that night as we lay in my bed.

"Mmmm."

I said it again, tracing a finger along her arm.

"Why do you keep saying my name?"

"Because it's beautiful. I've known Brianna's, but never a Brenna."

"Well, congratulations to you." She rolled off the bed and reached for her skirt. That skirt had been what started it all. I see a skirt and I want to know what's underneath it.

"Where are you going?"

The corner of her mouth lifted. "Do I look like the kind of girl who sleeps over on the first date?"

"No ma'am."

She fished around on the floor for the last of her clothes, and then I walked her to the door.

"Can I take you home?"

"No."

"Why not?"

"I don't want you to know where I live."

I scratched my head. "But you know where I live."

"Exactly," she said. She pushed up on her toes and kissed me on the mouth.

"Tastes like a *New York Times Bestseller*," she said. "Goodnight, Nick."

I watched her go and felt conflicted. Did I really just let a woman walk out of my house in the middle of the night and not take her home? I hadn't seen a car. My mother would have a coronary. I knew so little about her, but there was no question that she wouldn't take well to me galloping after her on my imaginary steed. And why the hell didn't she drive? I walked back into the kitchen and started cleaning up our dinner plates. We had only made it through half of the sushi before I leaned across the table and kissed her. She hadn't even acted surprised, just dropped her chopsticks and kissed me back. The rest of our night was impressively graceful. I credit her with that. She undressed me in the kitchen and made me wait to take her clothes off until we reached the bedroom. Then she made me sit on the edge of the bed while she undressed herself. Her back never touched the sheets. A true control freak.

I put the last of the dishes in the dishwasher and sat at my desk. My thoughts were coming at me fast. If I didn't get them down, I'd lose them. I wrote ten thousand words before the sun came up.

A week later we took our first trip into Seattle together. It was her idea. We rode in my car since she said she didn't have one. She looked nervous sitting in the front seat with her hands folded in her lap. When I asked her if she wanted me to put on the radio she said no. We ate Russian pastries from paper bags and watched the ferries cross the sound, shivering and standing as close as we could get to each other. Our fingers were so greasy when we were done we had to rinse them off in a water fountain. She laughed when I splashed water in her face. I could have written another ten thousand words just from hearing her laugh. We bought five pounds of prawns from the market and headed back to my house. I don't know why the hell I asked for five pounds, but it sounded like a good idea at the time.

"You have one of these," I said, as we were cleaning the prawns together at my kitchen sink. I ran my finger laterally along its body, pointing out the dark line that needed to be cleaned out. She frowned, looking down at the prawn she was holding.

"It's called a mud vein."

"A mud vein," she repeated. "Doesn't sound like a compliment."

"Maybe not to some people."

She de-headed her shrimp with a flick of her knife and tossed it in the bowl.

"It's your darkness that pulls me in. Your mud vein. But sometimes having a mud vein will kill you."

She set down the knife and washed her hands, drying them on the back of her jeans.

"I have to go."

"Sure," I said. I didn't move until I heard the screen door slam. I wasn't upset that my words had run her off. She didn't like to be found out. But she'd be back.

NICK'S BOOK

She didn't come back. I tried to tell myself that I didn't care. There were plenty of women. Plenty. There were women everywhere I looked. They all had skin and bones, and I'm sure some of them even had silver streaks in their hair. And if they didn't have a silver streak in their hair I'm sure I could convince them to put it there. But there is something about the process of convincing yourself that you don't care that just confirms even more that you do. Every time I passed the window in my kitchen I found myself looking up to see if she was standing in the rain, judging the weeds poking out of the driveway. I looked at those weeds so much that eventually I went out there in the rain and pulled them up one by one. It took me all afternoon and I got a nasty head cold. I was cleaning up my driveway for a woman.

I wanted to go look for her, but she'd told me little to nothing about herself. I could hold the five things she'd said in the palm of my hand, and still find plenty of room. Her name was Brenna. She came from the desert. She liked to be on top. She ate bread by pulling off little pieces and placing them in the center of her tongue. I had asked her questions, and she had skillfully turned them back on me. I had been eager to give her answers—too eager—and in the process I'd forgotten to collect answers from her. She had played me like a narcissistic trombone. Tooting, tooting, tooting my own horn. She must have been thinking what a fool I was the entire time.

Toot, toot.

I went back to the park, hoping to run into her again. But something told me that day in the park was a fluke. It wasn't her day to be there, and it wasn't mine. We met because we needed to, and I'd gone and screwed it up by telling her she had a mud vein. I thought she knew. *God.* If I had another chance with her, I'd never talk again. I'd just listen. I wanted to know her.

I sat in front of my laptop and wrote more words than had come to me in years—all at once. They just strung themselves together and I felt like a writing god. I had to have more of this woman. I'd write a library full of books if I had a year with her. Imagine a lifetime. She was meant for me. I cleaned out my weeds, I cleaned out my closets, I bought a new table and chairs for my kitchen. I finished my book. E-mailed it to my editor. I lingered some more at my kitchen window, industriously washing and rewashing my dishes.

It was Christmas before I found her again. Actual Christmas—the day of tinsel and turkey and colorful paper wrapped around goodies we don't want or need. I have a mother and a father and twin sisters with rhyming names. I was on my way to their house for Christmas dinner when I saw her jogging along the barren sidewalk. She was headed for the lake, her fluorescent sneakers blurring beneath her. She was a flash of speed. Her legs were chorded with muscle. I'd bet she could outrun a deer if she tried. I sped up and pulled into the empty lot of an Indian restaurant about half a mile ahead of her. I could smell the curries seeping from the building: green and red and yellow. I hopped out of my car and crossed the street, planning to cut her off before she reached the lake. She would have to go through me to get to the trail. I looked bolder than I felt. She could tell me to go to hell.

By the time she saw me it was too late to pretend she hadn't. Her pace slowed until she was bent at the knees in front of me. I watched the way her back rose and fell. She was breathing hard.

"Merry Christmas," I said. "Sorry for interrupting your run."

She glared at me from her bent position, confirming my guess that she didn't want to see me.

"I didn't mean to upset you the last time you were at my house," I said. "If you'd given me the chance to apologize I wo—"

"You didn't upset me," she said. And then, "I finished my book."

Finished her book? I gaped. "In the three weeks I haven't seen you? I thought you'd barely started."

"Yes, and now I've finished it."

I opened and closed my mouth. It took me a year to complete a manuscript, and that didn't include the time I spent on research.

"So when you just left like that…?"

"I knew what I had to write," she said, like it was the most obvious thing in the world.

"Why didn't you say something? Call me?" I felt like a clingy high school girl.

"You're an artist. I thought you'd understand."

I was wrestling with my pride to tell her that I didn't. I'd never in my life run out on dinner to finish a story. I'd never felt even a chord of passion strong enough to drive me to do that. I didn't tell her because I was afraid of what she would think. Me—New York Times Bestseller of over a dozen sappy novels.

"What did you write about?" I asked.

"My mud vein."

I got a chill.

"You wrote about your darkness? Why would you do that?"

There was nothing pretentious about her. No show, no thriving to impress me. She didn't even try to guard the ugly truth, which made every one of her words feel like a cold dousing of water to the face.

"Because it was the truth," she said, so matter of fact. And I fell in love with her. She didn't have to try to be anything. And everything that she was was something that I was not.

"I missed you," I said. "Can I read it?"

She shrugged. "If you want to."

I watched a trickle of sweat wind down her neck and disappear between her breasts. Her hair was damp, her face flushed, but I wanted to grab her and kiss her.

"Come with me to my parents'. I want to have Christmas dinner with you."

I thought she was going to say no and I'd have to spend the next ten minutes convincing her. She didn't. She nodded. I was too afraid to say anything as she walked with me to my car, in case she changed her mind. Without any objections, she climbed into the front seat and folded her hands in her lap. It was all very formal.

As soon as we were on the road, I reached for the radio. I wanted to put on Christmas music. At least prepare her for the Christmas crack she was about to experience at the Nissley house. She grabbed my hand.

"Can you leave it off?"

"Sure," I said. "Not a fan of music?"

She blinked at me, then looked out the window.

"Everyone is a fan of music, Nick," she said.

"But not you…?"

"I didn't say that."

"You implied it. I'm begging for a detail about you, Brenna. Just give me one."

"Okay," she said. "My mother loved music. She played it in our house from morning 'til night."

"And that made you dislike it?"

We pulled into my parent's driveway and she used the distraction to avoid answering my question.

"Pretty," she said as we slowed to a stop.

My parents lived in a modest home. They'd spent the last ten years making upgrades. If she thought the outside was pretty I couldn't wait to see what she thought of my mother's pink granite kitchen counters, or the fountain depicting a peeing boy they installed in the middle of the foyer. When I lived at home we'd had linoleum and plumbing that only worked a tenth of the time. She made no comment about the giant reindeer lawn ornaments, or the wreath almost the size of the front door. She hopped out without any reservation and followed me to the house of my very happy childhood. I looked at her before I opened the door, dressed in running clothes, her hair messy and stuck to her face. What type of woman jumped in the car with you on Christmas Day to meet your family, without putting on a cardigan and a dress? This one. She made every woman I'd ever been with feel insignificant and fake. This was going to be fun.

"Is this you, Senna?"

He was looking at me intensely. I didn't know what he was thinking, but I knew what I was thinking: *Damn Nick and his book.*

I could barely … I didn't know how to … My thoughts were trembling out of my hands.

"You're shaking," Isaac said. He set the book on the nightstand and poured me a glass of water. The cup was one of those heavy plastic things, the color of too many colors of Play-Doh mixed together. It grossed me out, but I took it and sipped. The cup felt too heavy. Some of the water spilled down the front of my hospital gown, plastering it to my skin. I handed the cup back to Isaac, who set it aside without taking his eyes off my face. He put each one of his hands over mine to steady them. It absorbed a little of my shaking.

"He wrote this for you," Isaac said. His eyes were dark, like he had too many thoughts and they were filling him up. I didn't want to answer.

There was no mistaking the similarities in name—Senna/Brenna. There was also no mistaking the actual story itself. The fine line that squiggled between fiction and truth. It made me sick that Nick told the story. Our story? His version of our story. Some things should be buried and left to rot.

I pointed to the book. "Take it," I said. "Throw it away."

His eyebrows drew together. "Why?"

"Because I don't want the past."

He stared at me for a long minute, then picked up the book, tucked it under his arm and walked for the door.

"Wait!"

I held out my hand for the book and he walked it back to me. Opening the cover I flipped to the dedication, touching it softly, running my fingers over the words … then I ripped it out. Hard. I handed the book back to Isaac, with the jagged page clutched in my fist. Stone faced, he left, the soles of his shoes sucking on the hospital floor. *Thwuup ... Thwuup … Thwuup.* I listened until they disappeared.

I folded the page over and over until it was the size of my thumbnail, square upon square upon square. Then I ate it.

I was discharged a week later. The nurses told me that normally a double mastectomy patient went home after three days, but Isaac pulled strings to keep me there longer. I didn't say anything about it as he handed me my prescriptions in a paper bag, folded over twice and stapled. I shoved the bag into my overnight bag, trying to ignore the rattling sound of the pills. Trying to ignore how heavy the bag was in general. I supposed that it was easier for him to keep an eye on me here rather than at my house.

He moved surgeries around and took the afternoon off to take me home. It annoyed me, and yet I didn't know what I'd do without him. What did you say to a man who inserted himself as your caretaker without your permission? *Stay away from me, what you're doing is wrong? Your kindness freaks me out? What the hell do you want from me?* I didn't like being someone's project, but he had his wits and car, and I was laced with painkillers.

I wondered what he did with Nick's book. Did he toss it in the trash? Put it in his office? Maybe when I got home it would be sitting on my night table like it had never left.

A nurse wheeled me through the hospital to the main doors where Isaac had parked his car. He walked slightly ahead of me. I watched his hands, the fat of his palm beneath his thumb. I was looking for traces of the book on his fingers. *Stupid.* If I wanted Nick's words, I should have read them. Isaac's hands were more than Nick's book. They'd just reached into my body and cut out my cancer. But I couldn't stop seeing the book in his hands, the way his fingers lifted the corner of the page before he turned it.

He put on wordless music when we got in his car. That bothered me for some reason. Perhaps I expected him to have something new for me. I tapped my finger on the window as we drove. It was cold out. It would be like this for another few months before the weather would crack, and the sun would start to warm

Washington. I liked the feel of the cold glass on my fingertips, like tiny shocks of winter. Isaac carried my bag inside. When I got to my room my eyes found my nightstand. There was a clear rectangle cut in the dust. I felt a pang of something. *Grief?* I was feeling a lot of grief; I had just lost my breasts. It had nothing to do with Nick, I told myself.

"I'm making lunch," Isaac said, standing just outside my room. "Do you want me to bring it up here?"

"I want to shower. I'll come down after."

He saw me staring at the bathroom door and cleared his throat. "Let me take a look before you do that." I nodded and sat down on the edge of my bed, unbuttoning my shirt. When I was finished, I leaned back, my fingers gripping the comforter. You'd think I'd be used to this by now—the constant gawking and touching of my chest. Now that there was nothing there I should feel less ashamed. I was just a little boy as far as what was underneath my shirt. He unwound the bandages from my torso. I felt the air hit my skin and my eyes closed automatically. I opened them, defying my shame, to watch his face.

Blank.

When he touched the skin around my sutures I wanted to pull back. "The swelling is down," he said. "You can shower since the drain is out, but use the antibacterial soap I put in your bag. Don't use a sponge on the stitches. They can snag."

I nodded. All things I knew, but when a man was looking at your mangled breasts he needed something to say. Doctor or not.

I pulled my shirt closed and held it together in a fist.

"I'll be downstairs if you need me."

I couldn't look at him. My breasts weren't the only thing torn and ripped. Isaac was a stranger and he had seen more of my wounds than anyone else. Not because I chose him like I did Nick. He was just always there. That's what scared me. It was one thing inviting someone into your life, choosing to put your head on the train tracks and wait for imminent death, but this—this I had no control over. What he knew, and what he'd seen about me brought so much shame I could barely look him in the eyes. I tiptoed to the bathroom, glancing once more at the nightstand before shutting the door.

Someone could take your body, use it, beat it, treat it like it's a piece of trash, but what hurts far worse than the actual physical attack is the darkness it injects into you. Rape works its way into your DNA. You aren't you anymore, you're the girl who was raped. And you can't get it out. You can't stop feeling like it's going to happen again, or that you're worthless, or that anyone could ever want you because you're tainted and used. Someone else thought you were nothing, so you assume that everyone else will as well. Rape was a sinister destroyer of trust and worth and hope. I could fight cancer. I could cut chunks out of my body and inject poison into my veins to fight cancer. But I had no idea how to fight what that man took from me. And what he gave me—fear.

I didn't look at my body when I undressed and stepped into the shower. It wouldn't be me in that mirror. Over the last few months my eyes had emptied out, become hollow. When I happened upon my reflection somewhere, it hurt. I stood with my back to the water, like Isaac told me, and my eyes rolled back in my head. This was my first shower since the surgery. The nurses had given me a sponge bath, and one had even washed my hair in the little bathroom. She'd pushed a chair right up against the rim of the sink and had me bend my head back while she massaged little bottles of shampoo and conditioner into my hair. I let the water run over me for at least ten minutes before I had the nerve to reach up and soap the empty place below my collar bone. I felt…nothing.

When I was finished, patted dry and dressed in pajama pants, I called Isaac upstairs. Some of my steri-strips had come loose. I stood quietly as he worked to fit new ones on, my wet hair dripping down my back, my eyes closed. He smelled like rosemary and oregano. I wondered what he was making downstairs. When he was done, I slipped on a shirt and turned my back to him while I buttoned up the front of it. When I turned back around Isaac was holding the hairbrush I'd tossed on the bed. I'd been unsure of how to lift my arms high enough to work out the tangles. Pouring shampoo on my head had been one thing, brushing felt like an impossible feat. He gestured to the stool in front of my vanity.

"You're so strange," I said, once I was seated. I was working hard to keep my eyes on his reflection and not look at my face.

He glanced down at me, his strokes gentle and even. His fingernails were square and broad; there was nothing messy or ugly about his hands.

"Why do you say that?"

"You're brushing my hair. You don't even know me, and you're in my house brushing my hair, cooking me dinner. You were a drummer and now you're a surgeon. You hardly ever blink," I finished.

His eyes looked so sad by the time I finished that I regretted saying it. He ran the brush through my hair one last time before setting it on the vanity.

"Are you hungry?"

I wasn't, but I nodded. I stood and let him lead me out of my room.

I glanced once more at my nightstand before I followed him to the food.

People lie. They use you and they lie, all the while feeding you bullshit about being loyal and never leaving you. No one can make that promise, because life is all about seasons, and seasons change. I hate change. You can't rely on it, you can only rely on the fact that it will happen. But before it does, and before you learn, you feel good about their stupid, bullshit promises. You choose to believe them, because you need to. You go through a warm summer where everything is beautiful and there are no clouds—just warmth, warmth, warmth. You believe in a person's permanence because humans have a tendency to stick to you when life is good. I call them honey summers. I've had enough honey summers in life to know that people leave you when winter comes. When life frosts you over and you're shivering and layering on as much protection as you can just to survive. You don't even notice it at first. The cold makes you too numb to see clearly. Then all of a sudden you look up and the snow is starting to melt, and you realize you spent the winter alone. That makes me mad as hell. Mad enough to leave people before they left me. That's what I did with Nick. That's what I tried to do with Isaac. Except he wouldn't leave. He stayed all winter.

The seasons split at the seams: spring, summer, fall and winter. I've always pictured them as giant sacks filled with air and color and smell. When it's time for one season to be over, the next seasons splits open and pours over the world, drowning its tired and waning predecessor with its strength.

Winter was over. Spring split and burst forth, spilling warm air and bright pink trees all over Washington. The sky was blue, and Isaac was trimming back the bushes in front of my house. A branch caught my arm the week before as I was walking to my front door and made me bleed. Isaac thought I cut myself. I could see the way he examined it. When he deemed my wound to be too curvy to come from a knife's blade, he went searching for shears in my garage. Normally I hired a landscaping company to do the yard work, but here was my doctor, hacking away at my little spruce trees.

I watched him through the window, flinching every time his arms flexed and the shears took a new branch in their mouth. If he accidentally hacked off a finger I'd be responsible. There were leaves and branches littered around his tennis shoes. I was never really hot enough in Washington to be dripping with sweat, but Isaac was damp and exhausted. You couldn't tell Isaac not to do something. He didn't listen. But, winter was over and I was tired of being his project. He was like a fixture here. On my couch, in my kitchen, trimming my hedges. The air was warm and the change had come. Nick used to tell me I was a daughter of winter—that the grey streak in my hair proved it. He said when the seasons changed, I changed. For the first time I think he was right.

"When are you going home?" I asked when he came inside. He was washing his hands at the kitchen sink.

"In a few minutes."

"No, I mean for good. When are you going home and staying home?"

He dried his hands, took his time doing it.

"Are you ready for me to?"

That made me so angry. He always answered my questions with a question. Infuriating. I wasn't a child. I could take care of myself.

"I never asked you to be here in the first place."

"No." He shook his head. "You didn't."

"Well, it's time for you to leave."

"Is it?"

He walked straight at me. I braced myself, but at the very last second he veered to the left and breezed right past where I was standing. I closed my eyes as the air that he stirred wrapped around me. I had the strangest thought. The strangest. *You're never going to smell him again.*

I was not a smell person. It was my least favorite sense. I didn't light candles, or wander into a bakery, drawn in by the scent of the bread. Smell was just another sense that I wrestled into my white room. I didn't use it, I didn't care about it. I lived in a white room. I lived in a white room. I lived in a white room. *But* … I was going to miss Isaac's smell. Isaac was smell. That was his sense. He smelled like spices and the hospital. I could smell his skin, too. He just had to be a few feet away from me and I could catch the smell of his skin.

"Isaac." My voice was full of conviction, but when he turned to face me, hands in pockets, I didn't know what to say. We stared at each other. It was awful. It was painful.

"Senna, what do you want?"

I wanted my white room. I wanted to never have smelled him or heard the words to his music.

"I don't know."

He took a step backwards, toward the door. I wanted to step toward him. I wanted to.

"Senna…"

He took another step back, like he wanted me to stop him. *He's giving me a chance,* I thought. Three more and he would be out the door. I felt the pull. It was in the hollows behind my kneecaps, something tugging me to him. I wanted to reach down and still it. Another step. Another.

His eyes were pleading with me. It was no use. I was too far gone.

"Goodbye, Isaac."

I took it as a loss. I thought so anyway. It had been a long time since I had mourned a person—twenty years, to be exact. But I mourned Isaac Asterholder in my own way. I didn't cry; I was too dry to cry. Every day I touched the spot where Nick's book used to sit on my nightstand. Dust was starting to fill the space. Nick was something to me. We shared a life. Isaac and I had shared nothing. Or maybe that wasn't true. We shared my tragedies. People leave—that's what I was used to—but Isaac showed up. I sat in my white room for days trying to clear myself of all the color I was suddenly feeling: red bikes, lyrics with thorns, the smell of herbs. I sat on the floor with my dress pulled over my knees and my head curled into my lap. The white room couldn't cure me. Color stained everything.

Seven days after he walked backwards out of my house I went to the mailbox and on my way back, found a CD on my windshield. I clutched it to my chest for an hour before I slipped it into my stereo. It was an intense crescendo of lyrics and drums and harp and everything he was feeling—and I was, too. The most remarkable thing was that I was feeling.

It ripped at me until I wanted to gasp for breath. How could music know what you were feeling? How could it help you name it? I went to my closet. There was a box on my top shelf. I pulled it down and ripped off the lid. There was a red vase. Bright. Brighter than blood. My father sent it to me when my first book was published. I thought it was terrible—so bright it hurt my eyes. Now, my eyes were drawn to the color. I carried it to my white room and set it on the desk. Now there was blood everywhere.

I searched for a song for days. I was new to the wonders of iTunes. I went back to Florence Welch. There was something about the intensity of her. I found it. I didn't know how to transfer it to one of those generic CD's he used. But I found out. Then I drove to the hospital, the disk on my lap the whole time. I stood for a long time next to his car. This was a bold move. It was color. I didn't know I had any color. I put the brown envelope on his windshield, and hoped for the best.

His songs reminded me of swimming, which somehow I'd forgotten.

He didn't come right away. He probably wouldn't have come at all if he hadn't seen me at the hospital a few weeks later. I'd gone to sign some of the financial paperwork for my bill. Insurance crap. I only saw him briefly—a few seconds, tops. He was with Dr. Akela. They had been walking down the hall together, their identical white coats differentiating them from the other humans milling around the nurses' station—two demi-gods in a sea of humans. I froze when I saw him, felt a feeling only drugs can give you. He was headed for the elevator, same as me. *Oh great, this is going to suck.* If there were people in the elevator I could scoot to the back and hide. I waited hopefully, but when the doors slid open the only people inside were on the poster advertisement for erectile dysfunction. *We should do this more often,* the slogan said. A handsome, athletic couple in their late forties, woman looking coy. I jumped in and hit the lobby button with my fist. *Close!* It did. Thankfully, it did, but before the doors sealed shut Isaac appeared in the gap. For a second it looked like he was going to hold a hand between the doors, force them to open. He drew back instead, the shock sketched around his eyes. He hadn't been expecting to see me today. *We should do this more often,* I thought. It all happened in a dizzy three seconds. The time it takes for you to blink, blink and blink. But I didn't blink, and neither did he. We locked into a three second staring contest. We couldn't have said any more in those three seconds.

When you spend extraordinary amounts of time pushing someone away, their reaction to your apology tends to be slow. I imagined so, anyway. That's how I wrote it in my stories. He came a week later. Since then I'd put away the red vase, gone back to craving white.

I was at the mailbox when his car pulled into my driveway. I felt.

You feel.

When had that started happening again? I waited with the stack of junk mail clutched in my hands. He stepped out of his car and walked to me.

"Hey," he said.

"Hi."

"I'm headed to the hospital, but I wanted to see you first." I took it. I missed him. *You miss Nick*, You know Nick. You don't know this man.

I pushed that away.

We walked up to my house together. When I closed the door behind us, he took my mail from my hands. I watched as he set it on the table next to the door. A single, white envelope slipped off the edge and slid to the floor. It skidded to a stop behind Isaac's right heel. He turned to me and took my face in his hands. I wanted to keep looking at the safe white of that envelope, but he was right there, making me look at him. His gaze was slicing. Sluicing. There was too much emotion. He kissed me with color, with drumbeat, and a surgeon's precision. He kissed me with who he was, the sum of his life—and it was all encompassing. I wondered what I kissed him with since I was only broken parts.

When he stopped kissing me I felt the loss. His lips, for a brief moment, touched my darkness, and there was a glimpse of light. His hands were still in my hair, touching my scalp, and we were only a nose apart as we looked at each other.

"I'm not ready for this," I said softly.

"I know."

He shifted positions until he had me wrapped up in his arms. A hug. This was far more intimate than anything I'd done with a man in years. My face was underneath his chin, pressed to his collarbone.

"Goodnight, Senna."

"Goodnight, Isaac."

He let me go, took a step back, and left. His impressions were so short and so acute. I listened to the hum of his car as it left my driveway. There was a small kick of gravel as he pulled onto the street. When he was gone everything was still and quiet as it always was. Everything but me.

PART THREE

ANGER AND BARGAINING

Out of the walls, music begins to play. We stand frozen, looking at each other, the whites of our eyes expanding with each beat. There is an invisible chord between us; there has been since Isaac saw my pain and accepted it as his own. I can feel it tugging as the music accelerates and Isaac and I stand immobilized by shock. I want to step into the circle of his arms and hide my face in his neck. I am frightened. I can feel the fear in the hollows of my mind. It's pounding like a doomsday drum.

Dum

Da-Dum

Dum

Da-Dum

Florence Welch is singing *Landscape* through our prison walls.

"Get warm clothes," he says, without taking his eyes from mine. "Layer everything you have. We are getting out of here."

I run.

There are no coats in the closet. No gloves, no thermal underwear—nothing warm enough to venture into negative ten-degree weather. Why didn't I notice this before? I push through the hangers in the closet, frantic. The music plays around me; it plays in every room. It's making me move faster. Those songs Isaac gave me, who knew about them? They were private … sacred to me; as unspoken as my thoughts. There are plenty of long-sleeved shirts, but most of them are thin cotton or light wool. I pull each one over my head until I have so many layers I am too stiff to move my arms. I already know it won't be enough. To get anywhere in this weather I'd need thermals, a heavy coat, boots. I pull on the only pair of shoes that looks warm: a pair of fur-lined ankle boots—more fashionable than practical. Isaac is waiting for me downstairs. He is holding the door open like he's afraid to let it go. I see that he doesn't have a jacket, either. He's wearing a pair of black gum boots on his feet. Something for rain or yard work. Our eyes lock as I walk past him, through the door and into the snow. I sink into it. Right up to my knees. Knee-high snow, that can't be good. Isaac follows me. He leaves the door open and we make it twenty feet before we stop.

"Isaac?" I grab onto his arm. His breath puffs out of his mouth. I can see him shivering. I am shivering. *God.* We haven't even been outside for five minutes.

"There's nothing, Isaac. Where are we?"

I spin in a circle, my knees brushing a pathway through the snow. There is only white. In every direction. Even the trees seem to be far off. When I squint I can see the glint of something in the distance, just before the tree line.

"What is that?" I ask, pointing. Isaac looks with me. At first it just looks like a piece of something, then my eyes follow it. I follow it until I spin and come back, full circle. I make a sound. It starts in my throat, a noise you'd make when surprised, and then it changes into something mournful.

"It's just a fence," Isaac says.

"We can climb it," I add. "It doesn't look that high. Twelve feet maybe…"

"It's electric," Isaac says.

I spin to look at him. "How do you know?"

"Listen."

I swallow and listen. A hum. Oh God. We couldn't hear that from behind the three inch plated windows. We are caged in like animals. There has to be a way around. An electrical wire we can cut… something. I look at the snow. It covers the trees beyond the fence and falls in a graceful white skirt down a steep ravine that drops off to the left of the house. There are no roads, no houses and no breaks in the cover of white. It never ends. Isaac starts walking back toward the house.

"Where are you going?"

He ignores me, his head down. The effort it takes to walk through the snow makes it look like he's climbing stairs. I watch as he circles around the back of the house, not knowing what to do. I linger for a few more minutes before following him, grateful for the path his struggle has cut for me. I find him facing what looks like a shed. Since there are no windows facing this way, it's the first time I am seeing what's back there.

There is a smaller structure to the right of it. The generator, I realize. When I look at Isaac's face I see that it's neither the shed nor the generator he's looking at. I follow his eyes past the structures and feel my breath seize. I stop shivering, I stop everything. I reach for his hand and we plow together through the snow, our breath returns, laboring from the effort. We stop when we reach the edge of the cliff. Laid out in front of us is a view so sharp and dangerously beautiful I am afraid to blink. The house backs right up to a cliff. One that our captor—our zookeeper—didn't give us windows to see. It seems like he's trying to tell us something. Something I don't want to hear. *You are trapped,* maybe. Or, *You're not seeing everything. I'm in control.*

"Let's go back inside," Isaac says. His voice is wiped clean of emotion. It's his doctor's voice; factual. *His hope just fell down that cliff,* I think. He heads back without me. I stay to look—look at the spread of mountains. Look at the dangerous drop-off that could turn a falling body into a sack of skin and liquid organs.

When I turn around, Isaac is carrying armfuls of wood from the shack and into the house. *It's not a house,* I tell myself. *It's a cabin in the middle of nowhere.* What happens when we run out of food? Fuel for the generator? I walk back toward the shed and peer inside. There are piles and piles of chopped wood. An axe rests against the wall closest to where I stand to the back of the shed are several large metal containers. I am about to go investigate them when Isaac comes back for more wood.

"What are those?" I ask.

"Diesel," he says, without looking up.

"For the generator?"

"Yes, Senna. For the generator."

I don't understand the edge in his voice. Why he's speaking to me like he is. I crouch down beside him and reach for the logs, loading my arms. We walk back together and stock the wood closet in the cabin. I am about to follow him outside for more when he stops me.

"Stay here," he says, touching my arm. "I'll do the rest."

If he hadn't touched my arm, I would have insisted on helping. But there is something to his touch. Something he is telling me. I crouch in front of the fire he's built until my shivering stops. Isaac makes a dozen more trips before our wood closet is full, then he starts piling logs in the corners of the room. *In case we get locked in again,* I think.

"Could we leave the door open? Wedge something in between the door jamb so it can't close?"

Isaac runs a hand along the back of his neck. His clothes are filthy and covered in a thousand flecks of wood.

"Would we be guarding it, too? In case someone closes it in the middle of the night?"

I shake my head. "There is no one here, Isaac. They dropped us off and left us here."

He seems to be torn about telling me something. This pisses me off. He's always had the tendency to treat me like I'm fragile.

"What, Isaac?" I snap. "Just say it."

"The generator," he says. "I've seen them before. They have underground tanks with a hose system attached."

I don't get it at first. A generator … no windows on the back of the house … a hose system to refill the diesel.

"Oh my God." I collapse on the couch and stick my head between my knees. I can feel myself gasping for air. I hear Isaac's footsteps on the wood floor. He grabs me by the shoulders and drags me to my feet.

"Look at me, Senna."

I do. "Calm down. Breathe. I can't afford to have anything happen to you, okay?"

I nod. He shakes me until my head snaps back.

"Okay?" he says again.

"Okay," I mimic. He lets me go, but doesn't step away. He pulls me into a hug and my face buries itself in the crook of his neck.

"He's been filling that tank hasn't he? That's why there are no windows on the back of the house."

Isaac's silence is confirmation enough.

"Will he come back? Now that we have the door open and can fill it ourselves?" It seems unlikely. Is it our punishment now that we figured out the code? A reward and a punishment: *you can go outside, but now it's only a matter of time before you run out of fuel and freeze to death. Tick-tock, tick-tock.*

He squeezes me tighter. I can feel how tense his muscles are underneath my palms.

"If he comes back," I say. "I'm going to kill him."

I haven't cut myself since the day I met Isaac. I don't know why. It might be because he made me feel things, and I didn't need a blade to feel anymore. That's why we do it, right? Cut ourselves to feel? Saphira would have said so. The dragon and her existential bullshit. *"Since humans can choose to be eitherrrr cruel or good, they arrre, in fact, neither of these things essentially."*

Now I am feeling too many things. I crave my white room. What was the opposite of cutting? Wrapping yourself in a cocoon and never coming out. I roll myself in the feather comforter on the attic bed—that's what we we're calling it—the attic. My room. The place where my kidnapper put me in pajamas and laid me. Laid me out to what? I don't know, but I'm starting to like it in the attic. I can't hear the music as well when I'm wrapped in feathers. *Landscape* has not stopped playing. The first of our songs. The one he gave to me to let me know he understood.

"You look like a joint," Isaac says. He hardly ever comes up here. I feel him touch my hair, which is sticking out of the top of my cocoon. I bury my face in the white and try to suffocate myself. I traded comforters with him. He took the red because I couldn't stand to look at it.

"There is something downstairs you should probably see," he says. He's touching my hair in a way that's lulling me. If he wants me to get up he's going to have to stop doing that.

I came straight up here after we carried the wood into the house and discovered the electric fence. Isaac must have found something more outside.

"Unless it's a dead body, I don't want to see it."

"You'd want to see a dead body?"

"Yes."

"It's not a dead body, but I need you to come with me." He unrolls me from my self-made joint, and pulls me to my feet. He doesn't let go right away. He squeezes where he holds. Then he pulls me along by my hand like I'm a child. I stumble after him. He leads me downstairs. To the wood closet. Pulling open the door, he holds me by the tops of my arms, forcing me to stand in front of him and look inside.

I see only the wood at first. Then he reaches over me with a pink Zippo and holds it as close to the inner wall as he can. Strange, I think, at first—there is writing on the walls. Some of the wood is obscuring it. I reach inside and move a couple of the logs over. I start shaking. He wraps his arms around my torso and squeezes, then leads me backwards to the sofa where I sit. Part of me wants to break away to go look some more, but I feel. I feel too much. If I don't stop feeling I'm going to explode. Pages of my book—over and over—wall-papered on the inside of the closet like a slap in the face.

"What does it mean?" I ask Isaac.

He shakes his head. "A fan? I don't know. It's someone playing games."

"How did we never notice that before?"

I want to press my fingers into the sides of his face and force him to look at me. I want him to tell me that he hates me, because for some reason he is here as a result of me. But he doesn't. Nothing he does is encumbered by blame or anger. I wish I could be like that.

"We weren't looking," he says. "What else are we not seeing because we aren't looking?"

"I have to read what's in there." I stand up, but Isaac pulls me back.

"It's Chapter Nine."

Chapter Nine?

I reach for it in my mind. Then I let it go. Chapter Nine hurts. I wish I hadn't written it. I tried to get the publishers to take it out of the manuscript before the book went to print. But they felt it was necessary to the story.

The day the book hit shelves, I sat in my white room, holding back my vomit, knowing that everyone was reading Chapter Nine and living my pain. I don't want to read it, so I stay sitting.

"Chapter Nine is—"

I cut him off.

"I know what it is," I snap. "But why is it there?"

"Because someone is obsessed with you, Senna."

"No one knew that was real! Who did you tell?"

I am screaming; so angry I want to throw something large. But the zookeeper didn't give us anything large to throw. Everything is bolted, sewn into the walls and floors like this is a dollhouse.

"Stop it!" He grabs me, tries to slow me down.

His voice is getting loud. I release mine, too. If he's going to yell I'm going to yell louder.

"Then why are *you* here?" I punch his chest with both of my fists.

He sits down abruptly. It throws me off. I was all geared up to fight.

"You've said those words to me so many times I've lost count. But this time it's not my choice. I want to be with my wife. Planning for our baby. Not locked up like a prisoner with you. I don't want to be with you."

His words hurt so bad. My pride keeps my knees stiff, otherwise I would have buckled from the pain. I watch him walk up the stairs, my heart pounding to the beat of his anger. I guess I was wrong about him. I was wrong about so many things with regard to him.

I am wrapped in my cocoon again when Isaac comes up with dinner. He brings two plates and sets them on the floor by the fire before unwrapping me.

"Food," he says. I lay on my back staring up at the ceiling for a minute, before throwing my legs off the side of the bed and slowly walking to his picnic.

He's already eating, staring at the flames while he chews. I sit on my knees as far away from him as I can—on the corner of the rug—and pick up my plate. The plate is square. There are squares around its edge. It's the first time I'm noticing. I've been eating off these dishes for weeks, but I'm just now observing things like color and pattern and shape. They are familiar to me. I touch one of the squares with my pinkie.

"Isaac, these plates…"

"I know," he says. "You're in a fog, Senna. I wish you'd wake up and help me get out of here."

I set my plate on the floor. He's right.

"The fence. How far does it run around the house?"

"About a mile in every direction. With the cliff on one side of us."

"Why did he give us that much room?"

"Food," Isaac says. "Wood?"

"So he means for us to take care of ourselves when the food runs out?"

"Yes."

"But the fence will keep the animals out, and there are only so many trees to cut down."

Isaac shrugs. "Maybe he intended for us to make it 'til summer. We'd see some animals then."

"There is a summer here?" I say it sarcastically, but Isaac nods.

"There is a short summer in Alaska, yes. But depending on where we are, there might not be one. If we are in the mountains it will be winter year round."

I don't long for the sun. I never have. But I don't like being told it has to be winter all year either. It makes me want to claw at the walls.

I fidget with the hem of my sweater.

"How much food do we have left?"

"Couple months' worth if we ration it."

"I wish this song would stop playing." I pick up my plate and start eating. These are Isaac's plates. Or were his plates. I only ate at his house once. He probably has the type of china now that married people have. I think about his wife. Small and pretty, eating off her china alone because her husband is missing. She doesn't feel like eating, but she's doing it anyway because of the baby. The baby they tried and tried for. I blink the image of her away. She helped save my life. I wonder if they've tied our disappearances together? Daphne knew some of what happened with Isaac and me. They had been seeing each other when he met me. He put everything on hold with her during those months he was keeping me alive.

"Senna," he says.

I don't lift my head. I'm trying not to crack. There is rice on my plate. I count the grains.

"It took me a long time…" he pauses. "To stop feeling you everywhere."

"Isaac, you don't have to. Really. I get it. You want to be with your family."

"We're not good at this," he says. "The talking." He sets his plate down. I hear the clatter of silverware. "But I want you to know one thing about me. *Want* being the key word, Senna. I know you don't *need* words from me."

I brace myself against the rice; it's all that stands between me and my feelings. Rice.

"You've been silent your whole life. You were silent when we met, silent when you suffered. Silent when life kept hitting you. I was like that too, a little. But not like you. You are a stillness. And I tried to move you. It didn't work. But that doesn't mean you didn't move me. I heard everything you didn't say. I heard it so loudly that I couldn't shut it off. Your silence, Senna, I hear it so loudly."

I set my plate down and wipe my palms on my pant legs. I have yet to look at him, but I hear the angst in his voice. I have nothing to say. I don't know what to say. That proves his point, and I don't want him to be right.

"I hear you still."

I stand up. I upset my plate; it topples.

"Isaac, stop."

But he doesn't. "It's never that I don't want to be with you. It's that you don't want to be with me."

I bolt for the ladder. I don't even bother using the rungs. I jump … land on my haunches. I feel feral.

"The life you choose to live is the essence of who you arrre."

I am an animal, bent on surviving. I let nothing in. I let nothing out.

DEPRESSION

I stink. Not the way you smell on a hot day when the sun toasts your skin and you smell like bologna. I wish I smelled like that. It would mean there was sun. I smell musty, like an old doll that has been locked up in a closet for years. I smell like unwashed body and depression. Yes. I slowly consider my stink and the awful way my grey streak hangs lank in my face. I don't bother to push it off my eyes. I stay curled under the blanket like a fetus. I don't even know how long I've been like this—days? Weeks? Or maybe it just feels like weeks. I'm composed of weeks, and days of weeks, and hours of weeks and days and minutes and seconds and…

I'm not even in the attic bed. It's warmer in the attic, but a few nights ago I took too many shots of whiskey and stumbled into the carousel room, only half conscious and holding in my sick. I was too dizzy to light a fire, so I lay trembling under the feather blanket, trying not to look at the horses. Waking up there was like having a night of drinking and then finding yourself in your bed with your best friend's boyfriend.

At first I was too shocked to move, so I just lay there paralyzed by shame and nausea. Not sure who exactly I felt like I was betraying by being in there, but felt it nevertheless. Isaac never came to find me, but considering that we were passing the bottle back and forth all night, he was probably just as sick as I was. That's what we do lately; we congregate in the living room after dinner to sip from a bottle that fits neatly in our hands. After dinner drinks. Except dinners are getting sparse: a handful of rice, a small pile of canned carrots. There is always more liquor in our bellies than food these days. I groan at the thought of food. I need to pee and maybe be sick. I run the tip of my finger back and forth, back and forth over the cotton sheets. Back and forth, back and forth until I fall asleep. *Landscape* is playing. It's always playing. The zookeeper is cruel.

Back and forth, back and forth. There is wallpaper to the left of the bed, of tiny carousel horses floating untethered through a creamy backdrop. Except they aren't angry like the horses attached to the bed. There are no flared nostrils and you cannot see the whites of their eyes. They have furling ribbons tied to their forelocks and cranberry colored jewels decorating their saddles. To the right of the bed is a baby blue wall and centered in the middle of it, a brick fireplace. Sometimes I look at the blue wall, other times I like to count the little carousel horses on the wallpaper. And then there are times I squeeze my eyes shut so tight and pretend I'm at home in my own bed. My sheets are different, and the weight of the blanket, but if I lie very still…

That's when things get a little crazy. I'm not even sure I want to be in my own bed. It was figuratively just as cold as this one. There is nowhere I want to be. I should embrace the cold and the snow and the prison. I should be like Corrie Ten Boom and try to find purpose in suffering. I get catatonic at that point. My thoughts, having run in circles for most of the day, shut down. I just stare until Isaac eventually carries in a plate of food and sets it on the table next to the bed. I don't touch anything. Not for days, until he pleads with me to eat. To move. To talk to him. I stare at one of the two walls and see how long I can go without feeling. I pee in the bed. The first time it's an accident; my bladder, stretched like a water balloon, reaches its limit. There's another time. In my sleep I roll away from it, find a new spot. I wake up closer to the fireplace, my clothes barely damp. It doesn't bother me. I'm finally in the place where nothing bothers me.

Spalsh

I squirm under hot water, writhing in shock. I come up gasping, trying to claw my way out of the tub. He dropped me in like a human bath bead. Water sloshes over the side of the tub and soaks into his pant legs and socks. I fight for a few more seconds, his hands holding me in the water. I don't have the energy to fight.

I let myself sink. The bath is so full that I can submerge myself completely. I sink, sink, sink into the ocean.

But there is no rest, because he grabs me under my arms and pulls me up to a sitting position. I gasp and grab the sides of the tub. I'm naked except for a sports bra and panties. He pours shampoo on my head; I bat at his hands like a child until his fingers find my scalp. Then I let him. My body, rigid a second ago, slouches as he rubs the fight out of my head. He washes me, using his hands and a sponge that looks like it came straight from a coral reef. Surgeon's hands rub across my muscles and my skin until I'm so relaxed I can barely move. I close my eyes when he rinses my hair. Both of his hands are holding my head up, cradling it so I don't sink beneath the water's surface. When they suddenly stop moving I open my eyes. Isaac is staring at me from above. His eyebrows are almost touching, so deep is his consternation. I reach up without thinking and cradle his cheek with my hand. I would be worried that he could see through my thin, white sports bra, but there is nothing to see. I'm practically a boy. I take my hand away and then I start to chortle. It sounds like a burst of madness. Why do I even wear a sports bra? It's so stupid. I should just walk around topless. I laugh harder, swallowing a mouthful of water as my body rolls to the side. I am choking—choking and laughing. Isaac pulls me up. Then all at once the sound and the choking are gone. I am Senna again. I stare at the wall behind the tap, feeling tired. Isaac grabs my shoulders and shakes me.

"Please," he says. "Just try to live."

My eyes are so tired. He picks me up out of the bath. I close my eyes as he kneels on the floor to dry me, then wraps me up in a towel that smells of him. I loop my arms around his neck as he carries me to the ladder. I squeeze his neck a little, just so he knows I'll try.

I come back to life a little bit. I have the hot and horrible thought that the carousel room tried to kill me. *No*. It's just a room. I tried to kill me. When my dark days recede, they come for Isaac. We take turns giving up, it seems. He locks himself in his room with the only bathroom, and I have to pee in a bucket and empty it around the back of the house. I leave him be, taking food to his room and picking up the empty plate. I keep the door to the carousel room closed. It stinks in there now. I washed the sheets in the bathtub the week before, and scrubbed at the mattress with soap and water, but the piss smell pervades. Isaac eventually comes out of his room and starts making our meals again. He doesn't speak very much. His eyes are always red and puffy. *Sow sadness, reap tears*, my mother used to say. We delve solely in sadness in this house. When will my reaping come?

Days, then a week, then two. Isaac gives me the silent treatment. And when there are only two people in the universe, silence is very, very loud. I lurk in his places: the kitchen, the carousel room where he sits against the wall and stares at the horses. I don't sleep in the attic room anymore; I curl up downstairs on the sofa and wait. Wait for him to wake up, wait for him to look at me, wait for emotions to implode.

One night I am sitting at the table … waiting … while he stands at the stove stirring something in a huge cast iron pot. We are running out of food. The freezer has seven plastic bags of indeterminate meat and about four pounds of frozen vegetables. All lima beans, which Isaac hates. The pantry is no less barren looking. We have one sack of potatoes and a two-pound bag of rice. There are some cans of ravioli, but I keep telling myself we will be out of here before I have to eat those. When he hands me my plate a few minutes later I try to catch his eyes, but they run from me. I push my plate away. The rim of my plate bumps against his. He looks up.

"Why are you treating me like this? You can barely look at me."

I don't expect him to answer. Maybe.

"Do you remember how we met?" he asks. I get a chill.

"How could I not?"

He runs his tongue across his teeth before leaning away from his food. He's certainly looking at me *this* time.

"Do you want the story?"

"I want to know why you can't look at me," I say.

He rubs the tips of his fingers together as if to rub away grease. But there is no grease. We are eating dry rice with a little potato and ground beef mashed into it.

"I had a flight booked, Senna. On Christmas Day. I was supposed to leave that morning and go home to see my family. I was on my way to the airport when I turned my car around and went home. I don't fucking know why I did it. I just felt like I needed to stay. I went for a jog to clear my head and there you were, running out of the trees."

I stare at him. "Why didn't you tell me?"

"Would you have believed me?"

"Believed what? That you went for a jog instead of hopping on a plane?"

He leans forward. "No. Don't make me feel stupid for thinking that there is purpose. We aren't animals. Life isn't random. I was supposed to be there."

"And I was supposed to get raped? So that we could meet? Because that's what you're saying. If life isn't random then it was in someone's plan for that bastard to do what he did to me!" I am out of breath, my chest heaving. Isaac licks his lips.

"Maybe it was in someone's plan for me to be there for you…"

"To keep me alive," I finish.

"No. I didn't say—"

"Yes, that's exactly what you're saying. My savior, sent to keep the pathetic, sniveling, Senna from killing herself."

"Senna!" he slams his fist on the table, and I jump.

"When we found each other we were both pretty dead and defeated. Something grew despite that." He shakes his head. "You breathed life back into me. It was instinct for me to be there with you. I didn't want to save you, I just didn't know how to leave you."

There is a long pause.

Not even Nick did that. Because Nick didn't love me unconditionally. He loved me so long as I was his muse. So long as I gave him something to believe in.

"Isaac..." his name falls flat. There is something I want to say but I don't know what it is. There is no real point in saying anything at all. Isaac is married and our situation leaves little room for anything but survival.

"I need to go get some wood," I announce.

He smiles sadly, shakes his head.

I cook dinner that night. Red meat; I don't know what kind it is until I smell it in the skillet and know it's some type of game. Who took the time to hunt these animals for us? Bag them? Freeze them?

Isaac doesn't come down from his room. I put his plate of food in the oven to keep it warm and climb onto the kitchen table. It's big enough for two people to lie side by side. I curl up in the middle, my face turned toward the window. I can see the window above the sink, and in it the reflection of the doorway. The kitchen is his go-to place. I'll wait for him here. It feels good to be somewhere I'm not supposed to be. The zookeeper wouldn't care that I'm lying on his table, but in general, tables aren't for lying on. So, I feel mildly rebellious. And that helps. No it doesn't. Who am I kidding? I unroll myself from the ball I'm curled into and jump down from the table. Walking to the silverware drawer, I pull it back forcefully until the silver clatters. I eye its contents, examining the selection: long, short, curved, serrated. I reach for the knife Isaac uses to peel potatoes. I run the tip across my palm, back and forth, back and forth. If I press a little harder I can draw blood. I watch my skin dent underneath the tip as I wait for the puncture, the inevitable sharp pain, the red, red release.

"Stop it."

I jump. The knife clatters to the floor. I place my palm over the blood that is beading on my skin. It wells, then flows down my arm. Isaac is standing in the doorway in pajama bottoms and nothing else. I glance at the stove, wondering if he's come down because he's hungry. He walks briskly over to where I'm still standing and bends to pick up the knife. Then he does something that makes my brow furrow. He puts it back in my hand. My mouth twitches as he wraps my fingers around the hilt. I watch, numb and wordless, as he points the sharp end at the skin just above his heart. My hand is locked underneath his, gripping the hilt with trepidation. I can't move my fingers—not even a little bit. He uses his strength against me when I try to pull away, yanking my arm and the blade toward him. I see blood where the knife is pressing into his skin, and I cry out. He's forcing me to hurt him. I don't want to hurt him. I don't want to see his blood. He pushes harder.

"No!" I struggle to break free, pulling my body backwards. "Isaac, no!" He lets go. The knife drops to the floor between us. I stand, riveted, and watch as the red gathers and then trickles down his chest. The cut is no longer than an inch, but it's deeper than one I would have made on myself.

"Why would you do that?" I cry. That was so cruel. I grab the only thing I see—a dishtowel—and I hold it against the cut that we made together. He has blood running down his chest, I have it running down my arm. It's morbid and confusing.

When I look up for his answer he is looking at me intently.

"What did you feel?" he asks.

I shake my head. I don't know what he's asking me. Does he need stitches? There must be a needle somewhere around here … thread.

"What did you feel when that happened?" He's trying to catch my eyes, but I can't take my eyes from his blood. I don't want the life to bleed out of Isaac.

"You need stitches," I say. "At least two…"

"Senna, what did you feel?"

It takes me a minute to focus. He really wants me to answer that? I open and close my mouth.

"Hurt. I don't want you to hurt. Why would you do that?"

I am so angry. Confused.

"Because that's what I feel when you hurt yourself."

I drop the dishtowel. Nothing dramatic—it's just become too heavy to hold along with my understanding. I look down at where it lies between my feet. There is a bright red stain on one side of it.

Isaac bends to pick it up. He also picks up the knife and places it back in my hand. Grabbing my wrist, he leads me back to the table and firmly plants me in front of it.

"Write," he says, gesturing to the wood.

"What?"

He grabs the hand that's holding the knife. I try to pull away again, but his eyes still me.

"Trust me."

I stop fighting.

He presses the tip into the wood this time. Carves a straight line. "Write here," he says.

I know what he's telling me, but it's not the same.

"I don't write on my body. I cut it."

"You write your pain on your skin. With a knife. Straight lines, deep lines, jagged lines. It's just a different kind of word."

I get it. All at once. I feel grief for everything that I am. *Landscape* is playing in the background, a strange soundtrack, a constant soundtrack.

I look down at the smooth wood tabletop. Pressing down, I carve the line we made deeper. I wriggle the blade around a little bit. It feels good. I do it some more. I add more lines, more curves. My movement becomes more frantic each time the knife meets the table. He must think I've gone mad. But even if he does, he doesn't move. He stands behind my shoulder as if he's there to supervise my assault. When I'm done I toss the knife away from me. Both hands are pressed against my carvings as I lean over the table. I'm breathing hard, like I've just run six miles. I have, emotionally. Isaac reaches down and touches the word I've made. I didn't plan it. I didn't even know what it said until I watched his fingers trace it. Surgeon's fingers. Drummer's fingers.

HATE

"Who do you hate?" he asks.

"I don't know."

I do a short spin into his chest, forgetting that he's right behind me. He grabs the tops of my arms and clutches me against him. Then he wraps his arm around my head, forcing my face against his chest. The other is circling my back. He holds me and I shake. And I swear … I swear he's just healed me a little bit.

"I still see you, Senna," he says into my hair. "You can't ever stop seeing what you recognize as part of yourself."

A week later, *Landscape* stops playing. I am stepping out of my shallow, lukewarm bath when her voice cuts off in the middle of the chorus. I wrap a towel around myself and dart out of the bathroom to find Isaac. He's in the kitchen when I come careening around the corner still clutching the towel to my dripping body. We stare at each other for a good two minutes, waiting for it to start up again, thinking there is a kink in the system. But it never comes back. It feels like a relief until the silence kicks in. True, deafening silence. We are so used to the noise, it takes a few days to acclimate to the loss of it. That's what it's like to be a prisoner of anything. You want your freedom until you get it, then you feel bare without your chains. I wonder if we ever get out of here, will we feel the loss? It sounds like a joke, but I know how the human mind works.

Two days later the power goes. We are in darkness. Not just in the house. November has come. The sun will not rise on Alaska for two months. It's the ultimate darkness. There is nowhere to find light, except crouched in front of the fire as our logs dwindle. That's when I know we're going to die.

We eat the last potato sometime in late November. Isaac's face is so drawn I would syphon out my own body fat to give him if I had any.

"Something is always trying to kill me," I say one day as we sit watching the fire. The floor is our perpetual hangout, in the attic room—as close to the fire as we can get. Light and heat. Light and heat. The barrels of diesel in the shack are empty, the cans of ravioli in the pantry are empty, the generator is empty. We've chopped down the trees on our side of the fence. There are no more trees. I watched Isaac hack at them from the attic window whispering "Hurry, hurry…" until he cut them down and hauled the logs inside to burn. But there is snow, plenty of snow. We can eat the snow, bathe in the snow, drink the snow.

"It seems that way, yes. But so far nothing has been able to."

"What?"

"Kill you," he says.

Oh yeah. How easily the brain flits about when there is no food to hold it in place.

Lucky me.

"We are running out of food, Senna." He looks at me like he really needs me to understand. Like I haven't seen the goddamn pantry and fridge. We've both lost so much weight I don't know how I could ignore it. I know what we're running out of: food … wood … hope…

Isaac set the traps we found in the shed, but with an electric fence we're not sure how many animals can get to our side without frying themselves first. Our power is out, but the fence remains on. The hum of the electricity feels like a slap in the face.

"If our generator ran out of power, there must be another power source on the property."

Isaac puts another log on the fire. It bites gingerly at the wood, and I close my eyes and say, *hotter, hotter, hotter…*

"It's all been planned out, Senna," he says. "The zookeeper meant for us to run out of generator fuel the same week that we were plunged into permanent darkness. Everything that is happening has been planned."

I don't know what to say, so I say nothing.

"We have enough for another week, maybe, if we're careful," he tells me.

The same question as always ricochets through my brain. Why would someone go through all the trouble to get us here, only to let us starve and freeze? I ask my question out loud.

Isaac answers with less enthusiasm than I asked. "Whoever did this is crazy. Trying to make sense of crazy makes you just as crazy."

I suppose he's right. But I'm already crazy.

Three days later we run out of food. Our last meal is a handful of rice cooked over the fire in a pot that Isaac rigs with metal poles he found in the shed. It is barely soft enough to chew. Isaac gives me the larger portion, but I leave most of it on my plate. I don't care if I die hungry. The only truth is that I'm going to die. When they finally find my body I don't want them cutting me open and seeing half digested rice in my stomach. It feels insulting. Prisoners always get their choice of a last meal. Where is mine? I think of the potato skins I ate over the sink. It feels good now, to know that I didn't waste them. We ate coffee grounds last week for breakfast. It was almost funny at first, like something out of a horror, survival story, but when they clogged up my throat with their bitterness I wanted to cry.

I roll myself tighter into my blanket. It's so cold, but we only burn two logs a day. If we can just get past that fence we can hack at the trees to our hearts' content. Sometimes I see Isaac outside staring at it, his hands in his pockets and his head dipped back. He walks up and down with a screwdriver he found in the shed, holding it against the posts to see how far the spark jumps. I think he's hoping for a day the zookeeper forgets. We've already chopped down anything that can burn, including the shed itself. The doors in the house are made of fiberglass or we would have used those too. We've burned furniture. Isaac sawed and hacked at the beds until only the metal frames were left. We've burned books. *God*—books! We burned the puzzles, we even pulled down the Oleg Shuplya prints, first for their wooden frames, and eventually we'd tossed in the paper as well. I could call this situation my own personal Hell, but Hell is warm. I'd love to be in Hell right now.

Isaac comes into my room. I hear him near the fireplace. He's lighting my log. My one, precious log. We were saving it. I guess the time for saving has come to an end. Usually he leaves when he's done, goes to his own room, but the attic room is the warmest in the house and the only one left with a burning log. I feel the mattress shift under his weight as he sits next to my cocoon.

"Do you have any of that chapstick left?"

"Yes," I say softly. "In the closet."

I hear him walk to the wooden armoire and move things around. We have one pink Zippo left. It's on its last few drops of lighter fluid. We've been so careful, but no matter how careful you are, things eventually run out.

"Chapstick will keep the fire burning longer," he says. "It'll make it hotter, too."

Some part of my brain wants to know how he knows this; I have a snarky question on the tip of my tongue: *Did you learn that in medical survival school?* But I can't formulate the words to ask him.

"I'm going to sleep in here with you," he says, sitting on the bed. I open my eyes and stare into the whiteness of the comforter. The color white is so prevalent here. I was growing sick of it when everything went dark. Now I long for it. His weight lifts from the bed as he unrolls me. The minute the last of the blanket falls away, I begin shivering uncontrollably. I stare up at him from my back. He looks ragged. He's lost so much weight it scares me. *Wait.* Did I already have that thought? I haven't looked at myself in weeks. But my clothes—the ones the zookeeper left me—they hang and wilt over me like I'm a child wearing my mother's things. Isaac leans down and scoops me up. I don't know where he's getting his strength. I can barely hold my head up anymore. The blanket is still underneath me. He lays me on the ground in front of the fire and spreads the blanket out around me. I don't understand what he's doing. Then my heart starts to pound. Isaac stands over me. I'm between his legs. Our eyes lock as he lowers himself over me; first to his knees, then his elbows. I don't move. I don't breathe. I close my eyes and feel his weight, a little at first, then all at once. His body is warm. I moan from the shock of it. I want to wrap myself around him, absorb his heat, but I hold still. He pulls me up just enough to wrap his arms around my back. My eyes are still closed, but I can feel his breath on my face.

"Senna," he says softly.

"Hmmm?"

"Roll with me."

It takes me a minute to get it. The human brain works like a bad internet connection when it's freezing. He wants to be wrapped in the cocoon with me. I think.

I barely nod. My neck is stiff. He tucks the edge of the blanket around us and I tense myself. I feel brittle, like my bones are made of ice. His weight might crack me. We roll ourselves in the blanket and end up on our sides. I can feel Isaac's heat pressed against my front, and the fire's heat licking at my back. I realize he positioned me here on purpose to place me closest to the fire.

My hands are on his chest, so I rest my cheek there too. He still smells like spices. I start listing them all in my head: *cardamom, coriander, rosemary, cumin, basil…* After a few minutes my shivering becomes less. He reaches for my wrist. I don't know why. I don't really care. His thumb presses into my skin. He's taking my pulse, I realize.

"Am I dying, doctor?" I ask quietly. It takes energy to put those words together in the right order, and even while I say them my brain sees a pink spade lying on green, green grass.

"Yes," he says. "We both are. We all are."

"Comforting."

He kisses my forehead. His lips are cold, but his warmth is bringing me back to life. A little bit at least.

"When was the last time you let yourself feel?" his words slur like he's been drinking, but the alcohol is long gone, it's the cold that makes it that way.

I shake my head. For someone like me feeling is dangerous. There is nothing left to fear when you're already dying. I lift my face to relay my answer without words.

His hands find my face.

"Can I make you feel? One more time?"

I cling to him, my fists tightening on his shirt. My yes.

His mouth is so warm. We are shivering and kissing, our bodies firing off heat and desire. We are cold and we are weak. We are emotionally destroyed. We are desperate to feel each other, and to feel hope—to feel one last piece of living. There is nothing joyful or sweet in our mouths. Just frenzy and panic. I taste salt. I'm crying. A kiss unclogged my tear ducts, I think.

When we are done kissing we lie very still.

His lips move against my hair. "I'm sorry, Senna."

I tremble. *He's sorry? Him?* "For what?"

There is a million year pause.

"I couldn't save you this time."

I cry into his chest. Not because he couldn't. Because he wanted to.

I think I doze off. When I wake Isaac's breathing is steady. I think he's still asleep, but when I shift to change positions, he lifts his hands from my lower back and lets me move around until I'm comfortable again. We lie like that for hours. Until the fire burns out its last flame and I know the night has curved into day, even though day no longer shows her face. Until I want to sob from relief and grief. Until I remember all of the ineffable hurt from years ago that he salved with the tender way he loves. We are going to die. But at least I'll die with someone who loves me.

Isaac is touch. Why have I ever thought anything different? He held me once to soothe me from my nightmares, and now he is holding me to protect me from the cold. He touches right where it hurts, and then all of a sudden it doesn't hurt. Yes, Isaac is touch. I see the pink spade again. I can feel the grit of coffee grounds as I work them between my teeth. Then I see The Great Wall of China, and I know my brain is short circuiting, passing along images of things that are in my subconscious. When I see the table flash in my mind—the carved up, heavy, wooden table from the kitchen downstairs—I feel something true. It's like when I sleep and my brain tells me what to write. What is it about the table…? Then I see it, but I'm so tired I can't keep my eyes open. *Don't forget,* I tell myself. *You have to remember the table…*

The fire goes.

Our hearts are slowing. We are resolute.

I wake up. I am not dead. I push at Isaac's chest to wake him up. He doesn't move. His skin feels strange—cold and stiff. *Oh my God.*

"Isaac!" I shove at him with the little bit of leverage that I have. "Isaac!"

I press my ear to his chest. My hair is in my mouth, falling in my eyes. I can't reach the pulse at his neck; I'm trapped between him and the blanket. I'm going to have an asthma attack. I can feel it coming. There's not enough air in this blanket. All I can hear is my own frantic breathing. I have to unroll us, but he feels like a thousand pounds. I push him onto his back and struggle to get out of the blanket. Struggle to breathe as my airways constrict. I have to wiggle up and out. When I am free of the joint, the air hits me. It's freezing. I need it in my lungs, but I don't know how to get it there. I pull the blanket away from his face and press my fingers to his neck. I'm mumbling *please* over and over.

Please don't be dead.

Please don't leave me here alone.

Please don't leave me.

Please don't let me have this asthma attack right now.

I can feel a pulse. It's barely there. I roll onto my back and wheeze. It's a terrible sound. It's the sound of dying. Why am I always dying? I arch my back, my eyes roll. I have to help Isaac.

The table! … What was it about the table?

I know. I see it all—what I saw last night in my delirium. The table from my book. I wrote about it metaphorically; the concept that all great things are made around a table: relationships, plans for war, the meals that keep our bodies alive. A table is an image that represents life and choices. We see it in Camelot when King Arthur's knights gathered around the Round Table, and in the paintings of The Last Supper. We see it in commercials where families eat dinner, laughing and passing a basket of bread. I wrote about a table that was a well. I was at the bottom end of my relationship with Nick and I was trying to illustrate where we had gone wrong. We needed to come back to the table, draw life into our dying relationship. It was melodramatic and stupid, but the zookeeper brought it to life. Built it in our kitchen, and I refused to see it.

I roll onto my knees and crawl … to the hole. I make it halfway down before I fall. I don't know if the cold has numbed me or if my lack of air is consuming my senses, but I feel nothing when I crack against the wood. I crawl some more toward the stairs … toward the table. I … can't … breathe…

I am there. My scribbles in the wood are there. I can feel them with the tips of my fingers, but it's so dark. I go to the cabinet, under the sink, and find the industrial flashlight that Isaac won't let us use unless it's an emergency. I flip the switch and place it on top of the counter, pointing it toward the object of my interest. I stagger forward. I know what I need to do, but I don't have the energy to do it. Three steps feel like twenty. I stand sideways and place my hip just below the lip of the table. Planting one foot against the wall, and the other on the floor, I push. With all and everything.

At first there is nothing, then I hear the grating. It is louder than the hissing, rattling noise that is coming from between my lips. It is confirmation. It's enough to make me push harder. I push until the heavy wooden slab has moved off center and is wobbling and ready to fall. I stand back to watch. There is an impressive thud as it angles sideways and then tips over, landing upright between the base and the wall. I stumble forward and peer down. I am looking into a dark hole. It's a well. Or, sort of, because there is no water. There is something down the table/well. But I still can't breathe, and Isaac is dying. I have nothing to lose. I climb onto the bench and swing my legs over the side. Then I jump.

The fall isn't a long one. But when I land I hear a crack. There is no pain, but I know I've broken a part of my body, and in a minute, when the shock passes and I try to stand up, I'm going to know what part that is. There is light filtering in from the flashlight I left in the kitchen; it stabs gently at the darkness around me, but it's not enough. Why didn't I bring it with me? I feel around with my hands, above my head, to my left. The zookeeper is precise. If he gave me a dark hole, he will provide a light with which to see it. The floor is uneven—dirt. I am on my back. I reach lower. My fingers touch a metal cylinder the width of my forearm. I lift it, bring it to my face. A flashlight.

Neither of my arms is broken. *That's so good*, I tell myself. *So, so good.* But it means something else is broken. I am breathing again. Not normally, but better. The fall must have knocked the breath back into me, given my body some perspective. I grimace and mess with the flashlight until my fingers find the switch. It powers on with bold, white light. I direct the beam at my body, and my fear is confirmed. There is a bone sticking out of my shin, pink and white. As soon as I see it, the pain hits me. It envelops, folding me over, stretching me out. I writhe. I open my mouth to cry out, but there is no sound for this kind of pain. I have nothing in my stomach to vomit. So I retch instead.

I don't have time to waste, so while I retch I direct the beam around. My eyes water but I can make out piles of wood, bags of rice, cans and cans and cans of food, shelves of food. I pull off my shirt, it's just one of three I'm wearing. I make a tourniquet, tying it above my knee. I gasp as I pull myself up. *You're going to faint,* I think. *And there isn't time for that. Breathe!*

I drag myself to the wood. I have to make him warm. I have to bring him back. I'm not a doctor; I studied art history, for God's sake, but I know that Isaac has one foot in this goddamn cabin and one foot in the fog beyond. There is a bag of rice that has split open. I rip at the hole and quickly turn the bag over, emptying the rice onto the floor. Then leaning against the wall, I drop one, two, three logs into the sack. I grab a can of creamed corn off a shelf—it's the nearest thing to me—and toss that in, too. There is a steel ladder in the corner of room, propped against a wall. Despite the cold, I am sweating; sweating and shivering. The zookeeper left us everything we needed to survive another…what? Six months? Eight? It was sitting here all along while we starved, and we didn't know. I pass a metal box with a big, red medical cross on it. I rip open the door. Inside there are bottles, so many bottles. I grab for the aspirin, popping off the lid, I tilt my head back and let half a dozen pills slide into my mouth. There is a roll of gauze. I rip the package open with my teeth until the material unravels in my fingers. I bend down and wrap it around the bone, flinching, feeling hot blood on my fingers. I want to look at the bottles, see what he left us. *Isaac first.*

I scream when I open the ladder … it's stiff with cold and time, and it jars my lower body, shooting pain everywhere. I climb backwards, keeping my leg extended and using my arms and good leg to lift myself up each rung. My arms burn, dragging the sack with me. When I reach the top of the ladder I have to lift my leg over the side of the well. There is no way to get to the floor gracefully and without pain. *Your leg is already broken. What more can happen?* I glance at the bone: nerve damage, tissue damage, I could bleed to death, die of an infection. *A lot more, Senna.* And then I drop my good leg to the floor with my sack clutched against my chest and my eyes closed. I stand there for a second, shivering and wanting to die. Another flight of stairs, another ladder, then I'll be there. First, the can opener. *This is nothing,* I tell myself. *There is a bone sticking out of your leg. It can't kill you.* But it can. Who knows what type of infection I might get after this? My pep talk doesn't bring me comfort. If Isaac dies, his death will kill me. My leg is preventing me from getting to Isaac. *Ignore the leg. Get to Isaac.*

It's easier to sit on the stairs and lift myself backward, sticking my injured leg straight out while I use my arms and good leg to lift myself. I toss my sack up ahead of me. I feel every bump, every movement. The pain is so intense I am beyond screaming. It is taking concentration not to pass out. I'm sweating. I can feel fat rivulets rolling down the sides of my face and the back of my neck. I use the railing to lift myself up on the top step, then I hop to the ladder. This is going to be the hard part. Unlike the ladder in the well, this one angles straight up. There is nothing to lean on and the rungs are narrow and slippery. I sob with my face pressed against the wall. Then I pull myself together and drag myself up Mt. Everest.

I lay the logs. I light them. Just one at first, then I add a second. I put his head in my lap and rub his chest. I've done so much research as a writer; I know that when someone has hypothermia you're supposed to focus on building heat in the chest, head and neck. Rubbing their limbs will push cold blood back toward the heart, lungs and brain, making things worse. I know I'm supposed to give him the heat from my body, but I can't get my pants off, and even if I could I wouldn't know how and where to put my body with a bone sticking out of it. I feel so much guilt. So much. Isaac was right. I knew the zookeeper was playing a game with me. I knew it when I saw the lighters and the carousel room. But I shut down and refused to help him figure things out. I shut down. Why? *God.* If I'd put two and two together, we could have found that well weeks ago. If he dies it's my fault. He's here and it's my fault. I don't even know why. But I want to. This is a game, and if I want to get out, I have to find the truth.

THE CAROUSEL

There is a carousel in Mukilteo. It sits in a copse of evergreens at the bottom of a hill called The Devil's Backbone. The animals impaled on that ride are angry, their eyes rolling, heads kicked back like something has spooked them. It's what you would expect from a ride that sits on the devil's tailbone. Isaac took me there for my thirtieth birthday, on the last day of winter.

I remember being surprised that he knew it was my birthday, and that he knew where to take me. Not to a pretentious dinner, but to a clearing in the woods where a little bit of dark magic still lived.

"As your doctor, I have access to your medical records," he reminded me, when I asked how he knew. He wouldn't tell me where we were going. He loaded me into his car and played a rap song. Six months ago my music was wordless, now I was listening to rap. Isaac was a virus.

The Devil's Backbone is curved like a serpent; it's a steep rock path you half walk, half skid down. Isaac held my hand as walked, dodging boulders that jutted out of the ground like knobs on a spine. When we stepped into the circle of the trees, the moon was already hanging over the carousel. My breath caught. Right away, I knew there wasn't something right. The colors were wrong, the animals were wrong, the sentiment was wrong.

Isaac handed five dollars to an old man sitting at the controls. He was eating sardines out of a can with his fingers. He stuck the five dollars in the front pocket of his shirt, and stood to open the gate.

"Choose wisely," Isaac whispered as we crossed the threshold. I went left; he went right.

There was a ram and a dragon and an ostrich. I passed them by. This felt important, as if what I chose to ride on my thirtieth birthday said something. I stopped beside a horse that looked more angry than scared. Black with an arrow piercing its heart. Its head was bowed like it was ready for the fight, arrow or not. I chose that one, glancing over at Isaac as I swung my leg over the saddle. He was a few rows up, already on a white horse. It had a medical cross on its saddle and blood on its hooves.

Perfect, I thought.

I liked that he didn't feel the need to ride next to me. He took his decision as seriously as I took mine, and in the end we each rode alone.

There was no music. Just the swish of the trees and the hum of machinery. The old man let us ride twice. When it was over Isaac came over to help me down. His finger stroked my pinkie, which was still wrapped around the cracked pole that speared my horse.

"I'm in love with you," he said.

I looked for the old man. He wasn't by his post. He wasn't anywhere.

"Senna…"

Maybe he went to get more sardines.

"Senna?"

"I heard you."

I slid off my horse and stood facing Isaac. My hair was pulled up or I would have started messing with it. He wasn't very far from me, maybe just the distance of a single step. We were wedged in between two gory, death-infatuated carousel horses.

"How many times have you been in love, Doctor?"

He pushed his shirtsleeves up to his elbows and looked out at the trees behind my shoulder. I kept my eyes on his face so they wouldn't wander to the ink on his arms. His tattoos confused me. They made me feel like I didn't know him at all.

"Twice. The love of my life, and now my soulmate."

I start. I was the writer; the worder of words—and I rarely used the beaten up idea of a soulmate. Love was sinned against too often for me to believe in that tired old concept. If someone loved you as much as they loved themselves, why did they cheat and break promises and lie? Wasn't it in our nature to preserve ourselves? Shouldn't we preserve our soul match with as much fervor?

"You're saying there is a difference between those two?" I ask.

"Yes," he said. He said it with so much conviction I almost believed him.

"Who was she?"

Isaac looked at me.

"She was a bass player. An addict. Beautiful and dangerous."

The other Isaac, the one I don't know, loved a woman who was very different from me. And now Doctor Isaac is saying he's in love with me. As a rule, I try not to ask questions. It gives people a sense of friendship when you ask them things, and there is no getting rid of them. Since I can't seem to get rid of Isaac anyway, I deem it safe to ask the most pressing question. The one that only he could answer.

"Who were you?"

It starts to rain. Not predictable Washington drizzle, but fast, fat bullets of water that explode when they hit the ground.

Isaac grabs the bottom of his sweater and pulls it over his head. I stand very still even though I'm startled. He's shirtless in front of me.

"I was this," he said.

Most people marked themselves with scattered ideas: a heart, a word, a skull, a pirate woman with huge breasts—little parts that represented something. Isaac had one tattoo and it was continuous.

A rope. It wound around his waist and chest, looped around his neck like a noose. It wrapped twice around each bicep before coming to an end right above the words I've seen poking out from underneath his sleeves. It was painful to look at. Uncomfortable.

I understood. I knew what it was like to be bound.

"I'm this now," he said. He used two fingers to point to the words on his forearm.

Die to Save

My eyes go to his other arm.

Save to Die

"What does that mean?"

Isaac looked at me closely, like he didn't know if he should tell me.

"A part of me had to die in order to save myself." My eyes move to his left arm.

Save to Die

He saved lives to die to himself. To keep the bad part dead he had to be constantly reminded of the frailty of life. Being a doctor was Isaac's only salvation.

God.

"What's the difference?" I asked him. "Between the love of your life, and your soulmate?"

"One is a choice, and one is not."

I'd never thought of love as a choice. Rather, it seemed like the un-choice. But if you stayed with someone who was self-destructing and chose to keep loving, I suppose it could be a choice.

I waited for him to go on. To explain how I fit in.

"There is a string that connects us that is not visible to the eye," he said. "Maybe every person has more than one soul they are connected to, and all over the world there are these invisible strings." As if to make his point, his finger traced a black ribbon that ran through my horse's mane. "Maybe the chances that you'll find each and every one of your soulmates is slim. But sometimes you're lucky enough to stumble across one. And you feel a tug. And it's not so much a choice to love them through their flaws and through your differences, but rather you love them without even trying. You love their flaws."

He was talking about soulmate polygamy. How could you take something like that seriously?

"You're a fool," I breathed. "You don't make any sense."

I felt angry with him. I wanted to lash out and make him see how stupid he was for believing in such flimsy ideals.

"I make too much sense for you," he said.

I shoved him. He wasn't expecting it. The distance between us grew for just a second as his left foot took a step backward to keep his balance. Then I launched myself at him, throwing him against the painted horse at his back. Fury in fists. I pounded at his chest and slapped at his face while he stood and let me. *How dare he. How dare he.*

Every blow I delivered set my anger to a lower simmer. I hit him until it was gone and I was mostly spent. Then I slid down, my hands touching the metal diamonds of the carousel floor as my back rested against the hooves of the horse I'd ridden.

"You can't fix me," I said, looking at his knees.

"I don't want to."

"I'm mangled," I said. "On the inside and the outside."

"And yet I love you."

He leaned down and I felt his hands on my wrists. I let him pull me up. I was wearing a black fleece that had a zipper down the length of it. Isaac reached for my neck; grabbing the top of the zipper, he pulled it down to my waist. I was so shocked I didn't have time to react. Minutes ago he had been bare-chested, now I was. If I had nipples they would have peaked in the frigid air. *If.*

I am just scars and pieces of a woman. Isaac has seen me like this. In a sense he made me like this, with his scalpel and steady hands, but I still reached up to cover my chest. He stopped me. Reaching for my waist he lifted me up until I was sitting sideways in the saddle of my pierced horse. He opened my fleece the rest of the way, then he kissed the skin where my breasts used to be. He kissed softly, over the scars. My heart—surely he could feel my pounding heart. My nerve endings had been damaged, but I felt his warm lips and his breath move across my skin. I made a sound. It wasn't a real sound. It was air and relief. Every breath I'd ever caught came whooshing out of me at once.

Isaac kissed up my neck, behind my ear, my chin, the corner of my mouth. I turned my head when he tried to kiss the other corner, and we met in the middle. Soft lips and his smell. He'd kissed me once before in the foyer of my house, it had been a drumbeat. This kiss was a sigh. It was relief and we were so drunk from it that we clung to each other like we'd been waiting for a kiss like this our whole, entire lives. His hands wrapped around my ribcage, inside of my fleece. Mine were holding his face. He pulled me off the horse. I steered him toward the only bench on the carousel. It was a chariot, curved with a leather seat. Isaac sat. I sat on his lap.

"Don't ask me if I'm sure," I said. I pulled down the zipper on his pants. I was determined. I was sure. He didn't move his hands from my waist. He didn't speak. He waited as I lifted myself up, pulling off my jeans and climbing back onto his lap. I left my panties on. His pants were pushed mid thigh. We were clothed and we were not. Isaac let me do everything, and that's the way I needed it to be; half concealed, in the cold air, with the ability to climb off and leave if I wanted to. I felt less than I thought I would. I also felt more. There was no fear, just the vibrations of something loud that I didn't quite understand. He kissed me while we moved. Then once, when it was over. The old man never came back. We zipped our clothes, and walked back up the hill chilled and in a daze. There were no more words between us. The next day I filed a restraining order against him.

And that was the last of Isaac Asterholder and me.

I try to remember sometimes what his last words to me had been. If he said something as we walked up that hill, or on the car ride home. But all I remember was his presence and his silence. And the slight echo of, *and yet I love you.*

And yet he loved me.

And yet I couldn't love him back.

When I wake Isaac isn't there. I weigh my panic against the pain. I can only focus on one at a time. I choose my pain because it won't loosen its grip on my brain. I am familiar with heart pain—intense, excruciating heart pain, but I've never experienced a physical pain quite this exquisite. Heart pain and physical pain are only comparable in that neither relinquish their hold on you once they get rolling. The heart releases a dull ache when it is broken; the pain in my leg so acute and sharp it's hard to breathe.

I wrestle with the pain for a minute … two, before I discard it. I broke my body and there is no way to fix it. I don't care. I need to find Isaac. And that's when I think it: *Oh God.* What if the zookeeper came while I was passed out and did something to him? I roll slightly onto my side until I have some leverage, and try to drag myself up using my good leg. That's when I see my leg. The lower half of my pants has been cut away. The place where the bone was sticking out has been wrapped in thin gauze. I feel liquid running down to my foot as I move. I hold my hand over my mouth and breathe through my nose. Who was here? Who did this? The fire is burning. The fire I built would have given up the ghost by now. Someone had built it back up, fed it new logs.

I wobble where I'm standing. I need light. I need to—

"Sit down."

I start, jarred by the voice. I twist my neck around as far as it can go.

"Isaac," I cry out. I start to teeter, but he darts over and catches me. *Darts is a strong word*, I think. For a minute it looks like he is going to fall with me. I lift my hand up, touch his face. He looks terrible. But he's alive and walking. He lowers me gently to the ground.

"Are you okay?"

He shakes his head. "Alive's not enough for you?"

"You shouldn't be," I hiss. "I thought you were going to die." He doesn't acknowledge me. Instead he walks over to a pile of something I can't see in the dark.

"Look who's talking," he says, softly.

"Isaac," I say again. "The table…" All of a sudden I'm feeling hot … weak. The adrenaline, which carried me up the well, up the stairs, up the ladder, has run out.

He walks over to me, his arms full. "I know," he says, dryly. "I saw."

He's looking at my leg as he sets things down next to me. He's lining them up, double-checking everything. But every few seconds he looks at my leg again like he doesn't know how to fix it.

"Is that how this happened?"

"I jumped down the table," I say. "I wasn't thinking. The asthma—"

The corners of his mouth pull tight. "You had an asthma attack? While this happened?" I nod. I can only see his face with the dim light of the fire, but it looks as if it's paled.

"Your tibia is fractured. Your leg must have bent at just the right angle when you fell to cause the break."

"When I jumped," I said.

"When you fell."

He's working with his hands, opening packages. I hear little rips, the clatter of metal. I lean my head back and close my eyes. I hear little bursts of air, I think it's Isaac, but then I realize that I'm panting.

He looks straight at me. "You must have gotten my body temperature back up. You did everything right."

"What?" I'm dizzy. I want to hurl again.

"You saved me life," he says. He glances up at me at the same time I crack open an eye.

"I need to move you."

"No!" I grab his arm. "No, please. Just let me stay here." I'm panting. The thought of moving makes me sick. "There is nowhere to move me, Isaac. Just do it here."

Do what here? Was he really planning to operate on the floor of the attic room?

"There's not enough light," I say. The pain is intensifying. I'm hoping he'll forget this whole thing and let me die. He reaches round his back and brings out the flashlight from downstairs. When I was a little girl, my mother would have chided me for reading under that light, now Isaac is planning on operating with it.

"What are you going to do?" I do a quick survey of what he's brought with him. There are six rolls of what look like bandages, alcohol, a bucket of water, a needle and thread, a bottle of tequila. There are some other things but he's placed them on a baking sheet and covered them with what looks like a bandage.

"Fix your leg."

"Where's the morphine?" I joke. Isaac props my upper body under pillows he gets from the bed so that I'm in a half sitting position. Then he unscrews the lid from the tequila and holds it to my mouth.

"Get drunk," he says without looking at me. I chug it.

"Where did you find all of this?" I take a couple of deep breaths letting what I've already swallowed settle, and then I lift the bottle back to my mouth. I want to hear how he found my discovery. He speaks while the cactusy taste of tequila burns its way to my stomach in small gulps.

"Where do you think?"

I bite my lip. My mind is numb from the alcohol. I wipe away what's running down my chin.

"We were starving, and all along..."

"I have to operate," he says. Is it my imagination or are there beads of sweat on his forehead? The light is so vague it could be a trick of the eyes.

He screws the cap off of a bottle of clear liquid and before I can open my mouth to stop him, he uncovers the gauze and pours it over my wound. I brace myself to scream, but the pain isn't as terrible as I thought it would be.

"You could have warned me!" I hiss at him, rearing up.

"Hush," he says. "It's just saline. I need to clear away the dead tissue ... irrigate the wound."

"And then...?"

"Set the bone. It's been too long already ... the risk of infection ... your soft tissue..." He's mumbling things. Words I don't hold the meaning to: debridement ... osteomyelitis. He reaches up and wipes his forehead with his shirtsleeve. I'm going to have to set your bone. I'm not an orthopedic surgeon, Senna. We don't have the equipment..."

I stare at him as he leans back on his haunches. He has a face full of scruff, and a head of hair that is standing every which way. He looks so different from the doctor that operated on me last time. The cuts around his mouth deepen as he stares into my wound. *He's more scared than I am,* I think. This is his job, his profession—saving lives. He is an expert at saving lives. Yet, this is out of his area of expertise. There is no one to consult with. Isaac Asterholder is positioned at a keyboard instead of the drums, and he doesn't quite know where to put his hands.

"It's okay." I sound peculiarly calm. Detached. "Do what you can."

He reaches for the flashlight, holds it right above the gash.

"The tissue is red, that's good," he says. I nod though I don't know what he's talking about. The room has started to spin and I just want him to get on with it.

"It's going to hurt like hell, Senna."

"Fuck you," I say. "Just do it." I sob on the last word. Such a tough guy.

Isaac gets to work. He washes his hands in the bucket using an amber colored soap. Then he douses his hands and arms in alcohol. He pulls on a pair of gloves. He must have found them down the well with the other supplies. So the zookeeper left us gloves. For what? Surgery? For when we decided to spring clean? Maybe we were supposed to fill them with air and draw faces on them with markers. Our captor though of everything. Except morphine, of course. Somehow I know that one was on purpose. No pain, no gain. This guy likes us to suffer.

Isaac does it. Without warning. While I'm thinking about the zookeeper. This time I don't scream. I pass out.

When I come to, my leg is throbbing and I'm wasted. That's what you get when you pour half a bottle of tequila in your starving stomach. He is sitting a few feet away with his back resting against the wall. His head droops down like he's sleeping. I crane my neck trying to get a look at my leg. Isaac cleaned up most of the mess, but I can see dark spots on the floor around my body—blood. My leg is propped on a pillow, the area where the bone broke through my skin is wrapped in gauze. He's splinted the leg between what looks like slabs of wood. I feel good about the scar it'll leave. It'll be long and jagged.

Isaac wakes up. Once again I notice how terrible he looks. Last night I thought he was dead, and now here he is fixing me. This wasn't right. I want to do something to make him better, but I'm lying on my back, drunk. He gets up and comes to me. He half scoots, half crawls.

"You were lucky. The bone only broke in one part. It was a clean break so you didn't have any fragments floating around. But since it tore through the skin there could be nerve and tissue damage. There was no internal bleeding that I could see."

"What about infection?" I ask.

Isaac nods. "You could develop an infection in the bone. I found a bottle of penicillin. We will do what we can. The greater the damage is to the bone, soft tissues, nerves, and blood vessels, the higher the risk for infection. And since you were dragging yourself all over the house…"

I lean my head back because the room is spinning. I wonder if I'll remember any of this when the effects of the tequila clear.

"It's the best I could do," he says. I know it is.

He hands me a mug with a spoon sticking out of it. I take it, peering inside. He picks up his own mug.

"What is it?" there is a lumpy looking yellow fluid in the cup. It looks disgusting, but my stomach clenches in anticipation anyway.

"Creamed corn." He sticks the spoon in his mouth, sucks it dry. I follow suit. It's not nearly as bad as it looks. I have hazy memories of grabbing the can the night before, the way it dug into my hip as I climbed the ladder.

"Take it slow," Isaac warns. I have to force myself not to down the whole mug in one gulp. My hunger pain subsides ever so slightly, and I am able to focus solely on the other pain my body is feeling. He hands me four large white pills.

"It'll just dim it, Senna."

"Okay," I whisper, letting him drop them in my hand. He hands me a cup of water and I drop all four pills into my mouth.

"Isaac," I say. "Please rest."

He kisses my forehead.

"Hush."

When I wake up the room is warm. I've noticed that the highlight of most of my days here are waking up and going to sleep. It's what I remember most about *The Caging of Senna and Isaac*: wake up; go to sleep; wake up; go to sleep. There is little in between to make a difference; we wander … we eat … but mostly we sleep. And if we're lucky it's warm when we wake. Now there is a new sensation—pain. I look around the room. Isaac is asleep on the floor a few feet away. He has a single blanket covering him. It's not even long enough to cover his feet. I want to give him my blanket, but I don't know how to stand up. I groan and lean back against the pillows. The painkillers have worn off. I am hungry again. I wonder if he's eaten, if he's okay.

When did this happen? When did my thoughts shift to Isaac's needs? I stare at the ceiling. That's the way it happened with Nick. It started out with him loving me, him being obsessed with me; then, all of a sudden … osmosis.

The minute I started freely loving Nick he left me.

Three times a day Isaac makes a trip down to the well to get food and restock our wood. We use a bucket to relieve ourselves, and it's his job to empty that too. He goes carefully. I can hear his steps creaking across the floorboards until he reaches the landing, and then the *clomp, clomp, clomp* on the stairs. I lose his sound once he's down the well, but he's never there for more than five minutes, except when he's doing laundry or throwing our trash over the side of the cliff. Laundry consists of filling the bathtub with snow and soap and swishing the clothes around until you think they're clean. We never had a shortage of soap, there are stacks of white bars, wrapped in a filmy white paper on the bottom shelf of the pantry. They smell like butter, and on more than one occasion when I was bent over with hunger I thought about eating them.

Isaac takes the smaller of the two flashlights—the one I found when I fucked up my leg. He leaves me the big one. He leaves it right next to my bed and tells me not to use it. But as soon as I hear his socked feet on the stairs, my fingers reach down to find the switch that turns it on. I let the light flow. Sometimes I reach over and pass my hand across it, playing with the shadows. It's a sad, sad thing when the highlight of your day becomes five minutes with a flashlight.

One day when Isaac comes back, I ask him why he doesn't just bring everything up at once.

"I need the exercise," he says.

After a week, he comes up the stairs with a handful of green bandages.

"There's no infection that I can see around the wound. It's healing." I notice that he didn't say, *Healing well.* "The bone could still become infected, but we can hope the penicillin will take care of that."

"What's that?" I ask, nodding toward his hands.

"I'm going to put your leg in a cast. Then I can move you to the bed."

"What if the bone doesn't fuse together properly?" I ask.

He's quiet for a long time as he works with the supplies.

"It's not going to heal properly," he says. "You'll most likely walk with a limp for the rest of your life. On most days, you'll have pain."

I close my eyes. Of course. Of course. Of course.

When I look up again, he's cutting the toes off of a white sock. He fits it over my foot as gently as he can and pulls it up my leg. I force breath from my nostrils to keep from wailing. It must be one of his. The sock. The zookeeper didn't give me any white socks. He didn't give me anything white. Isaac does the same thing with a second sock, and then a third, until I have them lined from the middle of my foot to my knee. Then he takes one of the bandages from the bucket of water. It's not a bandage, I realize. It's rolls of a fiberglass cast.

He starts mid foot, rolling the cast around and around until it runs out. Then he plucks out a new roll and does it again. Over and over until he's used all five rolls and my leg is fully cast. Isaac leans back to examine his work. He looks exhausted.

"Let's give it some time to dry, then I'll move you to the bed."

We stay in the attic room, forgetting the rest of the house. Day after day … after day … after day.

I count the days we've lost. Days I'll never get back. Two hundred and seventy-seven of them. One day I ask him to drum for me.

"With what?"

I can't really see his face—it's too dark—but I know that his eyebrows are raised and there is a trace of a smile on his lips. He needs this. I need this.

"Sticks," I suggest. And then, "Please, Isaac. I want to hear music."

"Music without words," he says, softly. I shake my head, though he can't see me do it.

"I want to hear the music you can make."

I wish I could see his face. I want to see if he's offended that I asked him to do something he hated giving up. Or maybe if he's relieved to be asked. I just want to see his face. I do the strangest thing, then. I reach out and touch his face with my fingertips. His eyes close when I trace my way from his forehead, down over his eyes and around his lips. He's serious. Always so serious. Dr. Isaac Asterholder. I want to meet the drummer, Isaac.

He disappears for an hour. When he comes back his arms are stacked with things I can't make out in the dark. I sit up straighter in bed and my mind hums with excitement. He works in front of the fire so that he won't have to use the flashlight. I watch him unload what he's brought up with him: two buckets, one smaller than the other, a metal skillet and a metal pot, duct tape, rubber bands, a pencil and two sticks. The sticks look smooth—like real drumsticks. I wonder if he's been carving them secretly while he disappears downstairs every day. I wouldn't blame him. I've been wanting to carve my skin for days.

He is making things. I can't tell what they are, but I hear the rip of the duct tape every few minutes. He swears a couple times. It's a soundtrack: rriiiip … swear … bang … rriiiip … swear … bang.

Finally, after what seems like hours, he stands up to examine his work.

"Help me up," I beg him. "Just this once so I can see."

He puts another log on the fire, and reluctantly comes over to my bed. I mouth, *please, please, please, please.* He picks me up before I can protest the help and carries me to what he made.

I stare in wonder at his creation, my leg jutting in front of me awkwardly. He's taped the larger bucket to a makeshift stand he's made out of some logs. The smaller bucket sits upside down next to it. On the opposite side are the two pots—both faced down.

"What's that?" I ask, pointing to a mess of a thing on the floor.

"That's my pedal. I wrapped rubber around a pencil. I cut out the sole of one of my shoes for the actual pedal."

"Where did you get the rubber?"

"From the fridge."

I nod. Genius.

"That's my snare." He points to the smaller bucket. "And bass…" The larger one, turned on its side.

"Can you stand me against the wall? I promise I won't put weight on my cast."

He props me against the wall near to where his drum set sits. I lean back, thrilled to be out of bed and on my … foot.

Isaac sits on the edge of the window seat. He leans down to test his pedal, then he plays.

I close my eyes and listen to his heart. This is the first time—the very first time—that I am meeting this side of Isaac. After all these years. Without his permission I turn on the flashlight and aim it at him like it's a spotlight. He gives me a warning look, but I just smile and keep it on him. This moment deserves a little something special.

It's four days 'til Christmas. Give or take a day or two. I do my best to keep track, but I've lost days along the way. They dropped out from under me and messed up my mental calendar. *You're the one who went crazy and pissed herself like some dink in a mental institution.* Isaac says I was like that for a week. Which still makes it Christmas.

Christmas in the dark.

Christmas in the attic room.

Christmas drinking melted snow and eating pinto beans out of a can.

Christmas was when we met. Christmas was when the bad thing happened. The zookeeper will do something on Christmas. I know it. And that's when it hits me. It was sitting there in my subconscious the whole time.

I moan out loud. Isaac is downstairs so he doesn't hear me. And then I can't quite catch my breath.

"Isaac," I wheeze. "Isaac!"

I hate this feeling. And I hate how it hits me out of nowhere so that I can never be prepared. I don't know what's more overwhelming at this moment, the fact that I can't breathe, or the realization that was powerful enough to steal my breath away. Either way, I have to get to a nebulizer. Isaac found them down the table. He brought one up. Where did he put it? I look helplessly around the room. The top of the wardrobe. I get out of bed. It's a struggle. When I'm halfway there he walks in carrying our wood ration for the day. He drops his armload when he sees my face. He darts to the wardrobe and grabs the nebulizer. Then he's pushing it between my lips. I feel a cold rush; the vapor hits my lungs and I can breathe again.

Isaac looks pissed.

"What happened?"

"I had an asthma attack, idiot."

"Senna," he says, swinging me into his arms and carrying me back to the bed. "Ninety percent of the time your asthma attacks are stress induced. Now. What happened?"

"I didn't know I needed anything extra," I snap. "Other than being imprisoned in a house made of ice with my…"

I lose my words.

"Doctor," he finishes.

I twist my body so that I'm facing away from him.

I need to think. I need to form a structure for this theory. The Rubik's cube twists. Isaac gives me space.

I'm locked in a house with my doctor. He's right.

I'm locked in a house with my doctor.

I'm locked in a house with my doctor.

With my doctor.

Doctor…

Christmas comes. Isaac is very quiet. But I was wrong; we don't eat beans. He cooks us a feast over our little makeshift stove in the attic: canned corn, spam, green beans and, to top it all off, a can of pumpkin pie filling. For breakfast.

For a moment, we are happy. Then Isaac looks at me and says, "When I first opened my eyes and saw you standing over me, I felt like I took my first breath in three years."

I grind my teeth.

Shut up! Shut up! Shut up!

'We only knew each other for three months before this," I say. "You don't know me." But, even as I say it, I know it's not true. "You were just my doctor…"

He's wearing the expression of someone being slapped over and over again. I slap him once more to put an end to this.

"You took things too far."

He walks out before I can say any more.

I bury my face. "Fuck you, Isaac," I say into my pillow.

At noon the lights turn on.

Isaac's head appears through the trapdoor a minute later. I wonder where he's been. My bet is on the carousel room. He takes one look at my face and says, "You knew."

I knew.

"I suspected."

He looks incredulous. "That the power would come back?"

"That something would happen," I correct him.

I knew that the power would come back.

He disappears again, and I hear his steps pounding down the stairs. *Clomp, clomp, clomp.* I count them until he reaches the bottom. Then I hear the front door hit the wall as he swings it wide. I flinch at all the cold air he's letting in, then remember that the power is back. *HEAT! LIGHT! A WORKING TOILET!*

I feel impassive. This is a game. The zookeeper gave us light. As a gift. On Christmas Day. It's symbolic.

He thinks light came into my life on Christmas Day when I met Isaac.

"You're just a badly written character," I say out loud. "I'll kill you off, my darling."

When Isaac comes back his face is ashen.

"The zookeper was here," he says.

I get chills. They skitter up my legs and arms like little spiders.

"How do you know?"

He holds out his hand. "We have to go downstairs."

I let him pull me up. He doesn't like me to walk on the leg, which means he's making an exception, which means this is dirt serious. I use him as a crutch. When we reach the ladder he helps me sit on the floor. Then he climbs down first. He has me lower my injured leg through the hole first. It takes me ten minutes to get it right, to maneuver it while not falling over. But I am determined. I don't want to be in the attic a second longer. When both legs are through, he reaches for my waist. I think we're both going to fall, but he gets me down. *Steady hands,* I remind myself. *A surgeon's steady hands.*

He hands me something. It's a tree branch—almost as tall as I am—shaped like a wishbone. A crutch.

"Where did you get this?"

"It's part of our Christmas present."

He stares intently into my eyes, and motions for the stairs. A few weeks ago we were burning everything we could. There is no way this could have escaped our fire. I lean on my crutch as I hobble for the stairs. I want to scream at how long it takes to make it to the bottom. I look around. I haven't seen this part of the house since I broke my leg. I have a need to walk around, touch things, but Isaac pushes me toward the door.

It's dark outside. So cold. I shiver.

"I can't see anything, Isaac."

My foot is about to sink into the snow when my cast hits something.

They never found the man who raped me. There was never another report of a rape in those woods, or any woods in Washington. The police said it was an isolated incident. With blithe nonchalance, they told me that he had probably been watching me for a while and possibly followed me into the woods. They used words like "intent" and "stalker". I'd had those before: letters, e-mails, Facebook messages that went from high praise to intense anger when I didn't respond. None of them were men. None threatening enough to concern me. None with the tone of a rapist, or a sadist, or a kidnapper. Just angry moms who wanted something from me—recognition maybe.

But there was something I never told the police about the day I was raped. Even when they pressed me for more details. I couldn't bring myself to say it.

No, I didn't see his face.
No, he didn't have tattoos or scars.
No, he didn't say anything to me…

The truth was that he did speak to me. Or perhaps he just spoke. To God, to the air, to himself, or perhaps to some person who abandoned him. I can still hear his voice. I hear it when I sleep, whispering in my ear and I wake up screaming. From the moment he started to the moment he finished, he chanted one thing over and over.

Pink Zippo

Pink Zippo

Pink Zippo

Pink Zippo

It was an omission. Maybe he got away because of it. Maybe another woman will be raped because I could have done more. But in that moment, when you've been violated, your soul darkened for no reason other than someone's sadistic cruelty, you're only thinking about your survival.

I didn't know how to live with my survival, and I didn't know how to kill myself. Instead, I plotted what I'd do to him. While Isaac was feeding me, and pulling me out of dreams that made me thrash and scream, I was cutting up my rapist, throwing him into Lake Washington. Pouring gasoline over him and burning him alive. I was carving his skin like Lisbeth Salander did to Nils Bjurman. I took the revenge I would never get in my flesh and blood life.

But it wasn't enough. It's never enough. So I took revenge on myself for allowing it to happen. I felt worthless. I didn't want anyone who had worth to be near me. Isaac had worth. So I got rid of him. But here we were; locked up and caged. Starved. The man who chanted *Pink Zippo* might have been a stalker, but he had nothing, nothing on the zookeeper. You can stalk a woman's body, but this animal was stalking my mind.

My cast hits something. Isaac flicks the switch that turns on the bulb above the door. It's been so long since light and not darkness has been my companion that it takes a moment for my eyes to catch up. The zookeeper has indeed left me something; a box, rectangular in shape, it reaches my knees. The box is pure white, shiny and smooth like the inlay of an oyster shell. On its lid are red words, the letters look as if someone dipped a finger in blood words that look as if someone dipped a finger in blood before tracing them. *For MV.*

My reaction is internal. The very essence of me writhes as if I am an open wound and someone has poured salt over me like one of those snails the kid next door used to torture. I hobble forward and lean over the box. *Please God, please, don't let it be blood.*

Not blood.

Not blood.

My hand is shaking as I reach down to touch the words. I go for the V, slicing it in half. It has dried, but some of it chips away on the tip of my finger. I place my finger in my mouth, the flecks of red clinging to my tongue. All this, and Isaac has been a statue behind me. When I bend over, letting my crutch drop away, moaning in some sort of grief, I feel his arms circle my waist. He pulls me back into the house and kicks the door closed.

"Noooooo! It's blood, Isaac. It's blood. Let me go!"

He holds me from behind as I twist to get away from him.

"Hush," he says into my ear. "You're going to hurt your leg. You can sit on the sofa, Senna. I'll bring it to you."

I stop fighting. I'm not crying, but somehow my nose is running. I reach up and wipe it as Isaac carries me to the living room and sits me down. The couch is barely a couch. We hacked parts of it away to burn when we discovered that there was a wooden frame underneath the stuffing. The cushions are gouged; they sink beneath me. The back of the sofa is gone; there is nowhere to rest my back. I sit straight, my leg poking out in front of me. My anxiety climbs every second that Isaac is gone. My ears follow him to the door, where his breath hitches as he lifts the box. It's heavy. The door closes again. When he walks back into the room he's carrying it like a body, his arms stretched around its sides. There is no coffee table to set it on—we hacked that up too—so he places it at the floor by my feet, and steps back.

"What's *MV*, Senna?"

I stare at the blood, the part of the V that I smudged with my finger.

"It's me," I say.

He tilts his head forward. It feels like he's lining up our eyes. Truth. I'm going to have to feed him some truth.

"Mud Vein. I'm Mud Vein." My mouth feels dry. I want to purge it with a gallon of snow.

His eyes flicker. He's remembering.

"The dedication in his book."

Our eyes are connected, so I don't need to nod.

"Would he...?"

"I don't know anything anymore."

"What does it mean?" he asks. I lower my eyes away from his, and to the blood letters. *For MV*

"What's inside?" I ask.

"I'll open it when you tell me why the zookeeper addressed that box to Mud Vein."

The box is just out of my reach. To get to it I'll have to use something to pull myself up. Since the couch no longer has a back, there is nothing I can use for leverage. Isaac, I realize, is being very strategic. I take a breath; it is broken in half by a sob that never reaches my lips. My chest convulses as I open my mouth to speak. I don't want to tell him anything, but I must.

"It's the black vein that curves around the back of a shrimp. Nick called it the mud vein. You have to remove it to make the shrimp clean..." My voice is monotone.

"Why did he call you that?"

When Isaac and I ask each other questions it reminds me of a tennis match. Once you've sent one over the net, you know it's going to come back, you just don't know the direction.

"Isn't it obvious?"

He blinks at me. One second, two seconds, three seconds...

"No."

"I don't get you," I say.

"You don't get you," he shoots back.

We have resumed our eye transmissions. I'm glaring, but his stare is more candid. After a minute he steps over to the box and opens it. I try not to lean forward. I try not to hold my breath, but there is a white box with the words *For MV* stenciled on the lid in blood. I am aching to know what's inside.

Isaac reaches down. I hear the gentle whisper of paper. When his hand comes up he's holding a loose page that looks as if it's been torn from a book. The corners have soaked up some blood.

For MV

Blood soaked pages, for MV...

Who knew that Nick called me that, besides Nick himself?

Isaac starts to read. "The punishment for her peace was upon him, and he gave her rest."

I hold out my hand. I want to see the page, know who wrote it. It wasn't Nick; I know his style. It wasn't me. I take the blood-stained page, careful to keep my fingers away from the red parts. I read silently what Isaac read out loud. The page is numbered 212. There is no title or author name. I read through the rest of it, but I have the feeling that those are the words I was meant to see first. Isaac hands me another page, this one with a spot of blood the size of my fist blooming out from the middle of the page like a flower. The font is different, as is the size of the page. I rub it between my fingers. I know this feel; it's Nick's book. This is *Knotted.*

Isaac pushes the box closer to where I'm sitting so that I'm able to reach inside. The pages are all pulled from their binding, lined in four rows. I lift another page. The style lines up with the first book, lyrical with an old-fashioned feel to the prose. There is something strange about the writing, something I know I should remember, and cannot. I start pulling out pages at random. Separating the pages of Nick's book from the new one. I work quickly, my fingers lifting and piling, lifting and piling. Isaac watches me from where he leans against the wall, his arms folded, lips pursed. I know that underneath his lips his two front teeth slightly overlap. I don't know why I have this thought, at this time, but as I sort pages my thoughts are on Isaac's two front teeth.

I am about halfway through the box when I realize that there is a third book. This one is mine. My fingers linger over the bright white pages—white because I told the publisher if they printed on cream I would sue them for breach of contract. Three books. One written for MV, one written for Nick … but the third…? My eyes reach over to the unknown pile. Who belongs to that book? And what is the zookeeper trying to tell me? Isaac pushes himself off the wall and steps toward the pile that belongs to Nick.

"We have to finish reading this one," he says. My face drains of blood and I can feel a tingling along the tops of my shoulders as they tighten.

I hand him the pile. "It's out of order and the pages aren't numbered. Good luck." Our fingers touch. Gooseflesh rises on my arms and I look away quickly.

We work to set the books in order. Through the longest night, the night that never ends. It's good to have something to do, to keep you from waltzing down crazy street—not that we haven't already been there. It's a street you only want to visit a couple times in your life. We have power again … heat. So we take advantage by not sleeping, our fingers flying over pages, our brows creased with the strain. Isaac has Nick's book. I take on the task of the other two—mine and…? It seems that there are too many pages to make up only three books. I wonder if we will discover a fourth.

Even as I come across pages of *Knotted* and hand them to Isaac, it is the nameless book that catches my attention. Each page has a line that pulls at my eyes. I read them, re-read them. No one I know writes this way, yet it is so familiar. I feel a lust for this author's words. A jealousy at being able to string such rich sentences together. The first line keeps coming back to me with each subsequent line I read. *The punishment for her peace was upon him, and he gave her rest.*

I don't notice when Isaac disappears from the room to make us food. I smell it when he comes back and hands me a bowl of soup. I set it aside, intent on finishing my work, but he picks it up and places it back in my hands.

"Eat it," he instructs me. I don't realize how hungry I am until I reluctantly place the spoon in my mouth, sucking the salty brown broth. I set the spoon aside and drink from the bowl, my eyes still scanning the piles set neatly around me. My leg is aching, as is my back, but I don't want to stop. If I ask Isaac to help me move he will guess at my discomfort and force me to rest. I rub the small of my back when he's not looking, and press on.

"I know what you're doing," he says, as he leans over his pile of pages.

I look up in surprise. "What?"

"When you think I'm not looking, I am."

I flush, and my hand automatically reaches for my aching muscles. I pull back at the last minute and curl my hand into a fist instead. Isaac snickers and shakes his head, turning back to his work. I'm glad he doesn't press the issue. I pick up another page. It's my own. The story I wrote for Nick. Instead of putting it on its pile, I read it. True and trite. It was my call to him. The first line of the book went like this:

Every time you want to remember what love feels like, you look for me.

That line grabbed every woman who had ever offered their throbbing little heart to a man. Because we all have someone who reminds us of what love stings like. That unreliquished love that slips between our fingers like sand. The second line of the book confused them a little. It's why their eyes kept following my trail of words. I was dropping breadcrumbs for the disaster that was to come.

Stay the fuck away from me.

I only wrote the book because he wrote one for me. It seemed fair. Most people text, or call, or write e-mails. My love and I write each other books. *Hey! Here's a hundred thousand words of 'Why the hell did we break up anyway?'* It was Nick who had finally crippled me; it was Nick who took my belief away. And I decided sometime after I filed the restraining order against Isaac that it was a story worth telling.

When we broke up it was his choice. Nick liked to love me. I was not like him, and he valued that. I think I made him feel more like an artist because he didn't know how to suffer until I came into his life. But he didn't understand me. He tried to change me. And that was our destruction. And then Isaac read that book to me, perched on the edge of my hospital bed, my breasts sitting in a medical waste container somewhere. Suddenly I was hearing Nick's thoughts, seeing myself as he saw me, and I heard him calling to me.

Nick Nissley was perfect. Perfect looking, perfectly flawed, perfect in everything he said. His life was graceful and his words were whetted to poignancy—both written and spoken. But he didn't mean any of them. And that was the greatest disappointment. He was a pretender, trying to grasp what it felt like to live. So, he found me looking at a lake and grabbed me. Because I wore a shroud of darkness and he wanted desperately to understand what that was like. I was charmed for a while. Charmed that someone so gifted was interested in me. I thought that by being with him, his talent would rub off on me.

I was always waiting to see what he would do next. How he would handle the waitress who spilled an entire dish of pumpkin curry on his pants (he took his pants off and ate his meal in boxers); or what he would say to the fan who tracked him down and showed up at his door while we were having sex (he signed her book half leaning out the door with his hair ruffled and a sheet wrapped around his waist). He taught me how to write by simply existing—and existing well. I can't say for sure when it was that I fell in love with him. It might have been when he told me that I had a mud vein. It might have been days later when I realized it was true. But whatever moment it took for my heart to decide to love him, it decided swiftly, and it decided for me.

God knows I didn't want to be in love. It was cliché—men and women and their social conformities to celebrate love. Engagement pictures made me want to vomit—especially when they were taken on railroad tracks. I always pictured Thomas the Train rolling over them, his smiley blue face beaded with their blood. I didn't want to want those things. Love was good enough, without the three-layered almond/fondant wedding cake and the sparkly blood diamonds encased in white gold. Just love. And I loved Nick. Hard.

Nick loved wedding cake. He told me so. He also told me that he'd like for us to have one someday. In that moment, my heart rate slowed, my eyes glazed and I saw my entire life flash before my eyes. It was pretty—because it was with Nick. But I hated it. It made me angry that he'd expect me to live that way. The way normal people lived.

"I don't want to get married," I told him, trying to control my voice. We used to have this game we'd play. As soon as we'd see each other, we'd dialogue the physical description of what the other person looked like. It was a writer's game. He'd always start with, *button nose, limpid eyes, full lips, freckles.*

Now he was looking at me like he'd never seen me before. "Well, what do you want to do then?"

We were sitting on our knees in front of his coffee table, sipping warm sake and eating lo mein with our fingers.

"I want to eat with you, and fuck and see things that are beautiful."

"Why can't we do that after the wedding?" he asked. He licked each of his fingers and then mine, and leaned back against the couch.

"Because I respect love too much to get married."

"That's bitter."

I stared at him. *Was he kidding?*

"I don't think I'm bitter just because I don't want the same things you want."

"We can come to a compromise. Be like Persephone and Hades," he said.

I laughed. Too much sake. "You're not brooding enough to be Hades, and unlike Persephone, I don't have a mother."

My mouth clamped shut and I started sweating. Nick's head immediately tilted to the right. I wiped my mouth with a napkin and stood up, grabbing the containers of food and carrying them to the kitchen. He followed me in there. I wanted to kick him off my heels. Nick's mother was still married to his father. Thirty-five years. And from what I'd seen they were happy, uncomplicated years. Nick was so well balanced it was ridiculous.

"Is she dead?"

He had to ask twice.

"To me."

"Where is she?"

"Off being selfish somewhere."

"Aha," he said. "Do you want dessert?"

And that's what I liked about Nick. He was only interested in what you were interested in. And I was not interested in my past. He liked that I was dark, but he didn't know why. And he didn't ask. He definitely didn't understand. But for all of our differences he took me as I was. I needed that.

Until he didn't. Until he said that I was an emotional fort. Until nothing about me came easy, and he grew tired of trying. Nick and his words. Nick and his promises of never-ending love. I believed them all and then he left me. Love comes slow, but God does it go fast. He was beautiful—then he was ugly. I esteemed him, then I esteemed him not.

Dr. Saphira Elgin had tried to teach me to control my anger. She wanted me to be able to pinpoint the source of it so I could rationalize my feelings. Talk myself down. I can never pinpoint the source. It runs around and around in my body without a point of origin.

I blew her off. I always blew her off. But now I try to pinpoint it. I'm angry because…

Isaac is touch, and he is sound. He is smell and he is sight. I tried to make him a single sense like I did with everyone else, but he is all of them. He overpowers my senses and that is exactly why I ran from him. I was afraid of feeling brightly—afraid I would become used to the color and sounds and smells, and they would be taken from me. I was a self-fulfilling prophecy; destroying before I could be destroyed. I wrote about women like that, I didn't realize I was one. For years I believed that Nick left me because I failed him. I couldn't be what he needed because I was empty and shallow. That's what he insinuated.

"Why can't you love wedding cake, Brenna?"

"Why can't I take your darkness away?"

"Why can't you be who I need?"

But, I didn't fail Nick. He failed me. Love sticks, and it stays and it braves the bullshit. Like Isaac did. And I am mad at Isaac because he is all of that. And I am all of this. It's irrational.

We finish our project—the page project, as we call it. In the end we have four piles and only three books: Mine, Nick's, and the nameless book. The fourth pile is the thickest and the most confusing. I stack each one with care that is mostly habit, lining up the corners until none of the pages poke past each other. The problem is, there is nothing on the pages. Each one is bone white. I have the fleeting thought that the zookeeper wants me to write a new book, then Yul Brenner reminds me that my personal Annie Wilkes didn't leave me a pen. Can't write a book without a pen. I wonder if I can resuscitate the old Bic we used when we first woke up here.

It must be symbolic, like the pictures hung all over the house—pictures of hollow sparrows, and bearers of death. I stare at the piles of paper while Isaac makes us tea. I can hear the tinkle of the spoon as it hits the sides of the ceramic cup. I murmur something to the books spread out around me, my lips moving in incantation. We may have separated them, but without page numbers they are still out of order. How do you bring order to a book you've never read? Or maybe that's point of this little exercise. Maybe I'm supposed to bring my own personal order to the two books I've never read. Either way, I'm telling them to sort themselves out and speak to me. Voices have been, and always will be, too afraid to speak with as much volume as a book. That's why writers write—to say things loudly with ink. To give feet to thoughts; to make quiet, still feelings loudly heard. In these pages are thoughts that the zookeeper wants me to hear. I don't know why, and I don't care except to get out of here. To get Isaac out of here.

"Do you want to have children?" he asks me when he carries our tea into the room. I am startled by the randomness of his question. We don't talk about normal things. Our conversations are about survival. My hand trembles when I take the cup. Who could think about children at a time like this? Two pals just sitting around, chatting about their life expectations? I want to rip open my shirt and remind him that he cut off my breasts. Remind him that we are prisoners. People in our predicament didn't talk about the possibility of children. But still … because it is Isaac who asks me, and because he has given so much, I let my mind rove over what he's saying.

I once saw a toddler throw a fit at Heathrow Airport. Her older sister confiscated an iPhone from the little girl's hands when she threatened to send it flying across the floor. As with most children, the tiny girl, who teetered on fresh, newly-walking legs, had a loud, indignant response. She wailed, dropped to her knees and made an awful herky-jerky noise that sounded like an ambulance siren. It rose and fell in crescendo, causing people to look and wince. As she wailed, she slid backwards on the ground until she was lying face up, her knees bent underneath her. I watched in astonishment as her arms flailed about, alternating between what looked like the backstroke and an interpretive butterfly dance. Her face was pressed into an anguished scowl, her mouth still sending out those godawful noises, when all of a sudden she scrambled to her feet, and ran laughing toward a fountain a few yards away.

As far as I was concerned children had bipolar disorder. They were angry, unpredictable, emotional ambulance-sirens with pigtails, grubby hands and food-crusted mouths that twisted from smiles to frowns and back again as quick as a breath. No, thank you very much. If I wanted a three-foot warlord as my master, I'd hire a rabid monkey to do the job.

"No," I say.

He takes a long sip. Nods. "I didn't think so."

I wait for him to tell me why he asked, but he doesn't. After a few minutes it clicks together—*snap, snap, snap*—and I feel sick. Isaac hasn't been eating. He hasn't been sleeping. He hasn't been speaking much. I've watched him deteriorate slowly over the last week, coming alive only for the delivery of the white box. I suddenly feel less angry about his out-of-place question. More concerned.

"How long have we been here?" I ask.

"Nine months."

My Rubik's cube brain twists. More of my anger dissipates.

When we first woke up here he told me that Daphne was eight weeks pregnant.

"She carried to term," I say, firmly. I search my brain for something else he needs to hear. "You have a healthy baby and it comforts her to have a part of you with her."

I don't know if this comforts him, but it's all I know how to say.

He doesn't move or acknowledge my words. He's suffering. I stand up wobbling slightly. I have to do something. I have to feed him. Like he fed me when I was suffering. I linger in the doorway, watching the slight rise and fall of his shoulders as he breathes.

This is my fault. Isaac shouldn't be here. I've ruined his life. I never read Nick's book. Just those few chapters that Isaac read to me while sitting on the edge of my hospital bed. I didn't want to see how the story ended. That's why I swallowed it. But, now I do. I suddenly have the urge to know how Nick ended our story. What he had to say about the way things between us dissolved. It was his story that compelled me to write an answer, and get myself imprisoned in the middle of the fucking South Pole. With my doctor. Who shouldn't be here.

I make dinner. It's difficult to focus on anything other than the gift that the zookeeper left for me, but Isaac's hurt outweighs my obsession. I open three cans of vegetables, and boil pasta shaped like bow ties. I mix them together, adding a little canned chicken broth. I carry the plates to the living room. We can't eat at the table anymore, so we eat here. I call up to Isaac. He comes down a minute later, but he only pushes the food around on his plate, stabbing a different vegetable on each prong of his fork. Is this what he felt when he watched me slip into darkness? I want to open his mouth and pour the food down his throat. Make him live. *Eat, Isaac.* I mentally plead. But he doesn't.

I save his plate of food, setting it in the fridge, which doesn't quite work since he stripped off the rubber sealant to make a pedal for his drums.

I hobble up to the carousel room using my new crutch. The room smells musty and there is a faint sweet smell of piss. I eye the black horse. The one who shares my pierced heart. He looks meaner today. I lean into him, resting my head against his neck. I touch his mane lightly. Then my hand goes to the arrow. I grip it in a fist, wishing I could break it off and end both of our suffering. More than that—wishing I could end Isaac's.

My eyelids flutter as my brain trills. When did I decide that the zookeeper was a man? It doesn't fit. My publishing company has done research on my reader base, and it consists mostly of women in their thirties and forties. I have male readers. I get e-mails from them, but to go this far … I should see a woman. But I don't. I see a man. Either way, I'm in his head. He's just a character to me; someone I can't really see, but I can see how his mind works by the way he's playing games with me. And the longer I'm here, the more he's taking form. This is my job; this is what I'm good at. If I can figure out his plot, I can outsmart him. Get Isaac out of here. He needs to meet his baby.

I return to the books. Eye each one. My hand lingers over *Knotted* briefly, before settling on the unnamed pile. I'll start right here.

I read the book. Without the pages numbered, I am forced to read pell-mell. It's like jumping backwards into a snowdrift and not knowing how deeply you're going to sink. My life has always been filled with order, until I was taken and set aside to rot in this place. This place is chaos, and reading with no order is chaos. I hate it and yet I am too enslaved by the words to desist.

The book is about a girl named Ophelia. On the very first page I read, which could be 5 or 500, Ophelia has been forced to give her premature baby up for adoption. Not by her parents, as most stories go, but by her controlling, schizophrenic husband. Her husband is a musician who writes what the voices tell him to write. So, when the voices tell him to give his five-pound baby girl away, he strong-arms Ophelia by threatening both her and her baby's life.

On the next page I pick up, Ophelia is a girl of twelve. She is eating a meal with her parents. It appears to be a normal family meal, but Ophelia's inner dialogue is riddled with the kind of markers that herald a girl both strange and strangely old. She is angry with her parents for existing, for being such simple contributors to society. She compares them to her mashed potatoes then goes on to talk about their failed attempts to replace her with another baby. *My mother has had four miscarriages. I'd take that as God's way of saying you aren't supposed to fuck up any more kids.*

I cringe at this part, wanting to know more about Carol Blithe's broken uterus, but my page has come to an end, and I am forced to pick up a new one. It goes like this for hours, as I gather bursts of information about Ophelia, who almost seems like the anti-heroine. Ophelia is a narcissist; Ophelia has a superiority complex; Ophelia can't stick with anything for too long before becoming bored. Ophelia marries a man who is the antithesis of boring, and she pays for it. She leaves him eventually, and marries someone else, but then she leaves him, too. I find a page where she speaks about a china doll that she had to leave behind after divorcing her second husband. She laments the loss of the china doll in the most peculiar way. I gather these details until my brain is hurting. I am trying to sort through all of it, put it in order, when I come across the last page. She is self- actuating on the last page of the book. When I reach the final line, my eyes cross. *You will feel me in the fall*

I vomit.

Isaac finds me lying on my back on the floor. He stands over me with a leg on each side of my body, and hauls me to my feet. His eyes briefly explore the puddle of vomit beside me before he reaches up and feels my forehead. When he finds it cool, he asks me, "What did you read?"

I turn my face away.

"Nick's book?"

I shake my head.

He looks at the pile closest to where I was lying.

"Do you know who wrote it?"

I can't look at him, so I close my eyes and nod.

"My mother," I say. I hear his breath catch.

"How do you know?"

"I know."

I hobble into the kitchen. I need water to wash out my mouth. Isaac follows behind me.

"How do I know it wasn't you who did this?" He takes a threatening step toward me. I back into a bag of rice. It falls over. I watch, horrified, as the grains spill across the floor, flowing around my bare foot.

"I brought you here? You think I brought us here to starve and freeze? For what?"

"It was convenient that you were the one to cut me free. Why weren't you the one tied up and gagged?"

"Listen to yourself," I say. "It wasn't me who did this!"

"How do I know that?" His words are sharp, but he says them slowly.

I shift my feet and rice fills the spaces between my toes.

My chin trembles. I can feel my bottom lip shaking with it. I clutch it between my teeth.

"I guess you have to trust me."

He points to the living room where the chest is, where the books lay in piles.

"Your book, Nick's book, and now your mother's book? Why?"

"I don't know. I didn't even know my mother wrote a book. I haven't seen her since I was a kid!"

"You know who did this," he says. "Deep down, you know."

I shake my head. How can he possibly believe that? I have searched—wracked—my brain for answers.

He backs up, covering his eyes with his palms. His back hits the wall and he bends at the waist with his hands on his knees. It looks like he can't breathe. I reach a hand out to him, and then drop it to my side. It's no use. No matter what I say, I took his wife and baby away. I birthed this psycho's obsession.

Three weeks later, Isaac removes my cast. He uses a kitchen knife to cut it off. It's the same knife he carried around on our first day here. We are both wide-eyed and short of breath as the fiberglass falls away. What will we see? How much more broken will I be? In the end there is just a hairy, skinny leg that looks a little off. It reminds me of blood in a cup, a sweater in a bathtub, a rock in a mouth. It's just visually *off* and I can't tell why.

I still have to use my crutch, but I like the freedom I feel after all those weeks lying in bed. Isaac still won't speak to me. But the sun has returned. It rises again. We stop using the lights to save the generator from burning gas. I read all of *Knotted,* but surprisingly it doesn't hurt as much as the nameless book my mother wrote. I see Nick a little differently; less glimmer. It's his best work, but I'm left unimpressed with his love note.

Isaac carries the rest of the supplies up from the well at the bottom of the table. He fills the cupboards and the fridge and the wood closet. *So we don't have to climb down there anymore*, he tells me. It takes him all day. Then he puts the table back together. When he goes to his room I come down from the carousel room and creep into the kitchen. I'm still in my robe and my legs are cold. I feel naked without my cast. I press the back of my legs to the lip of the table, and hop up. I scoot back until I'm sitting, my legs hanging over the side. My runner's legs look spindly and weak. A scar runs like a seam across my shin. I trace it lightly with the tip of my finger. I'm starting to look like a stitched-up Emo doll. All I need are the button eyes. I reach up, slipping my hand into the opening at the top of my robe, running my fingers across the skin on my chest. There are scars there too. Ugly ones. I'm used to being disfigured. It feels like parts of me keep being taken; eaten by disease, hacked off, snapped in two. I wonder when my body will become tired of it and just give up.

I'll never be able to run like I used to. I walk with a limp. I haven't told Isaac, but my leg aches constantly. I like it.

It's dark in the kitchen. I don't want to put the light on and risk Isaac knowing I was in here. If he is trying to avoid me, I'll help him. But when I look up he's standing in the doorway watching me. We stare at each other for the longest time. I feel anxious. It looks like he has something to say. I think he's come to fight some more, but then I see something else in his eyes.

He takes the steps to reach me. One … two … three … four.

He's standing in front of my knees. My hair is wild and unruly. I can't remember the last time I brushed it. It's grown past where my breasts used to be. Now it's sort of a shawl across my upper body, so that even when I'm naked I don't have to see myself. I don't even bother to hide my white streak behind my ear like I usually do when Isaac is around. It curls in front of my eye, partly obscuring my vision.

Isaac pushes my hair over my shoulder and I flinch involuntarily. Then he puts his hands on my knees. Their warmth stings. He pushes outward, spreading my legs, then he takes a step forward until he's standing between them. He bends his head until our mouths are almost touching. Almost. The fingers on both of my hands are splayed on the tabletop behind me, balancing myself. I can feel the grooves of my carvings. The carvings Isaac helped me make. He doesn't kiss me. We have never spoken about the kiss we shared when we thought we were dying. He breathes into my mouth as his hands run up the length of my thighs. His hands feel like warm water running across my skin. I cold shiver. My robe is hiked up to the top of my thighs. When his palms leave my legs, I want to cry out, *No!* I want more of the warmth, but he reaches up and grabs both lapels of my robe, pulling it open and exposing my chest. I'm frozen. Numb. He touches my scars. My barren womanhood. *Frozen ... frozen ... frozen ...* and then I break open.

I gasp and grab his hands, pushing them away. "What are you doing?"

He doesn't answer me. He lifts his hands to my neck. Wherever he touches me there is heat. I roll my head back and his thumbs graze my jaw.

"What I want," he says.

I roll my head to the left to try to pull away from him, but he pushes his hand into my hair at the back of my head, and kisses the side of my neck until I'm shivering. He has me at a disadvantage; I'm trying to keep myself upright with one hand and push him away with the other. Eventually, my hand slips out from under me and we collapse on the table.

He kisses me. Hard at first—like he's angry—but when I touch his face he softens. It's when his lips drag slowly across mine, his tongue darting in and out of my mouth that I relax. My legs lift off of the table and my feet cradle his waist. Heat; heat on the arches of my feet, heat on my mouth, heat pressed between my legs. He reaches down and pulls my robe open all the way. I lift my arms out of the robe and wrap them around him. Then he rolls me until I'm on top of him. I sit up and he lifts me at the waist until I'm hovering above his erection. He's right there; the tip is touching me. All I have to do is push down and he will be inside of me. And I want him to be. Because I need to touch and be touched.

But Isaac is hesitating. He doesn't want to let go of my waist. He's thinking of his wife; I'm thinking of his wife. I'm about to tell him, *forget it,* when he abruptly releases his hold on my waist. Without him suspending me, and with no warning I slide onto him. I suck air loudly. It's a gasp if I've ever heard one. One minute I'm empty, the next I'm full. A deep, slow panic. He does not belong to me. What am I doing? I try to climb off him, but he grabs my wrists and rolls on top of me, pinning me down. He kisses me slowly with both hands pressed against the sides of my face, all the while moving slowly in and out of me.

"I want to be with you," he says into my mouth. "Stop it."

So I stop it. I let him kiss and stroke and touch and I don't fight him. We've only had sex once; in the rain, on the carousel, with me on top. Now, it doesn't feel so much like sex. It feels intimate. I've never done what we are doing. Not with anyone. Not even with Nick. I've never laced my hands in a man's hair and breathed into his mouth with abandon, and wanted him to be as deeply inside of me as he could—because it felt more real that way. And a man has never buried his face into my neck and moaned, like every movement inside of me is worth a reaction.

But we are here on the table, rocking against each other and having the kind of sex that is breathless and tender and hard all at the same time. He is touching me everywhere. His fingers roving over my chest and back and thighs. It makes me feel like I am something beautiful rather than this atrocity that life has turned me into. And while Isaac is inside of me I forget everything. I forget that I am a captive, and that bones have been broken, and that we've almost died. I forget that he has a life with someone else. I forget that I was raped and that I have no breasts. I forget that I fight so hard not to feel anything. Isaac is making love to me, and all I feel right at this moment is valued.

He carries me up to his bed, and lays me down on the mattress. I can feel him trickling down my thigh as he climbs into bed and stretches out beside me. *Hold me,* I think. Only words in my head, but Isaac turns his body and folds himself around me. I crush my eyes together.

Pitter patter, pitter patter…

Fear, light footed, dances around me. She whispers seductively in my ear. We are lovers, fear and I. She calls to me, and I let her in.

Go. I tell her. Let me go, let me go, let me go, let me go.

"Tell me a lie, Isaac."

His fingertips trace a curlicue on my shoulder.

"I don't love you."

He cannot see my face, but it writhes: eyelashes, lips, the cutting of lines across my forehead.

"Tell me a truth, Senna."

"I don't know how," I breath.

"Then tell me a lie."

"I don't love you," I say. I sink beneath the weight of it all.

Isaac stirs behind me, and then he is leaning over me, his elbows on either side of my head.

"The truth is for the mind," he says. "Lies are for the heart. So let's just keep lying."

I kiss the man I lie to. He kisses me with truth. I am set free.

Two days later Isaac gets sick. It's the kind of sick that scares me. At first when I question him, he tells me that nothing is wrong. But then the tiny beads of sweat start to collect on his brow and upper lip like condensation. I narrow my eyes at him as we eat. He's clearly forcing down his food. His skin looks like wax—shiny and colorless.

"Okay, doctor," I say, setting down my fork. "Diagnose yourself, and then tell me what to do."

My voice is light, but something in my gut is telling that this is bad. We don't have any more antibiotics. We don't really have any more anything. I checked our supplies earlier: a couple tubes of burn cream and a surplus of bandages and alcohol wipes. We've been trying to save the power and use the logs from the well, but we are running low on those, too. I realize I've been waiting too long for Isaac's answer. He's staring at his plate, not really seeing anything.

"Isaac..." I touch his hand and my eyes grow wide. "I'd say you have a fever."

My lips feel dry. I flick my tongue over the top of them while considering Isaac's fever. "Let's get you upstairs, okay?"

He nods.

An hour later he is trembling uncontrollably. I've shaken like this—I can remember each time. But my trembling was emotion. The body deals with attacks the same way—emotional or not. Isaac was always the one to make it go away. I can't do the same for him. What he needs is beyond what my body can do for him.

I can't get him to wake up. He never told me what to do. His body says he's hot—too hot—but this cabin is a freezer. Do I keep him warm, or cool him down? I sit next to him and try to pray. If I lean close to his face I can feel the heat rising off his skin. No one taught me how to pray. I don't know who I'm praying to: an obese god who is always grinning? A god with a woman's head that sits on a man's body? A god with holes in his hands and feet? I pray to whichever it is. My mouth moves with words—begging, pleading words. I've never spoken to God before. I partly blame him for the bad that's happened to me. I say I don't, but I do. I'm willing to never blame him again if he just saves Isaac.

I think he's heard me when Isaac's shaking suddenly stops. But when I lower my head to his mouth his breathing is shallow. I pray directly to the God with the holes in his hands. He seems like the one to talk to. A God that understands pain.

"That's Isaac," I tell him. "He helped me, and now he's here. He didn't do anything to deserve this. And he shouldn't have to die because of me." Then I appeal directly to Isaac.

"You can't do this again," I tell Isaac. "This is the second time. It's not fair. It's my turn to almost die."

I lean down and touch my forehead to his. I want to lie on him and take his heat, but now is not the time for being cold. I pull my head up and stare down at him. I'm afraid to leave him and go look for medicine. We closed off the hole below the table weeks ago. But maybe he forgot something. Maybe there is still medicine down there: a pill in the dirt. A miracle in a dark corner. I know it's a long shot, but I can't just sit here and do nothing. I kiss him on the mouth and stand up.

"Don't die," I warn him. "I'll chase right behind you if you do."

If he can hear me, threatening him with my death will work. He will hold on just to keep me alive. I dart out of the room and head for the kitchen. The tabletop is easier to push aside this time. I'm stronger. I grab the flashlight and climb down the ladder he left in place. There are still grains of rice scattered across the floor from the day I knocked the bag over. They pierce my socks and make my toes curl up. The floors and shelves are bare. I run my hands along the back of them, feeling for any lucky leftover. I catch a splinter in my palm and pull it out. The metal box with the medical cross on it bolted to the wall is open. There is nothing on the shelves but dust. I grab the box and try to rip it off the wall, but the box is bolted down. My muscles are more inefficient than my anger.

"I can't even rip something off the wall right!" I yell at nothing.

I stick my fingers in my hair and pull until it hurts. First, I feel helpless, then I feel hopeless, then I feel overwhelming grief. I can't handle it. I don't know what to do with myself. I fall to my knees and clutch my sides. I can't do this. I can't. I want to die. I want to kill. All of my feelings are coming at once.

You're selfish, I hear a voice say. Isaac is dying and you're thinking about how you feel.

The voice is right. I stand up and dust the rice off my knees. Then I climb back up the ladder; the only indication I'm on overload is the trembling of my hands.

I go back to the room to check on Isaac. He's still breathing. That's when I remember the book I found in the chest, at the base of the carousel bed. It always struck me as strange that our captor would put that book in the same house with a doctor.

I shove open the lid to the chest and see the book lying at the bottom. There is a single puzzle piece resting on its cover. I dust it away. This was the only book I saved when we burned everything to keep warm. It makes no sense why I'd save it. I had Isaac to answer my medical questions. Isaac to stitch me up. I saved it for myself. Because on some level I knew the zookeeper put it here for me. My stomach clenches. I flip through the index. Page 546. *Fever.*

The part I am looking for is highlighted. In pink. It's a coincidence, I think. An old textbook bought at a yard sale or something. This person couldn't possibly have known that Isaac would spike a fever that could kill him. Could he? I suddenly get chills. I look up, and when I do, I'm eye-to- eye with the black horse. I drop the book.

This is a game. This move is mine. I go to the wood closet. There is no more shed; Isaac started storing the tools in the Chapter Nine wood closet. I pull the axe from where it is propped, ignoring the glossy pages that run up and down the inner walls. I touch the tip of my finger to the blade. Isaac kept it sharpened. *Just in case. Just in case Senna loses her mind and needs it*, I think. I make my way up the stairs and turn right into the carousel room. The book is facedown on the carpet where I dropped it. An ungraceful splat on the floor. I kick it aside and look at my horse. Right in the eye. This horse and I bonded once upon a time over an arrow through the heart. I feel as if it betrayed me. Made me love it with its bone saddle and death tokens and morbid obesity—morbesity. Fattened me up for the fall.

"Give me what he needs," I say. "I'll do whatever you want. Just give me what he needs." And then, "Checkmate."

I lift the axe and don't stop lifting the axe until my arms are jello-fied and my teeth are clanging together hard enough to deliver a headache, and the horse is just a mess of jagged, ripped metal. It reminds me of the inside of a Coke can I once cut open with a knife.

Now he can't see us anymore. Why did it take me so long to figure that out?

I lie beside Isaac, still as stone. I can hear the wind whipping the snow around outside. There is no window in Isaac's room. It's on the side of the house that faces the cliff and the generator shed that the zookeeper didn't want us to see. But across the hall is the carousel room, and the noise filters in from there. It sounds like a blizzard. I'm unconcerned. I'm already cold. I'm already hungry. I'm already hopeless. I'm stuck in reverse; always trying not to die.

I lift my head and check his breathing. Shallow. He needs fluids. I hold a cup of melted snow to his lips, but it just runs out of his mouth when I try to make him drink. I read the highlighted portion in the book and I do everything it tells me. Though there isn't much. Cool cloth to the forehead—we are in the arctic. Keep room at cool temperature—we are in the arctic. Cover him with a light blanket, doesn't matter if it's made of fur—we are in the arctic. Fluids. That's the most important thing, and I can't get him to swallow anything. There is nothing I can do.

He starts to mumble, his eyelids flickering from the turbulence of his dream. They are just words that drop off before he can finish them. Tormented moans and gasps intermingling with the chattering of his teeth. I lean my ear close to his lips and try to make out what he's saying, but as soon as I do, he stops. I am scared. I am really fucking scared. He's probably calling for his wife. And all he has is me.

"Hush," I tell him. "Save your pluck." Though I get the feeling I'm really telling me.

I fall asleep for a bit. When I wake up my body is pressed against Isaac's. I went looking for his heat while I slept. I'm too afraid to move. If he's hot, he's still alive. He makes a noise in the back of his throat. Relief floods. I get up and light a fire. I try to gather its heat in my palms as I wiggle my fingers toward the flames. Every few minutes I look over my shoulder to check on the rising and falling of his chest. It's barely a rise and fall. It's more of a little flutter.

Then I get an idea. I get up and grab the cup of water from the bedside table. The cup is cool against my hand. I climb onto the bed and throw a leg over his waist until I am straddling him. I keep my weight off his body by suspending myself on my knees. I just need enough leverage to get to his lips. Staring down at his gaunt, skeletal face, I take a deep sip of the water. This is probably a stupid idea, but there is no one to witness it. I bend my head down until my lips are touching Isaac's. It feels as if I have my mouth pressed against an overheated car engine. His lips part automatically. I push the water into to his mouth and keep my lips firmly pressed to his to keep it from rolling out. I feel his throat move, feel it push the water down, down, down his esophagus. I imagine that I can hear the tinkle as it drops into his empty stomach.

I do it again. The second time doesn't go as well as the first; water spills down the side of his face and he sputters a little, but I keep trying. When Isaac has swallowed a shot glass worth of the melted ice, I roll off of him and lie staring up at the ceiling. After the hours I've spent being helpless this feels like an accomplishment. One of epic proportions. It used to be that if I finished a book I'd feel accomplished. If I landed on the *New York Times* bestsellers list I'd feel more accomplished. If they made a movie out of the bestseller I'd feel like I was the essence of accomplishment. Now if the man I'm imprisoned with swallows a mouthful of water, I want to sprint around the room in victory.

My limbs and brain are flaccid. I repeat the process every twenty minutes. If I try too often he starts to choke. I'm so terrified that his heart will stop I keep my palm pressed to his chest to feel the lazy thud.

"You keep him alive," I tell it. "Keep beating."

Ugh. My tear ducts are burning. I fist my hands and rub my eyes like a child. I need to refill the water in the cup. I could slip around the corner to the bathroom, but the water from the faucet is brown and tastes like copper. Isaac and I usually drink the snow. My mouth is dry and my throat feels coarse. I haven't wanted to drink the water in the cup. I don't want to leave him, but the need to drink, to pee, to get more snow moves me off the bed.

I make my way down the stairs, grabbing my sweatshirt from the banister. Isaac's rubber boots are at the front door. I slip my feet into them and plod to the kitchen to grab a pitcher for the snow. The pitcher is below the sink. I duck down to retrieve it. When I come back up, I glance out the window to assess the snowstorm. That's when I see him.

The zookeeper calls me into the snowstorm. I knew he'd come eventually. You don't put on a show like this and not expect applause. I see him outside the kitchen window; a dark shadow against the white snow. He's facing me, but there is snow and wind and it's swirling around in cold chaos. It's like I'm looking at a grainy television picture. He stands there for at least a minute, until he knows I've seen him. Then he turns and walks toward the cliff. My hands grip the edge of the sink until my wrists ache from the pressure. I have no choice but to go out there and follow him.

Isaac is unconscious, his body overheating. I leave my pitcher on the counter, pocket an inhaler and then I take the knife. The little one he left me on the first day I woke up in this Hell. It was a gift. I want to thank him for it. I slip it into my pocket and step outside, veering right. Five steps into the swells of snow and my leg is aching. I am shivering and my nose is running. I glance back at the kitchen window, afraid Isaac will wake up and call for me. What if his heart stops while I'm gone? I push away these thoughts and focus on my pain. Pain will carry me through; pain will help me focus.

All I can see is his back; the silhouette of him against the white, white snow. A black coat hugging narrow shoulders and hanging down to the backs of his knees. He's facing the cliff as I walk toward him. If he's close enough maybe I can push him off and watch him crack on the bottom. I search for the direction he came from: a car, another person, a break in the fence where he could have slipped through. Nothing. My legs want to stop when I'm a few feet away. This is a heavy thing—meeting your captor. I am afraid. I am afraid the fuse in my bone will snap apart as I struggle to push through the last few yards of snow. I take my last step and

I am beside him. I don't look. My own hood is pulled up around my face so that I can't see left or right unless I turn my head. It's snowing into the hole in front of us. The flakes are heavy and dense. They fall quickly. The knife is out of my pocket, the blade pointed toward the body to my left.

"Why?" I ask.

Snow fills my eyes and mouth and nose until I feel like I'm going to choke on it.

There is no answer so I turn to face my captor, ready to stick the blade in his throat.

Her throat.

I drop the blade and stumble backwards. I almost fall except she reaches out and catches me.

I scream and thrash out of her hands.

"Don't touch me!"

My leg. Oh God—my leg. It hurts.

"Don't touch me," I say again. Calmer this time.

I start to cry. I feel like a little kid, so uncertain, so lost. I want to sit down and process this.

"Doctor," I say. "What is this?"

Saphira Elgin turns back to the cliff. It looks like a big bowl filling up with flour.

"You don't remember?" She sounds disappointed. I sound like I can't breathe. I pull the inhaler from my pocket, eyeing her red lips. I don't remember her being so tall, but maybe I've become more bent from the weight of this.

"Why would you do this, Saphira?" I'm shaking violently and I'm light headed.

Dr. Elgin shakes her head. "I can't tell you what you already know."

I don't understand. She's obviously crazy.

"You can save him. Send him back to his wife and baby," she says.

I'm quiet. I can't feel my toes.

"How?"

"Say the word. It's your choice. But you have to stay."

I feel an ache in my chest. Saphira sees the look on my face. Grins. I recall the dragon in her, the way her looks seem to regard my soul.

"Can you do it? It brings you pain to part with him."

"Shut up! Shut up!" I cover my ears with my hands.

I feel everything on my skin. I'm boiling over. I want to attack her, and sob and scream, and die all at once.

"You're sick," I hiss. I raise the hand with the knife, and she makes no move to stop me or step away. I drop my arm to my side. Save Isaac and die here.

"Yes. If that's my only choice, yes. Take him. He's sick and we don't have any more medicine." I grab her arm. I need her to take him with her. "Now! Get him to a hospital."

Where did she come from? Maybe if I can overpower her I can get to her car. Get help. But even as I think this, I know I am too weak, and I know she did not come alone.

She watches my struggle with interest. I'm so cold. I have so many things to ask: the box, my mother … the *Why? Why? Why?* But I am too cold to speak.

"Why?" I ask again.

She laughs. Her breath blows snow away from her mouth. I watch the flakes shoot horizontally and then continue their dance to the ground.

"Senna," she says. "You are in love with Isaac."

I don't know it until the words are out of her mouth. Then I know it, and it feels like someone has sucker punched me.

I'm in love with Isaac.

I'm in love with Isaac.

I'm in love with Isaac.

What happened to Nick? I try to pull up my feelings for Nick. The feelings that imprisoned me for a decade, chaining me to a rotting corpse of a relationship. All I did for years was punish myself for not being what he needed. For failing the person I loved the most. But out in the freezing cold, with the blizzard swirling around me, and my kidnapper's liquid eyes probing my face, I can't remember the last time I thought of Nick. Isaac happened to Nick. But when? How? Why didn't I know it was happening? How could my heart switch allegiances without me knowing?

Doctor—no, I won't call her a doctor after what she's done—Saphira looks smug.

I'm so cold I can't be anything but cold. I can't even muster anger.

I rest my hand on the outside of my pocket where my inhaler is. I don't want to have to use it again.

"Take him," I say again. "Please. He's very sick. Take him now." My voice is frantic. The wind is picking up. When I turn my head I can't see the house anymore. I'll do anything she says, so long as she saves Isaac.

She takes a syringe out of her pocket and hands it to me.

"Go say goodbye to him. Then use this."

I take the syringe and nod, though I don't think she can see me through the snow.

"What if I put this in your neck right now?"

I can feel her grinning.

"Then we'd all die. Are you ready for that?"

I'm not. I want Isaac to live because he deserves it. I wish he could tell me what to do. I was wrong about the zookeeper. I didn't expect this. I profiled my kidnapper, but I never hung the face of Saphira Elgin on him. She changes everything; because of her knowledge of me, she has the ability to outplay me.

I clutch the syringe. I can't see the house, but I know the direction it's in. So I walk. I walk until I see the logs. Then I walk running my frozen hands along the logs until I reach the door. I swing it open and collapse on the bottom stair, shivering. It's warmer in here, but not warm enough. I climb the stairs. Isaac is in his room where I left him. I add a log to his dwindling fire and crawl into the bed with him. He's burning up; his skin is the heat I crave so badly. I press my lips against his temple. There is a lot of grey there now. We match.

"Hey," I say. "Do you remember that time you showed up every day to take care of a perfect stranger? I never really thanked you for that. I'm not really going to thank you now either, because that's not my style." I press closer to him, cup his cheek in my hand. The hair prickles my palm. "I am going to do something to take care of you for once. Go see your baby. I love you." I lean over and kiss him on the mouth, then I roll out of bed and climb up to the attic room.

I feel nothing…

I feel nothing….

I feel everything.

I look at the needle for a long time, balancing it in the palm of my hand. I don't know what will happen when I do this. Saphira could be lying to me. She could have a more sinister plan now that Isaac is out of the picture. What's in the syringe could kill me. Maybe it'll make me sleep and she'll leave me here to die. I'd be grateful for that. I could fight back. I could wait and push this needle into her neck and take my chances with getting Isaac out of here myself. But I don't want to risk his life. He has no idea Saphira is responsible for bringing us here. Her taking him out of here and getting him help will put her at the risk of being discovered. I push the needle into the vein in my hand. It hurts. Then I stand with the back of my knees pressed against the mattress, spreading my arms wide. *This is what it feels like to love,* I think. It's heavy. Or maybe it's the responsibility that comes with it that's heavy.

I fall backwards. For the first time I feel my mother in the fall. She chose to save herself. She couldn't bear the weight of love—not even for her own flesh and blood. And in that fall, I feel her decision to leave me. It rocks my heart and breaks it all over again. The first person you are connected to is your mother. By a cord composed of two arteries and a vein. She keeps you alive by sharing her blood and her warmth and her very life. When you are born, and the doctor severs that cord, a new one is formed. An emotional cord.

My mother held me and fed me. She brushed my hair gently, and told me stories about fairies that lived in apple trees. She sang me songs, and baked me lemon cakes with rose frosting. She kissed my face when I cried and made little circles on my skin with her fingertips. And then she abandoned me. She walked out like none of that meant anything. Like we were never connected by a cord with two arteries and a vein. Like we were never connected by our hearts. I was disposable. I could be left. I was a broken- hearted little girl. Isaac broke the spell she put me under. He taught me what it was to *not* be left. A stranger who fought to keep me alive.

I scream aloud. I roll to my side and grab my shirt, bringing the material up to my face, pressing it against my eyes and nose and mouth. I cry ungracefully, my heart hurting so exquisitely I cannot hold in the ugly noises that rise from my throat.

I once read that there is an invisible thread that connects those who are destined to meet, regardless of time, place, or circumstance. The thread may stretch or tangle, but will never break. As the drugs dull me, I can feel that cord. I close my eyes, choking on my own spit and tears, and I can almost feel it tug and pull as she takes Isaac.

Please don't let it break, I silently plead to him. I need to know that some cords can't be cut. Then the drugs take me.

ACCEPTANCE

Isaac is not in his bed when I wake. He's not in the house. I check every corner, dragging my half useless leg behind me. My guess is that I've been unconscious for at least twenty-four hours, perhaps more. I step outside in Isaac's oversized clunky boots, sinking into the fresh snow. The blizzard has all but covered the lower half of the house. Snow piles in graceful sweeps of white. White, white, white. All I see is white. It looks like the house is wearing a wedding dress. If there were tire marks, they are gone now. I walk as far as I can before reaching the fence. I am tempted to touch it. To let the volts shake my body and send my heart to a screeching stop. I reach my gloves toward the chain link. My light wool gloves that do nothing to stave off the frigid air. *I might as well be wearing lace on my hands*, I think for the thousandth time.

Isaac is out. My hands pause midair. I have no idea if Elgin will take him to a hospital. My hands move an inch toward the fence. But if she does, he will live. And I might see him again. I drop my hands to my sides. She's crazy. For all I know she's locked him up somewhere else where she can play more of her sick games.

No. Dr. Elgin always did what she said she was going to do. Even if it meant locking me up like an animal to fix me.

The last time I had seen Saphira Elgin was a year past the date I filed a restraining order against Isaac. I'd been seeing her once a week for over a year. Our visits, that had started with her extracting one sliver at a time from the lockdown that is my mind, eventually became more relaxed. More pleasant. I got to speak to someone who didn't really care about me. She wasn't trying to save me, or love me to better health; she was paid (a hundred dollars an hour) to take an unbiased look into my soul and help me find the crickets. That's what she called them: crickets. The little chirping noises that were either alarms, or echoes, or the unspoken words that needed to be spoken. Or that's what I thought anyway. Turns out Saphira cared above and beyond her pay grade. She entered God's pay grade. Toying with fate and lives and sanity. But that last time, the last time I saw her, she'd said something that in hindsight should have been my clue in to her insanity.

I'd told her I was writing a new book. One about Nick. She'd become flustered at that. Not in the extreme outward way a normal person becomes flustered. I don't even know if I can pinpoint how I knew it upset her. Maybe her bracelets tinkled a little extra that day as she jotted notes down on her yellow pad. Or maybe her ruby lips pulled a little tighter. But I knew. I'd confessed to her that I'd messed everything up, but I wasn't sure how. When we ended our session she'd grabbed my hand.

"Senna," she'd said, "do you want another chance at the truth?"

"The truth?" I'd repeated, not sure of what she was getting at.

"The truth that can set you free..."

Her eyes had been two hot coals. I'd been close enough to smell her perfume; it smelled exotic like myrrh and burning wood.

"Nothing can set me free, Saphira," I'd said in turn. "That's why I write."

I'd turned to leave. I was halfway out the door when she'd called my name.

"Three things cannot be long hidden: the sun, the moon, and the truth."

I'd half smiled, and gone home and forgotten what she'd said. I'd written my book in the month after that meeting. I only needed thirty days to write a book. Thirty days in which I didn't eat or sleep or do anything at all but clack away at my keyboard. And after the book was finished and catharsis was complete, I'd never made another appointment to see her. Her office called and left messages on my phone. She eventually called and left a message. But I was finished.

"Three things cannot be long hidden: the sun, the moon, and the truth." I say it out loud, the memory aching in my brain. Is that where she had the idea? To put me in this place where for a time both the sun and the moon were hidden? Where like slow, seeping molasses I would discover the crickets of truth in my heart?

My zookeeper thought it kind to be my savior. And now what? I would starve and freeze here alone? What was the point of that? I hate her so. I want to tell her that her sick game didn't work, that I'm just the same as I've always been: broken, bitter and self-destructive. Something comes to me then, a quote by Martin Luther King, Jr. *I believe that unarmed truth and unconditional love will have the final word in reality.*

"Fuck you, Saphira!" I call out.

Then I reach out in defiance and grab the fence.

I cry out because of what I think is coming. But nothing comes. It's then that I acknowledge that there is no humming. The fence used to hum. My vocal chords are frozen, my tongue is stuck to the roof of my mouth. I unstick my tongue and try to lick my lips. But my mouth is so dry there is nothing to wet them with. I let go of the chain link and look over my shoulder at the house. I left the front door open, it's swung wide, the one dark spot beneath the veils of snow. I don't want to go back. The smart thing would be to go get more layers. More socks. I threw on one of Isaac's sweatshirts before I left, over the one I was already wearing. But the air cuts through both like they're made of tissue. I head back for the house, my leg aching. I throw on more clothes, stuff food in my pockets. Before I leave I climb the stairs to the carousel room. Kneeling in front of the chest, I search for the single puzzle piece that escaped the fire. It's there, in the corner, overlaid with dust. I place it in my pocket, and then I walk through my prison for the last time.

The fence. I lace my fingers through the wire and pull up. In Saphira's exit with Isaac, she might have overlooked turning the fence back on. If she comes back I don't want to be here. I'd sooner die free, cold and in the woods than locked up behind an electrical fence, turning into a human ice cube in that house.

Isaac's boots are big. I can't fit the toes into the octagons that make up the pattern of the fence. I slip twice and my chin bumps down the metal like something out of a Looney-Tunes cartoon. I feel blood running down my neck. I don't even bother to wipe it up. I am desperate … manic. I want out. I claw at the fence. My gloves snag on twisted pieces of steel. When I rip them away the metal catches the skin on my palm, ripping into the tender flesh. I keep going. There is barbed wire along the top of the fence, running in loops as far as I can see. I don't even feel the spikes when I grab onto one and swing my leg over the side. I manage to get both feet balanced precariously on the far side of the fence. The barbed wire wavers against my weight. I sway … then I fall.

I feel my mother in that fall. Maybe it's because I'm so near to the Reaper. I wonder if my mother is dead, and if I will see her when I die. I think all of this as I make the three-second spill to the ground.

One.

Two.

Three.

I gasp. I feel as if all the air in the world was pumped into my lungs, and then rapidly sucked out, lickety-split.

Right away I search myself. I can hardly breathe, but my hands are running over my limbs looking for broken things. When I am sufficiently comforted that *this* fall didn't break anything, I sit up, groaning, holding onto the back of my head like my brains are falling out. The snow broke my fall, but my head hit something. It takes me a while to get all the way to my feet. I'm going to have a huge knot … maybe a concussion. The good new is if I have a concussion I'll just pass out. No feeling wild animals rip my limbs apart. No feeling myself freeze to death. No eating tree bark and suffering the claws of hunger. Just a nice, bleeding brain and then … nothing. The bags of peanuts I put into my pockets are scattered around in the snow. I pick them up one by one as I bend my head back to look at the top of the fence. I want to see how far I fell. What is that—twelve feet? I turn toward the woods, my bad leg sinking low into the soft mounds of snow. It's hard to get it back up. I have worked a nice little path to the tree line when I suddenly turn back. It's only ten feet back to the chain link, but it's an arduous journey. I look one last time. I hate it. I hate that house. But it's where Isaac showed me a love that expects nothing in return. So, I can't hate it too much.

Please, please let him live.
And then I walk.

I hear the beating of helicopter blades.

Whump-Whump

Whump-Whump

Whump-Whump

I force my eyes open. I have to use my fingers to pry them apart, and even then I can't get them to stay cracked.

Whump-Whump

It sounds like it's getting closer. I have to get up, get outside. I am already outside. I feel the snow beneath my fingertips. I raise my head. There is a lot of pain. From my head? *Yes, I fell. Climbing over the fence.*

Whump-Whump

Whump-Whump

You have to get to a clearing. Somewhere they can see you. But all around me there are trees. I've walked so far. I am in the thickest of thickets. I can reach out and touch the nearest tree trunk with my pinkie. Did I stop here because I thought it would be warmer? Did I just collapse? I can't remember. But I hear a helicopter whipping the air, and I have to make them see me. I utilize the nearest tree trunk and pull myself to my feet. I stumble forward, heading in the direction I came from. I can see my prints in the snow. I think I remember a thicket just ahead. One where I could see the sky. It's farther than I thought, and by the time I reach it and tilt my head back, I can't hear the *Whump-Whump* quite as clearly as before. Not enough time to build a fire. I picture myself crouched in the snow whittling away at a pile of wood, and laugh. Too late to go back to the house, how long have I been out her? I've lost all concept of time. Two days? Three? Then I think it. Isaac is alive! He sent them. There is nothing to do but to stand in the clearing, head tilted up, and wait.

I am airlifted to the nearest hospital in Anchorage. There are already news trucks outside. I see flashes and hear slamming doors and voices before I am wheeled on the gurney through the back door and into a private room. Nurses and doctors in salmon-colored scrubs come rushing toward me. I am compelled to roll off the gurney and hide. There are too many people. I want to tell them that I'm fine. I'm a death escapist. There is no need for this many medical professionals or this many tests. Their faces are serious; they are concentrating on saving me. There's nothing really left for them to save.

Nevertheless, needles slide into my arms over and over until I can't even feel them anymore. They make me comfortable in a private room, with only an IV to keep me company. The nurses ask how I feel, but I don't know what to tell them. I know that my heart is beating and that I am not cold anymore. They tell me that I'm dehydrated, undernourished. I want to say, "No shit" but I can't form words yet. After a few hours they feed me. Or they try to. Simple food that my hollow stomach can handle: bread and something that is white and mushy. I push the food aside and ask for coffee. They say, "No." When I try to stand up and tell them that I'm getting my own, they bring me coffee.

The police come next. All official looking. I tell them I want to speak to Saphira before I speak to them. They want my statement; they're clicking the little buttons on the ends of their pens and pushing tape recorders at me, but I stare at them tight lipped until I can speak to Saphira.

"You can speak to her when you're well enough to come in to the station," they tell me. A chill runs through my body. They have her. Here.

"That's when I'll speak to you, then," I tell them.

A day before I am discharged I am visited by two doctors; one is an oncologist and the other an orthopedic surgeon. The ortho guy holds up the x-rays they took of my leg.

"The bone didn't heal straight, which is why you have pain when you put too much pressure on it. I've scheduled you for—"

"No," I tell him.

He brings his eyes to my face. "No?"

"I'm not interested in fixing it. I'll leave it how it is." I open the magazine on my lap to signal that the conversation is over.

"Ms. Richards, with all due respect, the irregular fusion of your bone that was caused by the accident will be something that pains you for the rest of your life. You will want to have the surgeries needed to repair it."

I close my magazine. "I like pain. I like when it lingers. It reminds a person of what they've lived through."

"That's a very unique perspective," he says. "But not practical."

I fling the magazine across the room. It flies with surprising force and hits the door with a healthy thud. Then I pull down my hospital gown—all the way—until the scars on my chest are exposed. He looks like he might pass out.

"I like my scars," I say. "I earned them. Now, get out."

As soon as the door shuts behind him, I scream. The nurses come rushing in, but I throw my water jug at them. At the rate I'm going they're going to put me in the psych ward.

"Get out!" I scream at them. "Stop telling me how to live my life!"

I am much nicer to the oncologist. She got my file from the hospital in Seattle and ran the yearly tests that I'd missed during my imprisonment. When she gives me the results she sits on the edge of my bed. It reminds me so much of Isaac that I feel overwhelmed. When she is finished she tells me that I am built to fight; emotionally and physically. I actually smile.

A few days later I am driven to the police station in the back of a police car. It stinks of mold and sweat. I am wearing clothes that the hospital gave me: jeans, an ugly brown sweater and green chucks. The nurses tried to comb through my hair, but eventually they gave up. I asked for scissors and hacked through the rope of it. Now it barely touches my neck. I look stupid, but who cares? I've been locked in a house for over a year eating coffee grounds and trying not to die of hypothermia.

When we reach the police station, they put me in a room with a cup of coffee and a bagel. Two detectives come in and try to take my statement.

"Not until I can speak to Saphira," I say. I don't know why it's so important for me to speak to her first. Maybe I think that they won't hold true to the bargain, and they'll keep me away from her. Finally, one of the detectives, a tall man who smells like cigarette smoke and says his *s*'s too softly leads me by the arm to the room where they are holding her. He tells me his name is Detective Garrison. He's in charge of this case. I wonder if he's ever seen action like this before.

"Ten minutes," he says. I nod. I wait until he closes the door before I look at her. She's ruffled. Her lips are bare of their usual deep red, and her hair is pulling out of a low ponytail. She's leaning her elbows on the table, her hands clasped in front of her. It's her typical shrink pose.

"What's wrong, Saphira? You look like an experiment gone wrong."

She doesn't look surprised to see me. In fact, she looks downright peaceful. *She knew she'd get caught. She wanted to. Planned it, probably.* The realization throws me off. I momentarily forget what I came here to do. I make my way over to the chair opposite her. It screeches against the floor as I pull it out.

My heart is racing. This isn't how I imagined this going. Her face blurs in and out of my vision. I hear screaming. No. It's my imagination. We are in a quiet room, painted white, sitting at a metal table. The only sound is silence as we sit contemplating one another, so why do I want to reach up and cover my ears?

"Saphira," I breathe. She smiles at me. A dragon's smile. "Why did you do this?"

"Senna Richards. The great fiction writerrr," she purrs, leaning forward on her elbows. "You don't rememberrr Westwick."

Westwick.

"What are you talking about?"

"You were institutionalized, my dear. Three years ago. At Westwick Psychiatric Facility."

My skin prickles. "That's a lie."

"Is it?"

My mouth is dry. My tongue is sticking to the inside of my mouth. I try to shift it around—to the roof of my mouth, the inside of my cheeks, but it sticks, sticks, sticks.

"You had a psychotic break. You tried to kill yourself."

"I would never," I say. I love death. I think about it all the time, but to actually act out a suicide is unlike me.

"You called me from yourrr home at three o'clock in the morrrning. You were delusional. You werrre starving yourself. Keeping yourrrself awake with pills. When they took you in you hadn't slept in nine days. You were experiencing hallucinations, paranoia and memory lapses."

That's not suicide, I think. But then I'm not so sure. I lift my hands off the top of the table where they are resting and hide them between my thighs.

"You were saying one thing overrr and overrr when they brought you in. Do you rememberrr?"

I make a noise in the back of my throat.

If I ask her what I was saying I'm acknowledging that I believe her. And I don't believe her. Except that I can hear screaming in my head.

"Pink hippo," she says.

My throat constricts. The screaming gets louder. I want to reach up and put my hands over my ears to quell the sound.

"No," I say.

"Yes, Senna. You were."

"No!" I slam my fist on the table. Saphira's eyes grow large.

"I was saying Zippo."

There is silence. All consuming, chilling, silence. I realize I was baited.

The corners of her mouth curl up. "Ah, yes," she says. "Z, for Zippo. My mistake."

It's like I've just woken up from a dream—not a good one—just a dream that concealed a reality I'd somehow forgotten. I'm not freaking out, I'm not panicking. It feels as if I'm waking up from a long sleep. I'm compelled to stand and stretch my muscles. I hear the screaming again, but now it's connected to a memory. *I'm in a locked room. I'm not trying to get out. I don't care about getting out. I'm just curled up on a metal cot, screaming. They can't get me to stop. I've been like that for hours. I only stop when they sedate me, but as soon as the drugs wear off, I'm screaming again.*

"What made me stop screaming?" I ask her. My voice is so calm. I can't remember everything. It's all in pieces; smells and sounds and overwhelming emotions that were there at once, making me feel like I was about to implode.

"Isaac."

I jar at the sound of his name. "What are you talking about?"

"I called Isaac," she says. "He came."

"Ohgodohgodohgod." I bend over at the waist, hugging myself. *I remember.* I've been falling, and now I've finally hit the ground.

Flashes of him coming into the room and climbing into the cot behind me. His arms wrapping around my body, until I stopped screaming.

I moan. It's an ugly, guttural sound.

"Why did I forget all that?" I'm still treating her like she's my shrink; asking her questions like she's sane enough to know the answers. *She's your zookeeper. She tried to kill you.*

"It happens. We block out things that thrrreaten to break us. It's the brain's best defense mechanism."

I'm struggling for air.

"This was all an experiment to you. You took advantage of your position. Of what I told you." All my gusto is gone. I just need answers so I can get out of here. *Get out of here and go where? Home,* I tell myself. Whatever that is.

"Do you remember what you asked me in our last session?" I stare at her blank faced.

"You asked, 'If there were a God, why would he let these terrible things happen to people?'"

I remember.

"With free will comes bad decisions; decisions to drink and drive and kill someone's child. Decisions to murder. Decisions to choose whom we love, whom we spend our life with. If God decided to never let anything bad happen to people, he would have to take away their free will. He would become the dictator and they would be his puppets."

"Why are you talking about God? I want to talk about what you did to me!"

And then I know. Saphira locking me in the house with Isaac, the man she believed was my safety and salvation, controlling the medicine, the food, what we saw, how we saw it—it was all her experimenting with free will. She became God. She'd said something once in one of our sessions: *Picture yourself standing on a cliff where you not only fear falling, but dread the possibility of throwing yourself off. Nothing is holding you back, and you experience freedom.*

The cliff! Why hadn't I seen it?

"Do you know how many people there are just like you? I heard it every day; pain, sadness, regret. You wanted a second chance. So I gave it to you. I gave you not the person you wanted, but the person you needed."

I don't know what to say. My ten minutes are almost over.

"Don't make out like you did this for me. You're sick. You're—"

"*You* are sick, my dear," she interrupts. "You were self destructing. Ready to die. I just gave you some perspective. Helped you to see the truth."

"What's the truth?"

"Isaac is your truth. You were too blinded by your past to see that."

I'm breathless. My mouth hangs open as I stare at her.

"Isaac has a wife. He has a baby. You act like you care so much, but you did this to him, too. Made him suffer for no reason. He almost died!"

Detective Garrison chooses that exact moment to come back. I want more time with her. I want more answers, but I know my time is up. He leads me to the door by my elbow. I look back at Saphira. She's staring into space, serene.

"He would have died without you, too," she says before the door closes. I want to ask her what she means, but the door swings closed. And that is the last time I ever see Saphira Elgin alive.

Detective Garrison is kind. I think this case is above his pay grade. He's not sure what to do with me—so he tries to feed me doughnuts and sandwiches. I eat none of it, but I appreciate the sentiment. There are six people in the room with me; two of them leaning against the wall, the others sitting. I give them my statement. I tell a tape recorder what the last fourteen months looked like; each day, each hunger pain, each time I thought one of us would die. When I am finished the room is quiet. Detective Garrison is the first to clear his throat. That's when I dare ask about Isaac. I've been too afraid up until now. Thinking his name alone hurts me. Hearing someone speak about him feels … wrong. He's been with me for all this time. Now he's not.

"Dr. Elgin got him over the Canadian border and took him to a hospital in Victoria. Took him is an ambitious word," he says. "She dropped him outside the Emergency room and drove off. He was unconscious for twenty-four hours before he finally started to come out of it. He grabbed a nurse by the arm and managed to say your name. The nurse recognized your name right away due to the media buzz you caused when you disappeared. She notified the police. By the time they got there Isaac was able to talk. He told them you were in a cabin somewhere near a cliff, but couldn't give them much more than that."

I am quiet.

"So he's okay?"

"Yes, he is. He's with his family in Seattle."

That hurts and brings me relief. I wonder what it was like meeting his baby for the first time.

"How did she do it? Get both of us to that house? Cross borders? She must have had help."

He shakes his head. "We are still questioning her. She took Isaac to the hospital in an RV. She was in the same RV when she tried to cross the border back into Alaska. When they searched her vehicle they found a false floorboard with a space large enough to hold two bodies. We think she drugged you and put you both in there. We don't know anything about help, we're still questioning her."

"Back into Alaska?" I ask. "She was coming back for me?"

He shakes his head. "We don't know."

I slam my fist on the table, frustrated. "What *do* you know?"

He looks affronted. I try to soften my face. This isn't his fault. Or maybe it is.

"How did you find me, then?"

"The Canadian police put out an APB on her vehicle. She was picked up at the border. She gave us the coordinates to the house where she was keeping you."

"Just like that?"

He nods.

"I don't get it."

"The house is on a large portion of land that she owns. Actually, large portion is an understatement. She owns forty thousand acres. Her late husband owned oil wells. He was also a conspiracy theorist. He published some books on Armageddon survival. We think he built the house out there as a result of those theories."

"You know all of that, but you don't know what she was going to do with me?"

"It's easy to find information that is already there, Ms. Richards. Extracting information from the human mind proves a little more difficult."

Maybe I underestimated soft *s* Detective Garrison.

"My mother…?" I ask. He cocks his head, his eyebrows drawing together. "Never mind." Perhaps she had no part in this. Perhaps Saphira found her and read her book without ever contacting her.

"I want to go home," I say, suddenly.

He nods. "Just a few more days. Bear with us…"

Nick is waiting for me when my flight lands in Seattle. I knew he would be. He contacted me through e-mail asking when I'd be coming home. He asked if he could be there. I sent him a quick response telling him the day, time, and flight number. When I come down the escalator to baggage claim, he doesn't see me right away. He looks nervous, which is unusual for him. I hide behind a huge potted plant, and peer at him through the leaves. My muse. My ten years wasted. It used to be that when I saw him my emotions would pitch a fever. I'd feel as if I were tumbling down, down, down, into something deep. Now he just looks like a guy in a trench coat with too much gel in his hair. No, that's unfair. He looks like a stew pot of memories; his hands are memories, his lips are memories, his body is a memory. But they don't entrance me like they used to. Either a year of imprisonment has left me more numb, or I've outgrown the love of my life.

"Where did your glimmer go, Nick?" I say through the plant. I am curious to know if it's still there. If I'll burst open the minute we make contact, like some quintessential love story.

He is sitting; a loner in an airport chair, watching the passers-by with apprehension on his face. It's a fine mental picture. Nick sees me as soon as I step out from my hiding place. When I walk toward him, he quickly stands. He embraces me without hesitation and with so much familiarity, my heart does a lurch. Maybe this is the spark.

He knows me. He knows what to say, what not to say. He speaks the language of my face, and waits for my expression to dictate his tone. That's what time does. It gives you space to learn each other. I soften into his embrace. It's no use fighting something like this.

"Brenna." He breathes my name into my hair.

I want to say his name, to return it, but my words are clotted in my throat.

"You ready?" he asks. "Do you have a bag?"

I shake my head. "I have nothing."

He takes my hand and leads me to the parking garage. He has a rental car. I fold into the front seat and stare at him. He is the only person I can stare at like this and not feel completely awkward.

The entire ride home I wait for him to ask me about it. Anything. Something. Anything. Why isn't he asking? It's unfair of me to expect it. Nick has never pried. He waits, and he knows that with me you can wait forever. But now I'm accustomed to something new. Funny how that can happen. Now I'm mentally begging him to ask me something. Anything. I feel the change in myself as the wheels of the car spray up water on the highway. When did that move in? I don't even know. In a house in the snow, probably. Where a surgeon sliced me open emotionally, and a musician brought me more color than I could handle.

It's summertime in Washington. More's the pity. When we reach my house there are reporters outside. They look sleepy until they see the car turn into the driveway. I wonder how long they have been camped here. I flew into Seattle under my real name to avoid this. Grabbing, scrambling, straightening hair, I look away from them and point Isaac toward the garage on one side of my circular driveway. *Nick.* I point Nick toward the garage. I rub my forehead. Since I don't have keys, we will have to go through the garage to get in the house. I tell him the code for the garage door, and he hops out and punches it in. They can't climb my driveway, but I hear them at the bottom, calling out my name.

Senna!

Senna Richards!

Did you know Dr. Elgin was behind your kidnapping?

Senna, tell us what it was like to—?

Senna, have you seen Isaac Asterholder since—?

Senna, did you think you were going to die?

Then the garage closes, muting their cacophony.

Boom!

Boom!

Boom!

Goes my heart…

Nick opens the door for me and we walk into my house. Dust fills my nose and mouth as I breathe in fourteen months of packed-up air. I touch the edge of his hand with my fingertip. He opens his fingers and entwines them with mine. He walks with me from room to room, and I feel like a ghost. He's never been in my house. Making money off of heartbreak is a good business to be in. When we reach the white room I jerk to a stop in the doorway. I can't go in. Isaac looks down at me. *Nick*. Nick looks down at me.

"What's wrong?" he asks.

Everything.

"This," I say, staring at all the white. Then, "Why did you come, Nick?"

We are on the edge of the white room. Technically a room that he created, inside of me and out.

He looks stricken. "Did you read my book?"

"Did you *mean* the book?" I spin back.

"Can we talk about this somewhere else?" He starts to step into my white room like he wants to take a look around. I grab his arm.

"We talk about this right here."

I want him on the brink of what he drove me to. I want to know what this is before I cross any more thresholds.

He leans against one side of the doorframe. I lean against the other.

"I was wrong. I was young and idealistic. I didn't realize…" He grimaces. "I didn't realize your value until it was too late."

"My value?"

"Your worth to me, Brenna. You spark things in me. You always have. I love you. I never stopped. I was just…"

"Young and idealistic," I repeat.

He nods. "And stupid."

I study him. Look at the white. Look at him.

"You have writer's block," I say. "You wrote the last book, and everyone freaked out. And now you have nothing else."

He looks startled.

"Tell me it's not true." I flick at the grey falling into my eyes. Then I think better of it, and let it drop back to cover them.

"It's not like that," he says. "You know we are good together. We inspire each other. Greatness comes when we are together."

I think about this. He is right, of course. We were great together. Some days I woke up playful. I wanted to laugh and flirt and be a love story. The very next day I couldn't stand being looked at or spoken to. Nick let me be. He spoke to me on the days I wanted to be spoken to. He left me alone when I shot eye daggers at him. We coexisted fluently and effortlessly. With him I can have companionship and love, and never have who I am questioned. We were great together. Until Isaac taught me something new.

I didn't want to be left alone. I wanted to be questioned. I needed it.

I didn't know I needed someone to dig into my heart and figure out why on some days I wanted to play, and why on others I craved solitude. I didn't even like it when he did it. It's a painful thing to look inside yourself and see the whys and the hows of your clockwork. You are a lot uglier than you think, plenty more selfish than you are ever likely to admit. So, you ignore what's inside of you. Thinking if you don't acknowledge it, it's not really there. Until someone unlikely comes along and cracks you. They see every dark corner, and they get it. And they tell you it's okay to have dark corners, instead of making you feel ashamed of them. Isaac wasn't afraid of my ugly. He rolled through the highs and lows with me. There was no judgment in his love. And all of a sudden there were fewer lows and more highs.

Nick loved me enough to leave me alone. Isaac knew me better than I knew me. I said I wanted to be left alone, he knew better. I said I wanted white, he knew better. He brightened me. He enlightened me. Because Isaac was my soulmate. Not Nick. Nick was just some great love. Isaac knew how to heal my soul.

"We were good together," I say to Nick. "But I'm not her anymore."

"I don't understand," he says. "You're not who?"

"Exactly."

"Brenna, you're not making sense."

"Do I ever?"

He pauses.

I shake my head. "I don't make sense to you. That's why you left me."

"I'll try harder."

"I have cancer. You can try as hard as you want, but I have cancer and I'm not going to be here in a year."

His face is a cocktail of woebegone and shock. "But … I thought … I thought you had the surgery."

I never told Nick about the surgery I had to remove my breasts, but my agent and publicist knew. Things get around in the writing world.

I was staining Nick's perfect, white idealism. Cancer happened, sure. But in Nick's world you beat it. Then you lived happily ever after.

"I have it again. It came back. Stage four."

He starts fumbling with sentences that he never finishes. I hear the words "treatment" and "chemotherapy" and "fight" and my heart grows tired.

"Shut up," I say.

Nick's glow is an ephemeral phenomenon. He's already looking like the same dumb fuck who thought I was too dark for his white room.

"It's too late for that. The cancer metastasized. While I was there. It came back. It's in my bones."

"There has to be something…"

He looks so terribly forlorn.

"You're trying to save me. But I'm not staying alive to be your muse."

"Why are you being so cruel?"

I laugh. A good belly laugh, too.

"Charm is clothed in narcissism, you know that? Get out of my house."

"Brenna…"

"Out!" I send my fists into his chest. "That's not my name anymore!"

"You're acting crazy," he insists. "You can't do this alone. Let me help you."

I scream. He created a monster, now he's going to meet her. Every little crevice.

"I am crazy! Because of you! I *can* do it alone. I've always done it alone. How dare you think I haven't."

He grabs my wrists, and tries to subdue me. I'm not having it. I rip away from him and walk to the center of my white room, rage rolling in waves. I can ride them, but someone's going to get hurt.

"You see this," I say, throwing my arms up, "this is you. You made me feel so much good, then you made me feel so much bad. So I decided to just stop feeling."

He's artist enough to understand me.

"What do you want me to say? I'm here now."

That's it. That's all he has to say and the truth hits me like an icy wind. My hair rises on its hackles. I feel flushed and bereaved.

I grab my head at the temples and squeeze with the heels of my hands. I am petrified. Never in my life have I been this afraid. Not of the cancer, not of being alone, not of my future or of my past. I am afraid of never seeing Isaac again. Of never having him hold me when life is so absolute in its unfairness that all I can do is scream. I turn to Nick. Nick, who is here now.

"Now?" I whisper, incredulous. "Now? Where were you when I was raped, or when I had my breasts cut off? Where were you when someone stole me away in the middle of the night and starved me in the middle of the goddamn arctic tundra?" I cut off the space between us and pound three hard times on his chest. "Where. Did. You. Go."

He's shaking. I'm dropping things on him like a hailstorm, but I don't give a fuck. I even say things like fuck now, because I don't want to waste another second on the white room way I lived my life. He's here now. But, Isaac was here then … and then … and then … and then.

"I was so hung up on you that I missed it," I say. I'm shaking so bad. I'm shaking worse than Nick, who looks like the weak, trembling leaf he's always been. I want to crush him between my fingertips.

"What did you miss, Brenna?" I don't like the way he says my name.

"Ahhh … agh…" I bend at the waist. Succulent, heavy tears drop right out of my eyes and onto the floor. *Splat.*

I cry now, I think. All the time. And it's so much fun.

"I missed my chance," I say, standing up straight and crushing the tears with the toe of my shoe. "With my soulmate."

Nick looks confused, then it comes. He sees his replacement, the guy locked in a house with his ex-muse.

"The doctor?" he asks, narrowing his eyes.

"Isaac. His name is Isaac."

"*I'm* your soulmate. I wrote that book for you." He looks like he's trying to convince himself, bobbing Adam's apple and all.

"You don't know the first thing about what it is to have a soulmate."

I feel such a pull toward Isaac I wonder if he's having this same fight with Daphne.

"It's time for you to leave," I say. It feels so good to say it. Because this time, I'm not even going to cry.

Before I shower, before I eat, before I crawl into bed and sleep off my fourteen-month nightmare, I call a cab. I have him pull into my garage, then I stand next to his window and check him out. Small guy, early twenties, bald by choice. I can see the shadows of where his hair should be. He's fighting that receding hairline with a shaved head. Defiant and a little ballsy, because we can all see why he's doing it. His eyes are wide and shifty; either the news vans freaked him out, or he's having withdrawals. *He'll do,* I think.

I climb into the front seat. "Do you mind?" I ask. But I don't really care if he says no. I buckle my seatbelt. "Take me to one of those stores with the lumber and the tools."

He spits out a couple options and I shrug. "Whatever."

We pull past the news vans and I smile at them. I don't know why except that it's kind of funny. I used to be famous for my books, now I'm famous for something else. It kind of constipates your mind; being famous for something that someone else did to you.

I make my cabbie wait while I run into the home fix-it store he chose. The building is expansive. I walk quickly past the lighting and the doorknobs until I find what I am looking for. I am there for thirty-five minutes while two employees see to my order. I have no purse or credit cards, just the wad of hundred dollar bills I shoved into my back pocket before I left the house. I kept them in an old cookie tin in my pantry for one day; a rainy day, a needy day, a day I just felt like blowing a wad of cash. Now there were only a few days left, so I figured it was time to spend. I toss three of the bills at the cashier and wheel my purchases out to the cab. I won't let him help me. I stack everything in the trunk, and climb back into the front seat.

My legs bounce all the way back. Flashes, doors, questions hurled up my driveway. Once again, I have him pull into the garage. He helps me this time, stacking everything just inside the door that leads into the foyer. I hand him the rest of the wad from my cookie tin.

"For one day," I say. His eyes bulge. He thinks I'm crazy, but hey, I'm handing him lots of money. He leaves before I can change my mind. I watch him pull out and quickly close the garage door. I grab an armload of my purchases and nudge the stereo with my toe as I walk past it. The first song Isaac ever gave me kicks on. It's loud. I make it louder until it's pounding through the house. I'm sure they can hear it outside: a one-man party.

I carry everything to the white room and pry off the lids of the cans with a butter knife: crimson, yellow, cobalt, bubblegum pink, deep purple—like a bruise—and three different greens to match the summer leaves. I stick my hand in the red paint first, and rub my fingertips together. It falls heavy, spilling on my clothes and the floor where I am kneeling. I scoop up more, 'til my hands are brimming. Then I throw it—a handful of red paint at my white, white wall. Color explodes. It spreads. It runs. I take more—I take all of the colors—and I stain my white room. I stain it with all the colors of Isaac, as Florence Welch sings me her song.

It's then that my phone rings. I don't pick it up, but when I listen to the message later that night, Detective soft *s* Garrison informs me that Saphira is dead. Dead by her own hand. *Good,* I think at first, but then my chest aches. He doesn't tell me how she did it but something tells me she opened her own veins. Bled out. She liked her patients to bleed out their thoughts and feelings; she would have chosen to go that way. Saphira and her god-complex would never have tolerated being tried in a court of law. She thought people were stupid. It would have been beneath her to be judged. I call him the next morning. There would be no trial. He sounds disappointed when he tells me, but I feel relieved. It's an end to the nightmare. I couldn't have handled months and months of a trial. Wasting my last days seeking human justice. I think I forgive her for believing she was God, I'm not sure God will.

Garrison informs me that there is an ongoing investigation into Saphira's accomplices. "Everyone we have questioned is shocked. She was well respected in the mental health community. No family in the country. No friends. She seems to have just snapped, lost touch with reality."

Who has time for friends when you're performing human experiments? I think.

"What about the blood on the books?" I ask. "Was it human?"

There is a long pause.

"The lab test indicated that it was animal blood. A ram or a goat, we can't be a hundred percent sure. We found your books in her home, along with your case file from-"

"I figured," I say quickly.

"There was something else," he says. "We found the footage of your time in the house."

I squeeze my eyes closed. "What are you going to do with it?"

"It'll go into evidence," he says.

"Good. No one will see it?"

"Not the media, if that's what you're asking."

"Okay."

"There is one more thing..."

How many more things could there be?

"Saphira had an apartment in Anchorage. We think that's how she got to you so quickly when Isaac was sick. She had been watching a recording of you and Doctor Asterholder. She was only able to see what was happening in the house when the power was on, and there was only sound in certain rooms. So there are gaps in the recordings. But, it was paused. I was hoping you'd be able to tell me something about the context of what I was seeing."

"What was it paused on?" I am breathless...sick. It never occurred to me that there were multiple cameras set up around the house.

"You holding a knife to Doctor Asterholder's chest."

I lick my lips. "He was holding a knife to his own chest," I say. My mind is ripping through what exactly Saphira was trying to tell me.

"It was the moment I changed," I say. "It was the reason she did what she did."

I look for my mother's book. I go the local bookstore and detail the plot to a wide-eyed girl of no more than eighteen behind the counter. She calls a manager to the front to help me. He looks at me earnestly while I repeat everything I just said to the girl. When I am finished, he nods like he knows just what I am talking about.

"The book I think you are talking about had a small run on the New York Times Bestsellers List," he says. I raise my eyebrows to his back as he leads me to the rear of the store and pulls a book off the shelf. I don't look at it as he hands it to me. I hold the weight of it in my hands and stare blankly at his face. I feel as if I'm about to see my mother face to face.

"You're the writer, the one who—"

"Yes," I say. "I'd like some privacy."

He nods, and leaves me. I have a feeling he's going to wherever managers go to tell everyone he knows that the kidnapped writer is here.

I take one of those breaths that make you burn on the inside, then I drop my head.

I see the cover—the words, the oranges and teals that make up the pattern of a woman's dress. You can only see the back of her, but her arms are spread wide, her blonde hair cascading down her back. *The Fall.*

The fall of my mother. I wonder if she wrote this for me. Is that too much to ask? An explanation for your abandoned daughter … your china doll? My mother is a narcissist. She wrote this for herself, to feel better for leaving me. I flip open the cover and search for a picture on the dust jacket. There is none. I wonder if she's still pretty. If she still wears flower skirts and headbands. She writes under the name Cecily Crowe. I grin. Her real name was Sarah Marsh. She hated the normalcy of it.

Cecily Crowe lives everywhere.
She does not believe in dogs or cats.
This is her first novel, and probably her last.

I close the book; slide it back into the space it came from. I have no desire to read it again, not even in order with page numbers. I got to know my mother in a discombobulated way. I am her china doll. She mourned me a little, but not enough. I can't fault her for running—I've been running my entire life; bad blood, maybe. Or maybe she taught me, and someone taught her. I don't know. We can't blame our parents for everything. I don't think I care anymore. It's just the way it is. I walk out of the store. I put her to rest.

Three months after I get home, I drive to the hospital to see Isaac. I don't know if he wants to see me. He hasn't tried to contact me since I've been back. It hurts after the emotional violence we experienced together, but it's not like I tried to contact him either. I wonder if he told Daphne everything. Maybe that's why…

I don't know what to say. What to feel. Relief because we both survived? Do we talk about what happened? I miss him. Sometimes I wish we could go back, and that's just sick. I feel as if I have Stockholm Syndrome, but not for a person—for a house in the snow.

I pull into a space and sit in my car for at least an hour, picking at the rubber on the steering wheel. I called ahead, so I know he's here. I don't know what it's going to feel like to see him. I held his body while he was dying. He held mine. We survived something together. How do you stand back and shake someone's hand in the real world when you were clutched together in a nightmare?

I fling open my car door and it cracks against the side of an already beat up minivan. "Sorry," I tell it, before stepping away.

The doors to the hospital slide open, and I take a moment to look around. Nothing has changed. It's still too cold in here; the fountain still sprays a crooked stream into air that smells deeply of antiseptic. Nurses and doctors cross paths, charts clutched against chests or hanging droopy from their hands. It all stayed the same while I was changing. I turn my face toward the parking lot. I want to leave, stay out of this world. No one but Isaac knows what it was like. It makes me feel like the only person on the planet. It makes me angry.

I need to talk to him. He's the only one. I walk. Then I'm in the elevator, sliding slowly up to his floor. He is probably doing rounds, but I'll wait in his office. I just need a few minutes. Just a few. I walk quickly once the doors open. His office is just around the corner and past the vending machine.

"Senna?"

I spin. Daphne is standing a few feet away. She is wearing black scrubs and a stethoscope is hanging around her neck. She looks tired and beautiful.

"Hello," I say.

We stand looking at each other for a minute, before I break the silence. I wasn't expecting to see her. It was stupid. An oversight. I didn't come here to make her uncomfortable.

"I came to see—"

"I'll get him for you," she says, quickly. I am surprised. I watch as she turns on her heel and trots down the hallway. Maybe he didn't tell her everything.

He won't speak to the news stations either. My agent called me days after I got back, wanting to know if I could write a book detailing what happened to me—to us. The truth is I don't know that I'll ever write another book. And I'll never tell about what happened in that house. It's all mine.

When I see him I hurt. He looks great. Not the skeleton man I kissed goodbye. But there are more lines around his eyes. I hope I put a few there.

"Hello, Senna," he says.

I want to cry and laugh.

"Hi."

He motions for his office door. He has to open it with a key. Isaac steps inside first and turns on the light. I cast a quick glance over my shoulder before walking in to see if Daphne is lurking anywhere. Thankfully, she's not. I can't bear her burdens on top of the ones I'm already carrying.

We sit. It's not uncomfortable, but it's not entirely tea and cookies either. Isaac sits behind his desk, but after a minute he comes and sits in the chair next to me.

"You're back to work," I say. "Couldn't stay away."

"I tried." He shakes his head. "I went to Hawaii and saw a shrink."

I sort of laugh at that one. "Brave."

"I know," he smiles. "The entire session was me trying not to tell her things that could get me kidnapped."

We get serious.

"How are you?" he asks cautiously. I appreciate the way he's tiptoeing around my feelings, but we are a little too crushed for such gentle sentiments. For the first time, I answer him.

"Shitty."

The corner of his mouth turns up. Just one corner. It's his trademark.

"That's better than being closed off, I guess," he says.

I feel emotion rush me—the intimacy, the awkwardness. I want to revolt against it, but I don't. It takes an awful toll on a person to fight down everything they're feeling. Elgin tried to tell me that once. The bitch.

"I heard about your prognosis…"

"I'm okay with it," I say quickly. "It just … is."

He looks like he has a million things to say, and he can't.

"I wanted to come see you, Senna. I just didn't know how."

"You didn't know how to come see me?" I ask, partially amused.

He looks at my eyes, in them. So sadly.

"It's okay," I say, slowly. "I get it."

"What do we do now?" he asks. I don't know if he's asking how we are supposed to live, or how we are supposed to finish this conversation. I don't ever know what to do.

"We live then we leave," I say. "Do the best we can."

He runs his tongue along the inside of his bottom lip. It puffs out and settles back down. It reminds me of when you're baking a cake and you open the oven too early. I toy with the jagged edges of my hair, glancing up at him every so often.

"Are things good? With you and Daphne?" I have no right to ask him, none at all. Especially considering that everything Elgin did was because of me.

"No," he says. "How can they be?" He shakes his head. "She has been supportive. I can't complain there, but it was like they gave me a month and then they wanted the old me back. They being my family," he tells me. "But I don't know how to be him. I'm different."

Isaac was always so honest with his emotions. I wish I could be like that. I feel as if I need to say something.

"I don't have anyone to disappoint," I confess. "I don't know if that makes it easier or harder."

He looks startled. His black scrubs wrinkle as he leans toward me. "You're loved," he says.

Love is a possession; it's something that you own from the layers of people in your life. But if my life were a cake it would be un-layered, unbaked, missing ingredients. I isolated myself too soundly to own anyone's love.

"I love you," says Isaac. "From the moment you ran out of the woods, I've loved you."

I don't believe him. He's a nurturer by profession and by person. He saw something broken and needed to heal it. He loves the process.

As if reading my thoughts he says, "You have to believe someone sometime, Senna. When they tell you that. Otherwise you'll never know what it feels like to be loved. And that's a sad thing."

"How do you know?" I ask, brimming with anger. "It's a big deal to say those words. How do you know that you love me?"

He pauses for a long time. Then he says, "I was offered a way out."

"A way out? A way out of what?" But I spit that out too soon. It's like a stone that drops between us. I wait for the thud, but it never comes because my brain loses its footing and the room tips and turns.

"What do you mean?"

"On the morning after we opened the door, I found a note in the shed with sleeping pills and a syringe. It said that I could leave. All I had to do was put you to sleep, inject myself, and I would wake up at home. The stipulations were that I could never talk about you. Not to police, not to anyone. I had to tell them that I had an emotional breakdown and ran away. If I told anyone about you, she said she would kill you. If I left you there, I could go home. I threw them over the side of the cliff."

"Oh my God."

I stand but my legs can't hold me. I sit again, burying my face in my hands. *Saphira, what have you done?*

When I look up, my soul is in my face, twisting my features. It's angry and sad.

"Isaac. Why would you do that?" My voice cracks. I know why Saphira did it. She knew he wouldn't leave me. She knew eventually he would tell me, and that in telling me, I would see everything clearly. I would see…

"Because I love you."

My face goes slack.

"I didn't leave you because I couldn't. I've never been able to." There is a pause and then, "Not unless you make me go. And if I'd known you better back then, I wouldn't have left you. I thought it was what you needed. But you didn't know yourself. I knew you. You needed me, and I let you push me out. And for that I'm very sorry."

He presses his lips together, and the vein in his head pops.

"I got another chance, too," he says. "She gave me another chance not to leave. So I took it."

"Are you saying Saphira—"

"I'm not saying anything about Saphira," he cuts me off. "She did what she did. We can't change that. Life happens. Sometimes crazy people kidnap you and make you a part of their personal psychological experiment."

The noise that comes from my throat is part laugh, part groan.

"She wanted to see what love would do if put to the test."

Love doesn't leave. It bears all things.

I don't know why Saphira wanted to test love. If it was to show me something, or to show herself. I wonder about that. Who she was. Who the man who built the house was to her. But she played with our lives, and I hate her for that. Isaac missed his daughter's birth, months of her life because of what Saphira did. We almost died because of what she did. But it changed me. The change that Isaac started, before I filed a restraining order to keep him out, Saphira Elgin finished in that house in the snow.

A part of me is grateful to her, and it makes me feel sick to admit that.

On the day I am scheduled to leave, I find a brown envelope on my windshield. I briefly think that I received a parking ticket somewhere, and failed to notice it until now. But when I lift my wiper and pull it away the paper is crisp, not something that's been sitting outside in the wet, Seattle air. It's also heavyish. My universe tilts. I spin in a circle looking for him in the trees and down the driveway. I know he's not here. I know that. But he was, and I can feel him.

Everything is boxed up in my house, including my sound system, so I turn the car on and push the silver disc into the car radio. It has just started to snow, so I open all of the windows and blast my heat so I can have the best of both worlds. I hit play, and hold on to the steering wheel. I'm about to careen off a cliff. I know it.

I can hardly breathe as I listen to the last song that Isaac will ever give me. I listen to it while my breath freezes and smokes into the air.

And while snow flies into the car windows.

And while my heart beats, and then aches, and then beats.

I listen to my soulmate's heart with saltwater seeping out of my eyes. He's speaking to me through a song. Like he always has. It's a hard thing to know that I'm never going to see him again or hear his music, which woke me up from a long, restless sleep. The shadows still chase me. And I know that when I wake up in the middle of the night screaming, he won't be there to climb in bed behind me and command them away with the complex way he loves me. The song crushes me. Our cosmic love, our cosmic connection.

Nick was wrong about me. Having a mud vein didn't kill me; it saved me. My vein drew Isaac. He was the light and he followed me into the darkness. He became the darkness, then he carried my burdens so I wouldn't have to. Isaac saved me from myself, but in the end, no one could save me from cancer.

I'm terminal. That's a funny word. Cancer can kill my body, but it can't kill me. I have a soul. I have a soulmate. We are vapors; here today and gone tomorrow. But before tomorrow comes I want to see color—the color threaded throughout Italy and France and Sweden. I want to see the Northern Lights. And when I die, I know there will be an invisible red thread connecting me to my soulmate. It can tangle, and it can stretch, but it can never break. When I die, I'll be in the light. And someday Isaac will find me, because that's what he is.

I put the letter in my mailbox and flip the little red flag up.

Dear Isaac,

I finally understand your tattoos. I never voiced how much they bothered me, but sometimes in that house in the snow, you'd catch me looking and I'd see the hidden smile on your face. You knew I was trying to work it out. When I asked you about it, you told me that we were all bound by something because we needed something to hold us together. What you wrap around your soul determines your outcome—that's what you said to me. But I didn't get it. I though that was crazy, until the day you held my hand, clamped over a knife, and pointed it at your body: both of us cutting into your skin.

You bore my burdens that hour. Does that make sense? You took my self-loathing and bitterness, my promise to pay back the world, and you pointed them at yourself. I loved you then. Because you saw me. It's the very instance that I woke up from a blinding, and knew that I was standing face to face with my soulmate. A concept I didn't believe in until your soul healed mine. The darkness that formerly commanded me yielded to your light. That's how I understood your tattoos. The ropes that bound me were no longer self-loathing and bitterness. They suddenly became you, but in a good way. I need those ropes to hold me together. I didn't want to hurt myself anymore because it hurt you.

Oh, God. I'm rambling. I just needed you to know.

Every minute you spent getting to know me, I got to know me. Forgive me for not recognizing our soul-likeness sooner, while we still had time. The nature of love is that it conquers. Hate. Even bitterness. Mostly, it conquers self-loathing. I was sitting in a white room hating myself, until you breathed life back into me. You loved me so much that I started to love myself.

Who would have thought that day that I was running out of the woods, I was running straight into the arms of my savior? Right out of an ugly life that had me conquered. I did not choose you, and you did not choose me. Something else chose for us. The snow covered me, and you covered me, and in that house—in pain, and cold, and hunger—I accepted unconditional love. You are my truth, Isaac, and you set me free.

We are all going to die, but I'm going to die first. In the very last second of my life, I will think of you.

Senna

ACKNOWLEDGMENTS

I guess I should start at the beginning. In 2012 Nate Sabin met me for the first time and called me, Mud Vein. After my initial shock receded, I realized that Nate was right; I did have a mud vein. It's my defining feature. Being that this book is dedicated to his wife, I'll just go ahead and thank the Sabin's for being the type of people who inspire me and call me out on my shit.

My dad, who has leukemia and is not afraid of anything. Thanks for the fearless gene. P.s. Sorry I have so many tattoos. I hope I can still go to Heaven.

Cindy Fisher, the best mother in the world. Our mansions will all sit in the shadow of yours.

Stephen King, thank you for teaching me how to write. You're a goddam genius.

My friend and assistant, Serena Knautz, you are shrewd as a snake and harmless as a dove. You put love into action. I adore you.

Sarah Hansen of Okay Creations, you are a true artist. This is the most beautiful cover I have ever seen. The vision was all you.

Marie Piquette, my editor, I, am, sorry, I, use, so, many, comma's.

Christine Estevez for always being on my team.

The blogging Jedi: Molly Harper of Tough Critic Book Reviews, Aestas Book Blog, Maryse's Book Blog, Vilma's Book Blog, Bec's of Sinfully Sexy Book Reviews, Madison Says Book Blog and Shh Mom's Reading Book Blog. Each of you gives blogging a different flavor. I appreciate each one of your voices and the time you take promoting my books. Vilma, that was the most beautiful review I've ever read.

I'd also like to thank Madison Seidler, Luisa Hansen, Yvette Huerta, Rebecca Espinoza and my little Nina Gomez for their input and friendship. Jonathan Rodriguez for assuring me every day that I'm a genius (even though I can't do fractions).

Tosha Khoury, I am so blessed to have you. You get me. You get what I write. I don't know anyone who believes in my books more than you.

Amy Tannenbaum, my tiny, tough, agent.

My vicious PLN army/gang, I love you! Sundae Coletti, Jennifer Stiltner, Robin Stranahan, Dyann Tufts, Robin Segnitz, Amy Holloway, Krystle Zion, Sandra Cortez, Nelly Martinez de Iraheta, Monica Martinez, Sarah Kaiser, Chelsea Peden McCrory, Dawnita Kiefer, Miranda Howard, Courtney Mazal, Yoss, Kristin McNally, Tre Hathaway, Shelly Ford, Maribel Zamora, Maria Milano, Fizza Hussain, Brooke Higgins, Paula Roper, Joanna Hoffman Dursi, Marivett Villafane, Amy Miller Sayler, and my favorite Kristy Garner. I wish I could list you all.

Since publishing my first book, I have met so many people who made me view the world differently. There is none more rare and precious than Colleen Hoover. She is a light shining in darkness. Thank you for loving Mud Vein, and for recognizing our red thread. You have no heart, and you have the biggest heart.

And finally, to the God who says: "Come to me, all who labor and are heavy laden, and I will give you rest." I live for you, mud vein and all.